DEATH-SIEGE!

Bodie slammed the bolt home and pushed Sara to the floor. The next instant sub-machine gun bullets rattled against the stout wood like flung pebbles.

Outside among his beloved flowers the vicar lay sprawled in death. On his face his last expression was implanted with the violence of his death.

That expression was one of shocked surprise.

Bodie rose to his feet. He looked hard at the women and saw what he expected to see. His lips firmed. This was not going to be an easy ride; yet there was nothing else he could do – not now.

'Round one,' said Bodie . . .

Also by Ken Blake in Sphere Books:

THE PROFESSIONALS 1: WHERE THE JUNGLE ENDS
THE PROFESSIONALS 2: LONG SHOT
THE PROFESSIONALS 4: HUNTER HUNTED

THE PROFESSIONALS:
Stake Out

KEN BLAKE

Based on the original screenplays by
Brian Clemens and **Dennis Spooner**

SPHERE BOOKS LIMITED
30/32 Gray's Inn Road, London WC1X 8JL

First published by Sphere Books Ltd 1978

TRADE
MARK

Set in Intertype Baskerville

Printed in Great Britain by
Hunt Barnard Printing Ltd.,
Aylesbury, Bucks.

THE PROFESSIONALS:

Stake Out

Chapter One

George Cowley opened his office door, switched off the light and lifted his foot to step out into the corridor. At that moment the telephone on his desk began to ring.

The brittle brr-brr filled the darkened office with sound. That special, demanding, imperious sound of a telephone ringing in a dark office made Cowley glance at his wrist watch.

The time was eight o'clock.

Light from the corridor shafted across the half-open door and picked out the marking on the tarnished wood:

HOME AFFAIRS (S) – GEORGE COWLEY – CONTROLLER C.I.5.

Without switching on the light, Cowley limped back across his threadbare carpet to the desk. He lifted the receiver.

'Yes – hello . . .'

That telephone had begun many problems for the chief of CI5. Far more to the point, it had been the instrument that had brought great grief to plenty of villains foolish enough to tangle with Cowley and his Squad, the Big A.

A tough, stocky, compact man, his craggy face with its network of lines retained most of the handsomeness that had both served him well and been the bane of his life over the years. His sandy hair was thinning a little now he was pushing fifty-five; but he could still handle himself in a rumble, gammy leg and all.

The quick bleeping on the phone ceased as the caller thumbed a coin into a paybox slot.

'Cowley . . . ?'

'Speaking.'

'Fraser. Listen – I'm on to something. Something big . . .'

'I saw your reports.'

'No. No. Not the drug business.' Fraser's voice was hushed, as though he was holding himself in. 'Something else. I ran across it by pure chance . . .'

Cowley gripped the receiver. 'Well, don't talk in riddles, man! What is it?'

A burst of noise rattled from the phone. It sounded like a line of empty trucks shunting on a dismal sooty railway line. In the phone box Fraser looked out through the glass, keeping a close watch on the Bowling Alley. The lanes were filled with bowlers going through the contortions that would lead to successful strikes. The balls spun and gleamed as they hurtled down the lanes. The ten pins were sometimes knocked askew, sometimes a few were left standing, isolated, ready for the second ball, and sometimes the ball would skid uselessly along the gutter. Fraser took it all in, the lights, the flash, the action, the girls in their short skirts, the people wandering about apparently aimlessly, watching the bowling or going to and from the bar or the cloakrooms. It was a familiar sight to him, for he'd been assigned this job and had stuck with it.

Patty walked in the door and Fraser, seeing her, allowed his lean body to slide down the glass until he was almost invisible. Patty was a dish, right enough, with long legs and a trim figure, with blonde hair that had not come out of a bottle. But she looked tense tonight, fidgety, and she stared about the Bowling Alley searching – always searching for something she would never find.

'I can't talk now,' said Fraser, hunched down. 'I'll meet you in the usual place in – ' He glanced at his watch. 'In fifteen minutes.'

Fraser replaced the receiver quietly and then, just

as quietly, eased out of the telephone booth.

In his office Cowley bellowed: 'Fraser? Fraser!'

But the line was dead.

Rattling the telephone bar did no good. Angrily, Cowley thumped the receiver back and, for only a moment, stood in thought. Then he headed out of the office and this time he limped with more purpose than before.

Something had got Fraser going and if there was one thing George Cowley insisted on it was always being in the picture. If something was going on with any of his agents he wanted to know it all and he wanted to know it fast.

Outside the Bowling Alley the brilliance of the neon lighting threw weird shadows over the car park. Fraser headed down on to the asphalt and threaded his way between the parked cars. He had fifteen minutes, and he was enough of a CI5 man to know damn well never to keep Cowley waiting.

Fraser found his car, a suitably unobtrusive Cortina picked out from CI5's motor pool, and fumbled in his pockets for the keys. A snazzy jazzed-up Avenger pulled into the park and a group of youngsters already kitted out for bowling tumbled out almost before the car halted. They were making a racket, laughing and joking, joking between themselves. The girls were squealing. The sounds bounced around between the rows of parked cars.

Bending to the car door Fraser found his keys.

A large form attired in a vulgar, bright check sports jacket appeared silently. The man eased in along the bonnet of Fraser's car, moving with bulky stealth to Fraser's unprotected back. The noise of the youngsters as they kidded and horse-played across to the Alley's doors took Fraser's attention. He glanced up.

The big man in the check jacket moved smoothly in front of Fraser. It was all very quick, very deadly.

The next moment Fraser was doubled up, clutching at his stomach. He was in abrupt and awful agony. The big man in the check sports coat moved sleekly away into the shadows between the garish neon lighting.

For a moment Fraser thought he would collapse.

The knife had gone in deep.

His guts were on fire. But the pain told him that he still had a few minutes yet – there was still time. He was a trained CI5 operative and his mind was bent obsessively on his mission.

With enormous effort he got the door open and struggled to pull himself into the driving seat. He shook with the agony and his face sheened sweat, garishly coloured as the neon lights shone emptily down. The youngsters had gone now and the quietness rang in his head.

He started the Cortina and put her in gear and then almost passed out as the car started with an uncontrolled jerk. But he did not stall, and the car rolled down the ramp. The lights of London spread around him, a wavering sea of flame, and the agony bit into him, deeper now, less edgy but more intense, as though all his insides were liquefying.

He saw his hands on the steering wheel.

His hands, the wheel, the gear lever, the door handle, all were smothered with greasy blood.

That was his blood, pumping out of him, leaching away from the knife wound.

He kept his foot on the accelerator and the Cortina weaved drunkenly down the road, between the lights, missing other cars by inches, but going on, going on . . .

Everything wavered in an out-of-focus nightmare. The lighted shops sped past, traffic lights were red or green and neither made much difference, the neon advertisements dripped colour and the whole blaze blended into a psychedelic chiaroscuro of light.

At the rendezvous in the sparsely-lit underground car park George Cowley tooled his immaculate Rover 3500 into a bay and switched off. He was in a perfect position to look up the descent ramp. His watch showed him fourteen minutes had elapsed since he'd taken Fraser's call. A minute later a frown creased down Cowley's craggy face.

Two minutes later he got out of the Rover and walked slowly across the concrete towards the mouth of the ramp. A car was coming. The engine note revved high, the snarl bouncing off the concrete walls. Again Cowley frowned.

Fraser's Cortina whirled into view, travelling fast, slicing down the ramp. Cowley moved a little forward expecting the car to stop. But the Cortina simply hurtled straight on, shooting from the descent ramp like a shell from a cannon, roared on to crunch headlong into a concrete wall.

The front of the car telescoped. The roof burst upwards. Broken glass spattered everywhere. The engine note died in the thunderous crash of the impact. The car skewered forward against the concrete, bending, collapsing, rending.

Fraser was slammed forward against the wheel and the car horn blared out, a long ghastly moan through the dimly-lit underground car park.

Cowley limped forward.

There was nothing he could do for Fraser now.

And whatever the agent had discovered was still locked away in the cells of his dead brain.

The flashing blue lights, the white ambulance, the blue-uniformed men, the stretcher and the red blankets, all these things occurred to celebrate the death of Fraser. Police began to measure up the scene of the accident. The crane truck would be along soon to remove the wreckage. Fraser was carried away.

Doyle and Bodie surveyed the scene.

Bodie's lean handsome face showed no trace of emotion as he spoke to his partner.

'He had a premonition, you know.'

'Fraser?'

'Fraser.' Bodie nodded. 'Always said he'd die one day.'

Doyle's round, fair-haired face also showed no readable emotion. His casual anorak and slacks were in marked contrast to the dark-haired Bodie's trim two-piece suit, cut by a very expensive tailor; but about these two limber, tough, rough young men clung that mystique of aggressive power channelled and contained, used by them instead of being allowed to use them. As George Cowley would grudgingly say, after a drink of pure malt Scotch – Bodie and Doyle were two of his best.

Now Doyle inclined his tousle-haired head a fraction.

'That's the safest prediction I've heard for a long time. I hope you didn't take any bets on it.'

'You know what I mean.'

'Yeah,' said Ray Doyle. 'I know what you mean.'

They watched sombrely as Fraser's body on the stretcher was carried away. George Cowley told the police officer in charge: 'I'd like his belongings, personal effects, everything . . .'

Doyle and Bodie were both well aware of the emotion in Cowley. They had all seen good men of the Big A shot down, killed, and they knew they'd never get used to it. This appeared to be an accident; but when you worked for CI5, which was dedicated to fighting domestic crime of the most serious kinds, accidents like this usually added up to murder.

'You were here when it happened, sir?' Doyle's flat voice remained perfectly neutral.

'I was.'

Bodie looked around the gaunt confines of the underground car park.

'He always used this place for a meet.'

Doyle said: 'Did he say anything?' As Cowley simply shook his head, Doyle went on: 'What was he working on?'

'Drug ring – undercover.' Cowley shook his head. 'Something big, he said. Fraser was on to something else. That's why he phoned me.'

Still talking in that soft, muted tone of voice, the three men made their way to their cars and drove back to the office.

The building leaned against the London night, grey and anonymous, just off Whitehall. The commissionaire checked everyone in and out, and commissionaires had been found dead at their posts, for this was the HQ of CI5 and the big villains of crime sometimes attempted to do what so many of their colleagues had failed to do. But Cowley and his team in the Big A survived and continued to wage war on crime. The whole place presented a run-down appearance, all except the forensic department, the operations room and the communications sections, which were equipped with the latest that money could buy. Even the motor pool had the look of a used-car lot, for among the Rolls and the Jaguars there was a plentiful sprinkling of beat-up Cortinas and anonymous Minis – undercover work demanded tools and motors for the job.

They ran the tape of Fraser's all-too brief telephone conversation.

At the point when Cowley's exasperated voice snapped out: 'Well, don't talk in riddles, man!' Bodie and Doyle heard that odd rattling succession of clicks and then the long screech. They exchanged baffled looks.

When Fraser's voice said: 'I can't talk now. I'll meet you in the usual place in – in fifteen minutes,' and Cowley's voice, harsh with impatience and strain, rapped out: 'Fraser? Fraser!' the tape ran on emptily.

Doyle said: 'That it?'

Cowley nodded. 'That's it.'

'That noise,' said Bodie. His eyebrows drew down. 'What was it?'

Doyle came back from the side table that held all the belongings the police had recovered from Fraser's body. He held out a pink slip. 'Here.'

Bodie took the pink slip, and realisation hit him.

'A ticket – a ticket to a Bowling Alley! Fraser was calling from – '

'And,' said Ray Doyle with satisfaction. 'We know which one.'

'Get over there and stake it out.' Cowley's order was an order, stark and functional.

'What are we looking for?' Bodie started to turn away.

'Don't ask me, Bodie. That's your job. What you're

trained for. Sniff hard, be alert, anything unusual . . . '

The two partners made for the door, Bodie, with his disgusted expression that sat so well on his darkly handsome face, saying : 'Stake out . . . !'

He caught Cowley's eye, and that eye was abruptly alert and keen and entirely chilling. Bodie, very rapidly, exited, saying as he did so : 'We're on our way, sir.'

The two men were arguing about just what the hell they were supposed to be doing at the Bowling Alley. Bodie was finely disgusted, looking over the action, the balls gleaming as they spun down the lanes, the bowlers full of energy, the big man at the counter serving new arrivals, the bar, the cloaks. He let his nostril curve up in disgust.

Doyle sighed.

'How many stake-outs have you been on, Bodie?'

'Not many.'

'You're lucky.' Doyle glanced about. 'Well, just look, listen, and learn.'

'Do nothing, you mean?'

'Look, what do you want us to do? *Announce* we're on a stake-out? Or maybe yell out : "Would anyone here like to confess?" '

Bodie favoured Doyle with a cold look. But the sense of what his partner said made him turn back to survey the Bowling Alley again. 'It could be a meeting place . . . But who is meeting who? And why?'

They moved unhurriedly along the cleared area immediately behind the lanes. The activity appeared normal. A man stood casually watching the bowlers. He continually flipped peanuts up from the plastic bag in his hand and his mouth caught them expertly, as a bird takes an insect on the wing. He was in his late thirties, casually dressed, and his face was of that vacuous variety to be seen and immediately forgotten.

But Bodie and Doyle had experience of men with anonymous faces . . .

'That guy with the peanuts?'

Bodie didn't answer. He was watching a powerfully-built Negro, dressed in sports shirt and slacks, alone on a lane. He was around thirty, with a strikingly handsome face, and by the way he let rip with the bowling balls he knew how to bowl. He was practising alone.

'Maybe the black fellow,' offered Bodie.

Before Doyle could reply, Bodie gripped his arm. 'No. Hold it.' He nodded his head. 'My money's on them.'

Two young girls in very short tennis-style skirts were playing on an adjoining lane. They laughed a great deal, although they, too, had played before. Their athletic figures made interesting shapes as they ran the three steps forward, skipped, and hurled. Bodie stared with that brooding, calculating look in his eyes. Doyle made a face; but he appreciated the free Amazon-like femininity on display.

'So why pull a face, Doyle? If we sit around we could wait forever.'

'Sometimes it takes forever.'

'Can you see anybody acting suspiciously?'

Doyle's face relaxed and he smiled. 'Yeah . . . *Us!* We're in a Bowling Alley and we're not bowling.'

Doyle moved towards the counter. 'Come on, let's play.'

Grumbling, Bodie started after his partner. 'We're here to watch, not play.'

'And if we don't play, *we'll* be watched.'

Still arguing the pair made for the counter where a big man served the soft shoes and provided answers to those with questions. He looked bored and yet, at the same time, tensed up as though waiting for something to happen that exhilarated and frightened him.

Bodie said: 'Play? For money?'

Doyle said: 'You ever played – ?'

Bodie countered with: 'Have you?'

Doyle smiled his wide smile that was almost a smirk.

'I asked first.'

Bodie nodded, making up his mind. 'Okay. Loser buys the drinks.'

Doyle's smile widened. 'You haven't played – '

'How do you know?'

'Deduction. Once a cop – if you had played it would be for bigger stakes.'

Bodie snorted. 'Deduction! Once a cop – always a stake-out expert. Come on, Doyle.'

An immensely fat man was playing with great energy at one of the lanes. The sweat sizzled off him; but he wore a thin pullover which strained across his gross bulk. Yet he had a real turn of athleticism and it was clear to Bodie and Doyle as they drifted past that the fat man could take care of himself in a brawl.

The constant movement and noise and the bright lights created interesting patterns among the players. Bodie and Doyle took long hard looks as they went, and yet to all appearances they were merely lounging around ready to start playing. Bodie bought the time for a couple of games and collected the soft shoes. They headed for the indicated empty lane.

They saw an attractive blonde girl with long legs and a trim figure wandering through the crowd and both admired her with the immediate acceptance of her femininity, yet Doyle said: 'That's a very edgy lady.'

'She's looking for someone, that's for sure.'

'And you think that someone could be you? You're on stake-out, remember.'

'How can I forget with you as a watchdog?'

Doyle picked up a ball from the dispenser. Bodie looked at it with marked disfavour.

'They must know we're beginners,' he said, 'they've given us balls with holes in.'

Doyle's look of disgust enchanted Bodie, who felt he had made his point.

And, all the time, their eyes kept up a ceaseless observation of the people about them. The noise cracked and rattled to the roof, the pins were knocked helterskelter and the rig swooped down like a flock of vultures to sweep away the dead men and replace them with ten brand new soldiers. The slow remorseless progress of the rig fascinated Bodie. He stood watching it until voices raised in argument made him half-turn.

The fat man and the handsome Negro were standing facing each other, and their tense attitudes spoke eloquently of passions being held in check.

Doyle nudged Bodie.

'Something to do with challenging him to a game, and the fat man declining. It takes all kinds.'

'Well away, Doyle. But something's eating fatso.'

'Whatever it is, we just watch.'

'We just watch. Great!'

'Cowley was right. Something is going on here, and Fraser's dead to prove it.'

A nondescript man wearing a raincoat moved past. His stomach bulged. The partners eyed him; but he turned away facing the two girls with their short skirts. Presently the man in the raincoat drifted off, his stomach bulging under the mack.

Bodie and Doyle turned their attention to bowling – briefly. Between each throw they would turn, yawning, stretching, reaching for the towel, and their eyes would rake out over the scene.

But nothing happened – at least, nothing they could see.

At the counter the attendant just finished up taking in the soft shoes from players who had finished their bowling stint for the night. He checked the sizes and racked them in the appropriate places. A telephone began to ring, a soft, discreet buzz, a small sound lost in the racket of the ten pins being hammered all over the place by the heavy and hard bowling balls. Bob glanced around first before reaching down under the counter for the telephone.

'Hello?'

The voice at the other end said: 'Bob?'

'Yes.'

'It's Frank. I'm still at Bedford. The merchandise is ready.' A slight pause, then: 'Have you dealt with Jack?'

Bob looked towards the doors, and around the area by the bar and the cloaks.

'No. He hasn't turned up yet.' Bob carefully looked away from the bowling lanes. 'But Number One's here.'

On the other end of the line in the big house in Bedford, Frank caught his breath. He looked about the room with its untidy clutter of printing equipment, a printing press, still wet with ink, leaflets scattered about. The wording was simple and direct and stentorian in its effect. KEEP AFRICA WHITE. This was the theme of the leaflets. Frank Turner knew they'd done a good job on the propaganda.

Frank Turner was an elegant man, neat and precise, dressed in a fawn safari suit. His tanned face showed a slight scarring under the chin. He was about forty and his voice held the faintest burr of a South African accent.

His gaze dwelt briefly on the leather carry-all standing on the table with the printing inks and the stacks of leaflets. The carry-all was of the kind used to transport bowling balls. He smiled, and the smile crinkled the corners of his eyes; but no warmth showed in their blueness.

'Then,' he said softly. 'It's tonight.'

'Just as well too,' said Bob.

The tone of Bob's voice alerted Frank Turner.

'Something went wrong?'

'Don't worry. We're in the clear. We must be, otherwise we would have heard something by now. Nothing happened that wasn't dealt with, finally. I'll tell you about it when you get here.'

'I'm leaving now – with the merchandise.'

'Good – hold on.' Bob screwed around over the phone receiver. 'It's okay. Jack's just arrived.' He replaced the phone.

Jack Saward walked through the open door into the Bowling Alley like a warmed-up corpse. He felt dreadful. There were pains in his head and chest, and his feet and hands felt numb. But he had done the job and he intended to collect. He staggered and put a hand on the wall to steady himself. He looked as though he was half-drunk. He sweated freely. He took a handkerchief from his pocket and mopped his forehead. Then he forced himself upright and headed for the Gentlemen's Cloakroom.

Bodie and Doyle took note of the latest arrival in the Bowling Alley as they took note of everyone and everything.

But they had to continue with the farce of bowling. Doyle hefted a bowling ball in his hands, finding the holes for his fingers and thumb. He squinted over the shiny black roundness at Bodie.

'How do you score?'

Then Doyle saw that Bodie was looking at the attractive blonde girl who was glancing up again at the big wall clock. She drifted past oblivious, it seemed, of the two. But Bodie was smiling.

'Oh, I just get lucky, I guess.'

Doyle snorted. 'Bowling! This kind of scoring!'

Bodie watched the blonde and then stared back at his partner. 'How do I know? Count up the ones you knock down, I suppose.'

As he spoke Jack disappeared into the Gentlemen's Cloakroom. Inside he staggered across to the line of sinks and leaned on the nearest. He stared at his reflection in the mirror. He looked awful. Sweating, pale, shaking, he looked a sick man.

Once Jack was safely inside the Gentlemen's Cloaks, Bob let out a sigh of relief. He bent and retrieved a brown manilla envelope, of the shape and size to contain folding money. Then he reached for his jacket hanging on a peg.

That jacket was very sporty, and was cut from a cloth of pronounced and vulgar checks.

Chapter Two

In the Gentlemen's Cloaks Jack stood gripping the sink and feeling as though the world had hurled itself at his head just as the bowling balls hurled themselves along the lanes in insensate fury to destroy the ten pins standing in so orderly a fashion. He really felt dreadful. The door opened but Jack did not turn around. Bob walked in and stood at Jack's elbow, staring at him in the mirror.

Then Bob took the money-sized envelope from his jacket pocket and placed it on the shelf below the mirror. The bright checks of the coat hurt Jack's eyes.

'You look terrible.'

'I don't feel so good.'

'Touch of 'flu, I'd say. It's all there.'

'That's what I'd say . . . Thanks.'

'Get yourself some aspirin and go to bed. You've earned it.'

When Bob left the cloakroom he almost bumped into a nondescript man who was in the act of tossing a peanut into the air and snatching it up with a nicely distended mouth. Bob glared and the peanut-eater moved away with an apology. Bob frowned after him. Then, thinking nothing of it, he went into the office through the door marked Private. Jack had done a good job, he'd been paid off, and now all they had to do was wait for Frank Turner to get here. Number One was here and so it was tonight. No doubts entered Bob's mind, no doubts at all.

Bodie, for one, was heartily sick of this so-called stake-out. He told Doyle so. 'What a waste of time this is.'

'I,' said Ray Doyle, 'have started to enjoy it.'

'How many do we play for?'

'Oh – two hundred and one?'

'That's darts.'

Doyle smiled. 'So why should bowls be any different?'

The door to the Gentlemen's Cloaks opened again and Jack staggered out. His face was like marble, dashed with sweat. He tottered forward. Then he pitched headlong on to the floor.

Bodie and Doyle reacted at once. This was something unusual. They headed the little group of concerned people who had gathered around the prostrate man. The man eating peanuts stopped flipping them into the air and the fat man also joined the group, moving with that deceptive ease he had displayed on the lane. Bodie bent over the unconscious man on the floor.

'Too much to drink, d'you think?'

Doyle shook his head. 'He's a hospital case.'

The plastic bag of peanuts disappeared into the nondescript man's pocket as he hurried forward.

'Can I help?'

Bodie did not look up. 'No. It's okay. We can manage.'

The fat man said: 'Better leave it to me. I have medical experience – '

'So,' said Bodie firmly, 'have we. We're students.'

'At Guy's Hospital,' amplified Doyle.

By simple inability to be deterred the partners lifted the unconscious man despite the protests of the others and started to help him out. He was in a bad way, that was clear. As they went, Doyle glanced back. He said, in a soft voice that Bodie instantly interpreted and responded to: 'Not everybody was interested.'

Through all the little excitement the handsome Negro had continued to play, hurling his bowling balls down the lane.

'Could be he doesn't want to get involved.'

'Could be,' said Doyle, 'he already is . . .'

As Bodie and Doyle carried the still form away the door marked Private opened. Bob appeared, smoothing down the lapels of his checked sports coat. He saw Jack being helped out by two strangers and a frown appeared between his brows. He almost started after them, and then stopped and looked at the Negro who was just picking up a towel to wipe his hands.

'What happened?'

The black man just was not interested. He went on wiping his hands. 'He fell over. Taken sick.'

Bob no longer wore a smile and his uncertainty made the look on his face even more that of a killer.

They took him to the private hospital and they cleaned him up and put him in a nice clean white bed and they examined him, and the doctor looked up from Jack and said: 'This man is dying.'

'Bad time to go,' said Doyle, and at George Cowley's sharp look, added swiftly: 'With five thousand pounds in your pocket.'

'Perhaps,' said Bodie, 'he thought you could take it with you.'

'And perhaps he'd just made a collection.'

Cowley nodded and spoke to the doctor. 'Have you made a diagnosis? Of the cause as well as the effect?'

Speaking in the tone of voice of one who knows whereof he speaks, the doctor said: 'Plutonium poisoning.'

Cowley looked startled.

'I'm quite sure.' The doctor looked down on his patient. As sure as I can be without all the tests. I've seen it before. Wrote a paper on it, as a matter of fact.'

Cowley digested the information. He did not like it all, not one little bit. He glared at his two alleged ace operatives.

'Plutonium! You get back to that Bowling Alley as fast as you can. Something's going on there. Fraser said: "Something big." Big enough to cost him his life, and big enough for this man to walk in there a dead man.'

In the bed Jack mumbled incoherently. Instantly Cowley bent, his head cocked, straining to listen.

'Swallows, I think,' said the doctor. 'Swallow – something about swallowing.'

Cowley frowned; but the dying man made no further sound. He swung back to see Bodie and Doyle waiting. 'Still here are you?' They started towards the door at once; but Cowley had a nasty little tickling feeling running up and down his spine. 'Hold it!'

They froze.

George Cowley glared at them. 'Take a back-up man with you this time. Charley Kent.'

They let Charley Kent drive.

He was a sociable man, as tough and rough as any in CI5, a contemporary of theirs, and a man you'd trust to have at your back in a fight. He was big-boned, and cheerful, and his face always contained that slight hint of naïveté, as though he was always surprised at the way of the world.

Kent wheeled the car into the Bowling Alley's car park and parked only a few spaces away from the bay where Fraser had been knifed. Doyle and Bodie alighted. They stretched their shoulders and looked at Charley Kent.

'Sit tight, Charley,' said Doyle.

'And,' said Bodie, 'if you're good we'll send you a lemonade out.'

As they moved off towards the lights spilling from the open doors, Charley Kent looked after them, and his face spelled out, loud and clear: 'It's all right for you, mates.'

The noise of the balls hitting pins sounded just the same as it had when they'd left, as it had when they'd listened to the tape of Fraser's last phone call. The clients looked the same, too. The man busily flipping up peanuts asked after the sick man, and so did Bob. Doyle and Bodie made non-commital answers, talking about a touch of 'flu and soon be out and not to worry.

Then the attractive blonde girl walked past, glancing up

at the big wall clock. Her face showed strain.

'Hi!' called Bodie. 'Hasn't he turned up yet?'

'Who?' She stared at Bodie distantly, yet he sensed at once the distancing was no stand-off, rather, it was the absence of relationship with the here and now. 'Hasn't who turned up?'

'Whoever it is you're waiting for.' He nodded towards the clock. The time was twenty minutes to ten. 'The clock's still right.'

The blonde girl walked away, and Bodie stared at her long legs and the way she walked, whilst Doyle sighed. 'Bodie . . .'

'I think,' said Bodie. 'I think I should go to work.'

'That's not what we're here for – '

'It could be exactly what we're here for.'

They stared at the girl as she moved past the crowds towards the counter.

'I was right before when I said she was one edgy lady.'

Bodie followed the girl discreetly and presently Doyle saw him talking to her and Doyle smiled. Good old Bodie did not appear to be making any progress. Bodie persevered.

'Who knows?' he said, all his warm personality in his smile. His dark eyes appraised her with friendly interest. 'I might be able to help.'

Suddenly, as though an inner light had turned on, Patty became pleasant for the first time, and the distant manner vanished as frost vanishes in the sun.

'Yes – yes, you might, at that.'

'Want a Coke?' At the refreshment bar Bodie went on: 'You play a lot, do you?'

'No, not really.'

'But your fellow does? The one you're waiting for?'

'Something like that.' Patty was a dental receptionist, and Bodie made the obligatory jokes about toothache and the pub on the way to the dentist affording a certain quick cure – until the next time. Patty grew more and more jittery. At last, as though coming to a decision that had cost her, she looked around to make sure they were not overheard. Then:

'Look – can we go for a walk?'

'Outside?'

'That's right. Outside.'

Bodie was now sure the girl was a mass of nerves and he wondered why. 'Sure,' he said. 'Why not?'

Outside the Bowling Alley the harsh neon lights cut lozenges and rectangles and bars of light through the shadows. The hum of passing traffic floated in; but the long brick wall of the Bowling Alley muffled a deal of the sound, and the shadows clustered, thick and dark and oddly welcoming.

Patty led the way swiftly past the car park where Charley Kent, taking a good long eyeful, smiled to himself as he saw Bodie and the girl. Some agents working for CI5 got all the luck . . .

At a black rectangle with a dimly-lit sign over it proclaiming that this was an exit, Patty turned in. She halted with a muffled cry and Bodie bumped into her.

In the exit doorway a young couple were closely locked in each other's arms, and the passion going on there made Bodie smile with a connoisseur's taste. Patty stalked on; but the gallant Bodie nodded, and with a quick: 'Sorry,' moved off after those long legs as Patty headed for the entrance to an alleyway leading off towards the distant street.

She halted and swung about, her face illuminated in a random shaft of neon lighting. Bodie came up to her and, before he was aware, Patty leaned forward and kissed him full on the mouth.

The kiss was sweet and Bodie, interested, forced himself not to respond – well, not too much. Then, immediately, Patty broke away, half-turning. She was panting.

'Is that what you wanted?' At Bodie's little grimace, a deliberate facial gesture which meant 'maybe' Patty, hurried on: 'If it isn't you can have whatever you want – for – twenty pounds.'

'Twenty pounds?'

'All right. Fifteen. You tell me.'

'Why?'

'Don't preach to me – just yes or no. Why? Because I need the money. That's why. The double-crosser didn't turn up.'

Patty was now overwrought, near hysteria, and yet she did not cry but flared into a spurt of anger. Bodie recognised the signs. He grabbed her by the wrist and pulled back her sleeve. He stared at her arm in the distant lights of the neons. Her white skin showed the unmistakeable signs of the needle.

'Your pusher – you were waiting for your pusher!'

'No. Johnny wasn't a pusher – ' She was gasping.

'Johnny?'

'He's just a guy I know. Fraser promised to deliver – '

'Fraser. You were waiting for John Fraser.'

'You know Johnny?'

Bodie's face had lost all its easy-going charm. He glared at Patty and some of his feelings made her start back as she saw them starkly revealed. 'Yes, I know Johnny. I should say I used to know Johnny.'

Bodie's grip tightened involuntarily.

'You're hurting me!' Patty tried to draw away. Bodie held her; but he gentled his grip. 'I hardly knew him – '

'You knew him.' Bodie breathed deeply. 'He was doing you a favour, bringing you a fix.'

'He wanted information – we made a deal. That's all.'

'What else did Johnny say?'

'Nothing.' At Bodie's movement, Patty cried out: 'Nothing. He was chasing swallows . . . '

'What?' Bodie produced his I.D. Card and showed it to Patty. Her terrified face crumpled. 'Okay, this is a bust.'

'A bust? But I don't know what he meant.' Patty's face broke up, and the tears started to run down her cheeks. 'He just said he was chasing swallows . . . '

When Charley Kent saw Bodie and the luscious blonde he had sense enough not to pass any comment on the girl's shattered appearance. He opened the car door and Bodie pushed Patty in. She collapsed on to the rear seat, her shoulders shaking.

'Take her back, Charley. Tell Cowley she was waiting for Fraser.' He looked into the rear of the car. 'And don't waste your time on him,' he said, meaning Charley Kent for the girl's benefit. 'He doesn't even know what twenty quid looks like.'

And Bodie slammed the car door with a crash.

The handsome Negro, Doyle and the fat man had at last agreed to play against one another. The fat man seemed to have overcome his reluctance to play with the black, and the game looked set fair to be interesting. Doyle had no hopes of doing anything worth while; but he was satisfied that he was keeping up his cover in the stake-out. Whilst Ray Doyle wondered what that hellion Bodie was up to with that voluptuous if edgy blonde out in the car park, he had to admit that he was getting hooked on bowling. He took the regulation three steps, and his lithe athletic body swung into a smooth co-ordination. He let the muscles pull as they willed, allowing a powerful body-motion to carry his arm away and under and just at the right moment release the ball. The black sphere sped down the lane, just a fraction off centre, beginning to curve, straightening up, catching the front pin just that perfect vector off centre. All the pins went flying.

It was a perfect strike.

Ray Doyle turned around from the line and walked back. He just could not stop the immense smile from spreading all over his face in fat satisfaction.

The Negro looked up. 'Bad luck, mister.' At Doyle's slow loss of the smile and his growing look of puzzlement, the black man explained. 'You had your foot over the line.'

Doyle looked hard at the line. 'I was nowhere near it!'

'It was a foul throw.'

Doyle's nostrils pinched in. Anyone who knew Ray Doyle would recognise the danger signals were flying.

'It was a good throw!'

The fat man chipped in, barely glancing at the Negro. 'He's right – '

'You keep out of it.' The Negro had had enough of fatso. 'I was watching – real close.'

'And I was throwing,' said Doyle in a voice close to a snarl.

Bodie, coming back into the alley saw the scene, saw the way the handsome black man and Doyle were facing each other. Bodie lifted his eyes heavenwards and started across, moving smooth and fast. Bodie could see his partner's face. Doyle had lost his show of temper. For those who did know the ex-policeman he was now menacingly quiet. But still those nostrils pinched in.

'Then, mister,' said the Negro. 'Throw again.'

'You tempt me, *Mister . . .*'

Bodie saw. He knew. He broke into a run and shouted. 'Doyle!'

At the shout Doyle half-turned to face Bodie. He took his eyes off the black man who abruptly exploded into action. A big black fist lashed out and slugged against Doyle's unprotected jaw. Doyle went over in a sprawling half-somersault and landed on the shiny floor in an untidy heap. The fat man took a pace back, and other onlookers hastily looked away. Bodie hauled up, standing over Doyle, and speaking quickly to the Negro.

'He's sorry – very sorry. He drinks a lot, you know. Carry on with your game. I'll try and sober him up.'

Bodie bent down over his partner as the Negro and the fat man, after a brief pause, turned back to resume bowling. Doyle struggled to a sitting position. His face looked highly interesting to the critical gaze of his opposite number.

'What,' ground out Doyle, 'are you doing?'

'I was just going to say that – '

'I would have killed him.'

'You would have killed him.'

'I got a strike. All ten pins.'

'So I see.' Bodie wiped a trickle of blood from the corner of Doyle's mouth, the full lips just a little split. 'And for ten pins you'd blow your cover? A little David like you smashing that Goliath into a multi-piece jigsaw puzzle. Now – how would that look?'

With the savagery ready to burst out of him in red roaring action, Doyle grated out: 'Very good at the moment.'

'On stake-outs,' Bodie told his partner, 'you're a seven-stone weakling – and you let people kick sand in your face.'

For a moment it seemed Doyle would insist on being an Atlas without benefit of the lessons; then he relaxed. He sighed and lifted a hand in acknowledgement. 'You're right. I'm a seven-stone weakling.'

Bodie reached down and hoisted Doyle to his feet. He made a performance out of it, gasping. 'You're an overweight seven-stone weakling, at that, Doyle.'

With Bodie at his shoulder, Doyle was shepherded across to the drinks refreshment bar. Bodie said: 'Ask me about the girl.'

'I never encourage your boasting.'

'She was waiting for Fraser.'

Doyle reacted. His lips pursed up. '*Was* she . . .'

'And just like the Plutonium man, she said – "Swallows . . ." '

'Swallows?'

'Swallows.'

The inquisitorial light in the Interrogation Room of CI5 did not shine with the blinding ferocity it could summon when used to question suspects of deep-dyed villainy. But it did shine undeviatingly upon Patty as Cowley asked her questions. He was not too rough. The blonde girl was clearly almost over the edge.

'I don't know, really,' said Patty, almost crying. 'Just – Swallows.'

'What else?' Cowley urged her, gently but persuasively.

Cowley felt the edginess on him, too. *Something* was going on, something big, as Fraser had said. And Fraser was dead. And there was a man dying of Plutonium poisoning. The answers to the vital questions had to be found, and found quickly.

'I was just going to meet him, that's all.' Patty dabbed at her eyes with a scrap of lace handkerchief. 'He spoke about – Bedford.'

'Bedford?'

'Yes. He said he was going there...'

The door of the Interrogation Room opened a fraction and Cowley's personal assistant, the delectable and icy-distant Betty appeared, carrying a file. She waited for her boss. Cowley looked up and saw her, the reflected light haloing his sandy hair and putting dedicated creases into his forehead. He smiled.

'We'll try this again later, Patty.' He moved to the door and allowed the woman agent to see to Patty. He eyed Betty.

At once she responded. 'The hospital tests confirmed it – it is Plutonium poisoning. And the man – Saward, Jack Saward – is an engineer. At the Atomic Power Plant at Pelbright.'

'Pelbright!' Cowley lost his smile and the muscles along his jaw tightened. 'Isn't there an investigation currently in progress there . . . ?'

'That's right.' Betty tapped the file, the fount of her knowledge. 'Twenty-five pounds of Plutonium went missing.'

Cowley nodded. He had the notion of what at least one part of the jigsaw was about now, and the more he put together the less he liked the picture that emerged. He went along to the private ward of the hospital of CI5 and entered quietly. The doctor was bending over the still form of Jack in the bed. His face was grave. Cowley went forward, and his face was grim and determined. He bent over the bed and stared calculatingly at Jack Saward. Jack was obviously dying. He was shrunken, a mere pale shell of a man.

Without preamble, Cowley said: 'It was to make a bomb, wasn't it?'

Jack did not reply. Cowley glanced up at the doctor. 'He can hear me?'

'I don't know.' The doctor was concerned.

Cowley bent to Jack again. 'We know you took the Plutonium. Where is it?' Jack stirred and moaned. 'Doctor,' went on Cowley in that gruff voice. 'You've *got* to make him talk.'

About to say that there was nothing left to mortal medicine that he could do, the doctor paused. Jack gulped a rattling breath and his head rolled. His lips glistened. He garbled out a few words, laboured, breathy, spoken with immense effort.

'Bedford. Must get – to – Bedford.'

The game between the fat man and the Negro proceeded; but it was clear to Bodie and Doyle, vaguely watching them as they watched everything, that the fat man's heart was not in it. Bodie yawned and put a hand up when the yawn was almost done.

'What time does this place close?'

'One fifteen. Why?'

'Because I've had enough, that's why.' Bodie jerked his head in the direction of the two girls in their short white tennis skirts. They had almost finished their last game and were skylarking around. The man in the raincoat with the protuberant stomach hovered on the sidelines. 'And I could think of a much better way of spending the night, Doyle.'

That sentiment was shared by Bob at the equipment counter. He watched the fat man and the Negro playing, only half-aware of those two tough-looking men on the periphery of his vision. When he caught the fat man's eye, Bob pointedly jerked his head up, staring at the big wall-clock. The time was half past eleven.

'I'm calling it a day,' said the fat man, and began to collect up his things.

The Negro looked disgruntled. 'But we haven't finished the game.'

The fat man managed to squeeze out a smile; but it was clear the smile hurt him somewhere deep. 'You're too good for me.' He pulled a roll of money from his pocket and peeled off a couple of notes. 'Here . . . '

The money changed hands and the black man, satisfied, stared for a moment, and then turned his back ready to collect his own bowling gear. Behind the Negro's back the fat man went through the pantomime of spitting on the floor.

Then he went off to the Gentlemen's Cloakroom.

He stripped off the thin sweater, pulling it up with an effort over the bulge of his stomach. He reached to hang it on a peg and then bent to run water into the basin. As the water ran in, splashing silver, the fat man looked at himself in the mirror. He ran a broad hand over his chin. He wore a T-shirt under the sweater. On the T-shirt had been machine-printed an emblem and a name.

The emblem was a flying bird.

The name was THE SWALLOWS BOWLING CLUB.

Chapter Three

Bodie had just had a brilliant typical Bodie idea. 'Why,' he asked Doyle, 'don't we just run everybody in . . . ?'

Doyle let his smile grow on his mobile lips, feeling the split there, and wincing. 'It would give Cowley a late night, questioning them all.'

'That's right. And we could go home.'

Doyle's smile grew despite the split lip. 'He'd be full of praise, too. Oh, I wouldn't want to take any of your credit for an idea as good as that, would I?'

Thinking, Bodie said: 'You'd admit it was me?'

'Grudgingly. With just the right touch of admiration.'

'You know, Doyle,' said Bodie, grimly, 'what you are, don't you?'

'I know what you *think* I am.'

Bodie finished up his cup of tea and took Doyle's empty cup ready to head back to the refreshment bar. Into the cleared area by the open doors Charley Kent walked in, just as though he owned the place and picked up Bodie and Doyle right away. He gave no sign that he knew them. Bodie nodded at Doyle.

'Must have a message from Cowley.'

Kent saw the door to the Gentlemen's Cloaks and started for it, moving easily, and Bodie took the two cups across to the refreshment bar. If things were going on in the Bowling Alley then there would be eyes watching, and the men from CI5 preferred to observe rather than be observed.

Light girlish laughter broke up from an adjoining lane

and the girls with their short skirts flaring pushed and jostled as they prepared to finish their extended series of games. Doyle, watching them, noticed the man in the raincoat with the stomach that looked as though a slimming diet would do him good. The man turned his back to Doyle, and moved slowly away.

Just before Bodie got to the cloakroom door he passed a man eating peanuts. Bodie filed away the interesting fact that the peanut eater had not, as far as he could see, actually laid a hand to a bowling ball, and had not actually let a ball go skimming down a lane to rattle into the ten waiting pins. Doyle had said you came to a Bowling Alley to bowl. But the peanut eater had not been bowling . . .

Pushing the door open, Bodie half-stood aside as the fat man came out, perspiring already despite his recent wash. He wore his thin sweater, rumpled up over his gut, and he gave Bodie a hard stare as he passed.

Bodie went inside. There were quite a few people here tonight he'd like to know more about. Cowley had a nose for trouble, like Doyle, a copper's nose. Something was going on; but for Bodie what that something was appeared to him as remote as the Moon.

Side by side at the basins, Kent and Bodie stared at each other's reflections in the mirrors.

'News?'

'Information from Cowley.' Kent rapidly filled Bodie in with the news on the Plutonium and the imminent death of Jack Saward. Bodie's eyebrows drew down.

'Cowley can't think the Plutonium's here, surely?'

'I don't think he thinks anything. Just that you should be brought up to date.'

Bodie felt the annoyance. 'This place was probably used for a pay-off, that's all. Though by who . . . ? For what . . . ? Anyway, we're just wasting our time now.'

'Cowley won't see it that way.'

'I know, I know. But I can't think why not.' Bodie reached out to dry his hands under the hot air blower. 'You said this Saward talked about Bedford?'

Kent nodded.

At the door, as a parting shot to vent his frustration, Bodie said waspishly: 'Bedford – that's where it's at.'

At the equipment counter the fat man was making a fuss about checking his stuff in. Bob ran with the play, being properly attentive. He leant forward and lowered his voice.

'Frank should be here anytime now.'

In the same lowered tone, the fat man said: 'If he doesn't make it you'd better phone me.'

'You going straight to Bedford?'

The fat man nodded. 'Straight to Bedford.'

With a final loud goodnight, the fat man headed for the exit. His gross bulk moved still with that deceptive speed. Leaning against the wall by the door the peanut eater, with a bored expression on his face, watched the fat man as he went out. The bag of peanuts was screwed up, with a harsh gesture of finality. The anonymous-looking man straightened from the wall and – just for a moment – the expression on his face was no longer anonymous. Not anonymous at all. He looked, for just that little moment, like a predator moving in for the kill.

Then he tossed the screwed-up plastic bag into a litter bin and followed the fat man out and into the car park.

By the time fatso had managed to climb into his car, with a deal of grunting effort, the peanut eater who no longer ate peanuts was waiting at the wheel of his own car. Smoothly he tooled the motor and followed the fat man's car as it headed out of the car park and turned north.

The two young girls bent over to collect up their belongings. Their short white tennis skirts rode up to reveal their briefs. Doyle and Bodie glanced across and then Doyle said: 'What did Charley want?'

'Nothing important –'

'Good. Tell me later.'

Doyle drew Bodie's attention to the nondescript man in the bulging raincoat. For a brief moment the raincoat flapped open and then as swiftly closed.

'He's been doing that all evening.'

'I was looking at the girls – '

'The raincoat, the raincoat.'

Once again the raincoat flapped open and as swiftly closed.

Bodie and Doyle moved.

Anything unusual, Cowley had said . . . Right, then . . .

The man in the raincoat positioned himself with a casualness he had long cultivated. He twitched the raincoat open again to reveal what had been causing the bulge. A reflex camera nestled on his stomach, hung by its strap around his neck. He was about to press the shutter when he became aware of two looming shadows, one at each shoulder. Startled, flustered, he looked up, not sure which side to look first.

Both sides spelled trouble.

Bodie said: 'Just the man we wanted to see.'

Doyle said: 'You do take family snapshots, don't you?'

Two powerful hands fastened on the man's arms. He was lifted so that his feet left the floor. Smiling, friendly, Bodie and Doyle began to carry the man to the exit.

He swallowed. His throat was very dry, all of a sudden.

'I can explain – '

'Any sudden noise or movement . . . ' said Doyle.

' . . . could result in a broken arm,' said Bodie.

Still smiling broadly, Doyle finished: 'Even two broken arms.'

With his feet just brushing the floor and no more, the camera bug was escorted outside.

Other people were moving out for the night, also, and Bodie had to release the man's arm. Doyle went on out holding the camera bug's arm and guiding him along, this time allowing him to use his own two feet. The man was quite shattered, all his worst fears materialised and gibbering at him.

Leaning against the wall the Negro watched Doyle gripping the raincoated man's arm.

The sneer in the black man's voice was very plain and very cutting.

'Found someone smaller than you, did you, mister?'

Doyle abruptly became aware of the Negro. He recalled that wild haymaker to the jaw. But he was on business and private matters would have to wait.

'Cool it, eh? I haven't got the time.' Doyle went to move on past.

'For the likes of me, is that it?'

Bodie had stood holding the door like a real gentleman for the last person. Now he saw what was developing – again – between the Negro and Doyle. Bodie hustled forward. 'Oh, boy!' he said. 'That's all we need!'

The Negro moved purposively towards Doyle. It was clear he wanted to finish what he'd begun in the Bowling Alley.

'Always looking for trouble, aren't you?'

'Doyle!' Bodie called. 'Show the man your I.D. Card.'

'Yeah,' said Doyle in that voice that came out like a subdued snarl. 'I will. When I'm good and ready.'

With that Doyle thrust the camera bug in the raincoat at his partner. Bodie grabbed. He sighed. 'This is no time to settle the score . . .'

But Ray Doyle was past worrying over that. For him, the score was going to be settled, here and now. The Negro was big, beautifully built, and he started in with another tremendous haymaker. Doyle let it pass and then stepped in and chopped, hard and low, into the Negro's guts. The black man let out a surprised whoof of air and backed away, only to come leaping in again with pummelling fists.

Very severely, Bodie said to the scared camera bug: 'Don't you try anything. He might want to start on you afterwards.'

Terrified, the camera bug swallowed down.

Doyle blocked the vicious blows, slipped the last and

then smashed a right forearm across the black's windpipe. He let him have the old one-two and the Negro staggered back. Careful not to mark that handsome black face Doyle cut the Negro up.

The raincoat shook as the camera bug watched.

'What's he trying to do?' he whispered.

'Make a jigsaw puzzle,' Bodie said.

The Negro was not finished yet. He couldn't understand why he hadn't flattened this guy yet, as he had before. Then a rocket exploded in his guts, a laser beam slashed across his throat again, and he couldn't breathe. Finally, at long long last, Doyle let fly with a spectacular punch to the jaw. The Negro flew back, collapsed in a heap, slid to the floor. Then, and only then, Doyle slowly brought out his I.D. card and flashed it into the glazing eyes.

Bodie, watching, let his eyes look heavenward. Ray Doyle!

George Cowley had kept busy with routine work as he waited for the reports from his agents to come in. He felt the old itchiness. Plutonium, a probable bomb, Bedford, something to do with swallowing – he just did not like the look or smell of this one. CI5 had been set up by Government order, and with the approval of police departments and Government departments responsible. The job had been spelled out as being to elevate criminal intelligence to the very sophisticated levels already existing in military intelligence, and thus to bring to bear an expertise similar to if not better than that used habitually by the modern criminal. Any kind of situation that affected the domestic security of the country was grist to the mills of the squad, the Big A – CI5.

Now Cowley looked up with an absent smile he tried to make more pleasant as his personal assistant walked in carrying a number of blown-up photographs. Betty was incredibly useful about the office, besides being dynamite in the pulchritudinous stakes, and an iceberg with it, and Cowley often had a quiet little period of amusement when he wondered just how some of his men made out with the delectable Betty – Bodie and Doyle, say. Particularly Bodie and Doyle.

Taking the photographs he spread them out and then put on his heavy-rimmed glasses.

Almost at once he felt the sense of outrage, of being on a wild-goose chase, flood through him. He raised an eyebrow; but his face remained perfectly grave.

Betty looked down on the photographs. She smiled, a small wan smile, not so much embarrassed as encompassing the frailties of little men in raincoats.

Cowley looked over his glasses at this particular little man in a raincoat. The camera bug sat on a hard wooden seat by the far wall and looked stricken. His hands were moist, his forehead was wet and his mouth was dry. And he desperately wanted to go to the lavatory.

'It's a hobby,' he said. He felt the desperation. He tried to explain. 'Just a hobby.'

Cowley did not reply. He looked down on the photographs that had been rushed here by Charley Kent and developed and printed at top speed in the darkrooms of CI5. He sighed.

Every photograph was of a pretty girl – but in almost every case the photograph took in merely the girl's legs, or bottom, in action poses as the girls bowled. The short white tennis skirts looked very fetching as they flared.

'Just a hobby,' mumbled the camera bug.

Betty looked from the corners of her eyes at the grave face of her boss. Not a muscle moved. If she expected a reaction, then George Cowley was not the man to give anything away.

Frank Turner had driven as fast as he dared from Bedford, but traffic snarl-ups where the engineers and navvies were putting in a new fly-over to carry a brand-new ring road had held him up. He left his car in the Bowling Alley car park and lifted the leather carry-all with great care. He held the gripped-handle in his fist and he felt like he was carrying the world.

He walked steadily across the lot towards the entrance.

Watching from a dark corner, Bodie and Doyle saw the squarely-built man leave his car and head for the Bowling Alley. They registered the carry-all of a type similar to others they had seen inside used for the transport of bowling balls.

Bodie yawned.

'I think we can call it a day.'

'Another ten minutes or so yet.' Doyle was never one to cop off duty early. His experience as a policeman, a constable, driving a patrol car, as a detective constable, had conditioned him into at least the knowledge that trouble blew up right at the moment when you relaxed.

Bodie sighed, and yawned again and nodded to the man carrying the leather bag as he went into the Bowling Alley.

'He won't have much of a game.'

Doyle looked across. 'You could be right.'

Inside the Bowling Alley Frank headed straight for the equipment counter. Bob's face relaxed as Frank appeared and the big man eased his shoulders in the brilliant checked sports coat.

'You're late,' Bob greeted the newcomer. 'Nothing wrong, is there?'

'No. Delayed, that's all.'

Frank lifted the leather carry-all and with great care placed it on the counter. Bob eyed it as a rabbit might eye a snake, fascinated, repelled, helpless . . .

'We had trouble earlier,' he said, at last. 'Just before you phoned.' At Frank's reaction he went on quickly. 'I knew we were safe. Nothing came of it.'

'Serious?'

'At the time I suppose it was . . . An agent. I had to – silence him.' Bob put a hand to the back of his belt. The knife snugged, cleaned and sharp and ready for the next interfering nosey-parker. 'And Jack Saward collapsed, too. He was taken to hospital – '

Frank's mouth opened and closed. Then, in his South African burr, he said harshly: 'Then we've failed. How can we go through with it now?'

'Failed? Nothing has happened. We're as safe as we ever were.' He put his hand on the carry-all. 'Anyway, there's nothing anyone can do now. Is it set?'

Frank nodded. His lips pursed up. Moving with a slow deliberateness that emphasised the importance of his actions, he unzipped the carry-all. He unzipped it only a short way and reached in a finger. The sound of a switch closing made a dry, final click.

'It is now.'

Bob lifted the carry-all carefully and placed it gently on a shelf. He let out a breath. His forehead was wet.

Frank looked around. 'Number One gone?'

'Yes, he left on time. All the literature will go out as planned.'

Frank nodded and started to turn away. Then he spoke over his shoulder, already in the action of leaving.

'You'd better leave soon. You know what kind of area that covers.'

'Yes,' said Bob, with deep feeling. 'Any time now.'

Frank walked steadily towards the exit. The feeling of relief at having got rid of the carry-all was compounded by the realisation of what he had set in train when he'd flicked that switch to ON. He tried not to run. He felt hot. He unbuttoned his safari jacket. He wanted to get away, well away, miles away . . .

Outside he headed for his car.

Watching the people leaving, Bodie and Doyle were about to call it a day as Bodie had cuttingly suggested more than once.

They saw the man who had gone in with the carry-all coming out without it. They looked at him as they looked at everyone. A random shaft of brilliant neonlight, yellow as a buttercup, fell on the man and his opened safari jacket.

He wore a T-shirt.

Bodie and Doyle saw the emblem on the shirt, saw the lettering.

They saw the swallow.

They saw THE SWALLOWS BOWLING CLUB.

Bodie and Doyle looked at each other just the once. One look, one fleeting glance, was all that was necessary. Here, at least, was one piece of this crazy jigsaw fitting into place.

Frank Turner crossed to his car, feeling hot, and unlocked the driving side door. He wanted to get away. He wanted out. He'd done his part, and done it well, and he believed in the causes which were the reason he had done what he had. He wondered briefly what could be the matter with Jack Saward. He hoped Bob wouldn't hang around too long. He opened the door and a man suddenly appeared before him, smiling, easy, relaxed.

'Can I beg a lift?'

Frank's startled look, about to be replaced by a look that would see this interloper off, abruptly congealed.

Another man, as tough as the first, appeared, flashing an official card.

'He's with me,' said the first man, as though that explained everything.

Between them, Bodie and Doyle got Frank into the back seat. Then they took over Frank's car. Bodie drove. Doyle sat in the back with Frank. Doyle was ready, instantly, to deal with any attempt by the fellow who belonged to the Swallows Bowling Club to leave the car.

As the car swished past the exit doors two girls appeared, giggling, drawing their coats about themselves as the two fellows they felt sure they'd picked up for the night followed. Bob moved out after them, holding the sweater one of the girls had forgotten and left lying on the seat by the lane.

He started to shout to the girls to hang on for the

sweater. Frank's car sped past. For an instant Bob could hardly believe what he was seeing. That was Frank's car. And there was Frank in the back seat next to a tousle-haired customer who looked as rough and tough as anyone Bob had met. He looked something like one of those two fellows who had been hanging about all night, having a go at bowling, the two who had taken Jack to hospital.

As the car sped past him, Frank looked out of the window.

He stared straight at Bob. In his face was a look of desperate helplessness.

Bob lost his smile. He felt shaken. He stood there, transfixed. Then, viciously, he shook himself and turned hurriedly back to the Bowling Alley.

He ran across to the equipment counter and yanked down the phone. He dialled and hammered with his fist on the counter. The ringing note stopped. A voice said 'Hello?'

Bob said: 'Tony? It's Bob. Get over here with Les.' Then he paused, and said: 'Could be big trouble. They've got Frank. Depends if he talks. Get over here and be prepared to put the boot in.'

Chapter Four

This time the Interrogation Room spotlight shone with greater brilliance. Its rays fell harshly on Frank Turner as he lolled in the straight-backed chair. But he had recovered his composure. His safari jacket was pulled straight and his hair was unruffled. He sat easily, his hard face showing his feelings of contempt for these little bureaucratic men of the Establishment. They'd done nothing for him or his country, except interfere. Now he and his associates had them over a barrel, and the sensation flooded a sense of power into Frank Turner. He smirked an arrogant smile, confident, poised, fancying himself in command of the situation.

George Cowley had dealt with people like Frank Turner before, and every time was different, every time you had to pull another rabbit out of the hat.

He flicked a propaganda pamphlet before him, letting the light runnel off the big black lettering: KEEP AFRICA WHITE.

'Keep Africa White,' said Cowley. 'And London dead. Is that it, Turner?'

Turner just didn't bother to answer. The job had been done, the demands made, and the due processes set in motion. The recalled memory of that switch going over with its final and chilling click made him sweat and tremble – and also made him glee with the sense of power. He was well away from that . . .

Bodie and Doyle stood silently in the shadows of the room, waiting for the chief to get to grips with this part of the problem. It had all been a messy business so far, with far too many suspects, not enough leads, and simple leg-work – a stake-out in this instance – bringing boredom and frustration. But they felt they were getting somewhere. This guy Frank Turner had some of the answers.

Cowley saw his two alleged ace agents standing by the wall. He scowled, glaring over the top of his heavy-rimmed spectacles.

'Are you still here?'

Quietly, Ray Doyle said: 'The Bowling Alley's closed now.'

Bodie stretched his broad shoulders and said to Doyle: 'He's letting us go home.' He started to move towards the door, smiling.

'Stay here!' Cowley's voice lashed out, cracking. 'Both of you!'

Without waiting for their reactions Cowley swung back to glare balefully upon Frank Turner. With a gesture of supreme contempt he screwed up the pamphlet in his broad capable hands. He threw the crumpled ball full in Frank's face.

'We know everything – everything – except the location of the bomb.'

The sneer in Frank's voice brought up the hackles of the CI5 men.

'Quite an exception . . .'

Cowley moved back and stood, pensively, surveying Frank. He spoke in a thoughtful voice. 'Cool customer . . . Just exactly what are you trying to achieve?'

Frank's smile broadened.

'I thought you'd read our pamphlet.'

That got to Cowley. His craggy face abruptly assumed that hard look that struck the cold horrors down those people unfortunate enough to have experienced Cowley's methods. He almost leaped forward and hit Frank Turner. But he controlled himself and then, opportunely, the phone rang. Doyle answered.

'Special Branch. For you, sir.'

Cowley took the phone and removed his spectacles, swinging them by one earpiece. 'Cowley here.' A pause. 'That's right, I called.' He nodded. 'I thought we might have got our wires crossed.' He cupped the mouthpiece, the glasses angling up and glinting in reflected light. He spoke across to Doyle and Bodie. 'They've had a man on the case all along.'

He uncovered the mouthpiece and said into it: 'We've got Frank Turner here. Yes. As you wish, then.' He put the phone down. The two CI5 agents looked at him questioningly. Cowley moved across to stand before Frank. He looked as though he was about to order the hangman to pull the lever.

'I don't know if you're interested, Turner. But your base at Bedford is about to be raided . . .'

The man who no longer needed to eat peanuts tooled his car quietly up the drive of the large old house outside Bedford. The night breathed quietly about him. He opened the door and got out and his right hand went under his coat. When it came out it held a Service automatic. It was perfectly clear that the ex-peanut eater was accustomed to handling guns.

Special Branch had called in the local police and weapons had been issued. The men were waiting. They began to walk up to the house, a line of dark shadows against the trees.

The raid was carried out meticulously, without fuss, a routine operation that, if it went wrong, could end up with guns blazing and blood splashing and men being killed.

The peanut eater kicked the door in and belted into the house. In the big room with its Printing Press and the litter of leaflets exhorting Africa to be white, the fat man from the Bowling Alley staggered up. He looked stricken as the police burst in after the first man with the big gun in his fist. The uniforms filled the room. The plain clothes men started their work. The fat man and his accomplice put their hands up. There was, really, nothing else they could do.

The reports came in. All satisfactory. George Cowley pulled his glasses off and stared challengingly at Frank Turner, who lolled with such contemptuous ease in the straight-backed chair in the Interrogation Room.

'Raided, Turner,' he said. 'All wrapped up.'

'It makes no difference to me.'

Cowley decided that a little of the contempt ought to be leached away from Frank Turner. He tapped his spectacles as he spoke. 'Oh, a political animal. You'll die for the cause. Well, I'll ask you just once more. Where is the bomb? The Plutonium bomb?'

Frank's sense of triumph made him smile with an insolence he was well aware would grate on the nerves of these little puppets of oppressive government unable to see which way their duty lay.

'You'll never find it.'

Ray Doyle's tousle-haired head moved into the rays of the lamp. His mobile lips were firm. He looked utterly determined.

Doyle said: 'It's at the Bowling Alley.'

Bodie nodded confirmation. The recollection came to both partners. Frank Turner in his safari jacket striding into the Bowling Alley with the leather carry-all, very late to find a game, and then returning, showing his Swallows T-shirt – coming out of the Bowling Alley without the carry-all.

Doyle told Cowley. Bodie agreed. Cowley looked up.

He started for the door and the two agents followed. Then George Cowley swung about. His face showed a tight unpleasant mask of fury, a fury controlled and contained and used, as he so often preached to new men. He jerked his head at Frank.

'*Bring him!*'

The Army bomb squad was on the way. The police were informed. But Cowley and his men knew this one was down to them. This was the kind of situation for which CI5 had been created. Cowley's Rover 3500 howled through the night streets, the lights whirling past in a streaming succession of colours. Already, this night, a car had been driven through waterfalls of light, with a dying man at the wheel. And now, again, a car was hurtling along in a race against time – and if the race was lost then all the men in the car were dead men – and many millions more . . .

The Bowling Alley lay in darkness save for a few security lights. The silence sat eerily on this place that had so recently been filled with laughter and shouts and the clack and rattle of bowling balls and the staccato clatter of ten pins being knocked helter-skelter. The shadows groped along the shining floor. The big wall clock ticked solemnly on. The time was nine minutes to two o'clock.

Tiny sounds obtruded on the scene, growing louder as the doors were bashed open and Cowley and his men came in.

Straight to the equipment counter Cowley led on, walking briskly, his shoulders squared. Bodie and Doyle flanked Turner, who looked about, suddenly uneasy, and yet hiding that, keeping up his intense feelings of satisfaction and triumph.

'Which one?' snapped Cowley, looking at the shelves.

Doyle indicated the leather carry-all they had seen Turner bring in and Cowley lifted it gently out and placed it on the counter. He unzipped it all the way. Gleaming steel was revealed in the slanting security lighting, dials and switches and meters – and a timing device that made George Cowley compress his lips.

With that granite look on his face, Cowley turned to Frank. He made a small motion towards the carry-all – towards the bomb.

'It's all yours, Turner . . .'

Frank's smile remained; but his voice was not altogether

steady. 'We had an agreement – all of us Swallows. If any of us was caught – in this situation – we swore we'd go up with it.'

Harshly, Doyle put in: 'Very idealistic, Turner. But this is for real.'

'How long have we got?' demanded Cowley.

Their eyes lifted and they all looked at the clock on the wall. The minute hand jerked around approaching two o'clock.

'Minutes,' said Frank Turner. 'Just minutes.'

'Minutes, eh?' said Bodie, aggressively. His eyebrows drew down and he glared at Frank. 'A few minutes, and then what? You'll be spread over an area of ten, fifteen, twenty miles?'

'And so will you!'

Cowley shook his head. 'Wrong!' He snapped his fingers. 'Keys!'

Doyle took the keys to the handcuffs Frank was wearing and threw them to Cowley. He caught them as a trout catches a fly.

'Hold him.'

Under Cowley's harsh orders, Bodie and Doyle unlocked one cuff and then relocked it around the central heating pipe that ran down the wall behind the equipment counter. The other cuff was clamped around Frank's ankle. He could reach the counter and the carry-all – and that was as far as he could reach.

Cowley regarded Frank with that baleful stare that would frighten a charging tiger. 'Maybe we'll have enough time to get away, maybe we won't. But we have a chance, Turner, a chance. Which is more than you'll get.'

'But you'll get a good view,' Bodie told Frank Turner. 'A very good view. We promise you that.'

The clock ticked away another minute.

Frank regarded them as they moved back from the counter. He licked his lips. These three hard cases – Cowley, the older was called, a real hard egg, and the dark smoothie Bodie, and the deceptively easy Doyle – they were going to leave him here. They meant it. His gaze swivelled to the leather carry-all. He knew what was in that. Jack Saward – well, Jack was out of it now, dead, he'd been told, of Plutonium poisoning. That was the way he'd go himself, Plutonium poisoning – although the poison would be shaped like a mushroom and he'd be spread out over twenty miles of London . . .

His mouth pained him and he realised he'd bitten through his lip. He crumbled. He crumbled in face of unrealised realities, harsh and cruel, thrust before him in a way he could not evade.

'Don't leave me here! Don't leave me!'

They halted, and turned back, and regarded him curiously, as they might regard a specimen under a microscope.

'Don't leave me – I'll try. I promise I'll try!'

Silently, the three CI5 men watched as Frank threw himself on the bomb. His agile fingers went to work. The sweat started out afresh on his forehead, thick, greasy drops. He blinked and cursed and his fingers shook and they mustn't shake, not if he was to stop himself being blown all the way back to the Cape . . .

Charley Kent walked up behind Bodie and Doyle; but he, too, like the others, remained silent. They concentrated on Frank who worked on the timing device, knowing what to do and desperately frightened that he would do it wrong, and shaking and slobbering and trying to concentrate a mind that kept shrieking at him that he was a dead man.

A voice spoke over that hushed scene. A hard voice, an edgy voice, a voice that sounded like ground glass grinding between millstones.

'Get your hands off it, Frank.'

Bodie and Doyle swivelled to stare. The door marked Private had opened silently and Bob stood there. His sports coat caught a security light's shaft and the brilliant vulgar checks shouted at them. In his hand the automatic gleamed, blue-black.

‘We swore an oath – a promise.’ Bob was worked up to the point of near-transformation. He was rock steady, hard, dedicated. ‘If we had to – we said we’d go with the bomb! Remember, Frank? Remember?’

From the shadows two large, hairy, plug-ugly men advanced. They were unarmed; but they looked the kind who could break a few ribs and legs and arms in a dust-up. They moved in for the kill.

Cowley glanced up at the clock. The minute hand trembled, shivered, and then jerked forward another notch towards doomsday.

Frank babbled almost incoherently: ‘We’ll all get killed.’

‘That’s up to you. Turner,’ snapped Cowley.

‘Wrong.’ Bob shook his head, reprovingly, chastisingly. ‘Very wrong. That’s up to me.’

Bodie and Doyle moved gently, hardly appearing to change position. The dark-haired man and the fair tousle-haired man looked – somehow – different from the two who had so rebelliously attempted to play at bowling and stake-out this place.

Doyle said: ‘When you’ve got to go –’

Bodie said: ‘You should be able to choose the way.’

Bodie tensed himself to hurl forward and try to get under the gun. The fellow with the garish sports jacket might be bluffed, put off balance for just the length of time necessary for Bodie to get him –

Doyle saw. He saw Bodie. He knew what his partner was going to do – correction – what his partner was going to try to do. And Doyle knew there wouldn’t be time.

A loose ten-pin ball lay to one side. It had been cracked around the thumb hole and was awaiting repair. Doyle saw it. He did not stop to think. To think was to act, and to act was to move. The bowling ball was in his hand, his fingers and thumb sought and found the grip holes without pause. The ball swung back, it flew forward and released. Spinning, glinting under the security lights, it rolled across the floor straight at Bob’s legs.

The hurtling bowling ball overtook Bodie who was running crouched and flat out. The ball spun past. Bob saw Bodie. He snouted the automatic around and the ten-pin ball struck him shrewdly across the shin. He let out a yell and the gun angled and let loose with the blam of a thirty-eight round. Charley Kent bellowed and spun about, clutching at his shoulder.

Then Bodie was on Bob with the pounce of the tiger.

The first of the two plug-uglies launched himself at Doyle as Bodie began to take Bob apart. Doyle turned from that bowling action, swung, ducked, avoided the massive blow and let rip with a swinging roundhouse that crunched into the heavy's jaw. The thug went over and hit shoulder first on the shiny floor. He skidded.

The other plug-ugly thought he could deal with the fellow with the craggy face and screwed-up eyes and sandy hair. He looked past it. Cowley snatched up a loose pin and brought the heavy plastic over and down and slugged the heavy across the side of the head. The thug simply went on and over and out.

Frank Turner took one horrified look, cast his gaze up at the clock. It was almost two o'clock. Almost zero hour.

Frenziedly he went back to his work on the timing device.

And, this time, his hands did not shake and he could see clearly with no sweat blurring his vision.

The two separate fights battled on. Both Doyle and Bodie knew they were up against real professional toughs. But they traded blows, blocked the incoming, used their feet, worked on their men. Eventually Doyle set up his man, slashed him across the throat, and then hit him cleanly.

The plug-ugly went over on to the bowling lane and slid. He slid all the way up the lane and crashed into the ten pins all set up to receive him. He lay there and he did not move.

Bodie and Bob tangled. Blood decorated Bob's face. Bodie hit him again, took a wild punch in the guts, whoofed, and set to work in earnest. He caught a smashing punch on his left forearm, twisted, got a grip, hurled Bob into a racked stack of chairs. The chairs tangled on to the floor. Bob staggered up, seized up a chair and hurled it at Bodie.

Bodie ducked. The chair clattered away. With a second chair gripped high, Bob plunged in. He brought the chair down wickedly. The metal legs raked for Bodie's face.

The chair whistled on past. Bodie went in low, drove a hard, skewering punch where it would do the most good, kicked Bob as he went down, landed a tattoo of punches on his face, and finished up with a right-hander to the temple.

Bob lay spreadeagled on the floor.

The ten-pin ball lay close. Bodie, breathing evenly, picked it up. He held it in both hands, his elbows in, ready to smash the ball down on to Bob.

But Bob lay there and he, too, no longer moved.

Charley Kent, his face whiter than usual, staggered up gripping his shoulder.

George Cowley held the gun he had whipped from the shoulder holster at the ready. He surveyed the scene.

'Finished, have you?'

He spoke to his men – but Frank Turner slumped back from the carry-all. He let out a great whooshing sigh of relief. The clock ticked on the last minute to two o'clock.

'Finished,' said Frank Turner. Then he sat down very sharply, on the floor, and started to shake.

Cowley holstered his gun as Doyle moved up to him. Bodie appeared still holding the ten-pin bowling ball.

'Good work,' said George Cowley, Chief of CI5. 'You can take the rest of the night off.'

He turned away to check on Frank Turner and noticed the ball in Bodie's hands.

With only the trace of a smile, Cowley took the ball. From where he stood he pivoted, took three precise steps and hurled the ball. It went on to the lane with a crash, spun, pelted down towards the pins.

Everyone stood watching as though mesmerised.

The ball hit the pins and cleared them all. A perfect strike.

Bodie and Doyle, hot with the memories of their own bowling feats, exchanged disgusted glances.

As one, they said: '*He'd* play for money!'

Chapter Five

Back in 1971 Ray Doyle was still a policeman, driving a patrol car in partnership with Syd Parker. They got on well together, for Parker was a veteran of the Force and had taken the young Doyle under his wing. Syd Parker was forty or so, never made sergeant, and accepting that with a philosophy that accepted much of unhappiness in life, sought for the consolations to be found in the human condition. Doyle liked him and his wife, Susan, who was pretty sick and needed a lot of attention and nursing. But Syd was a paragon there, and Doyle was always welcome.

Doyle was doing the driving, tooling Charley Victor Four along the dismal London street. The pubs were doing a roaring trade for the heat wave that had closed in on the city had given everyone a raging thirst. The sun belted down brassily. There was no wind. Just how much longer this was going on for, not even the weather men on the radio could say. But it was good for the cricket, that was for sure.

Charley Victor Four left that dreary street and the heat devils whirled up from the hot tarmac as the patrol car entered a smart residential suburb. Here the houses were set back from the road in greenery. But the trees and bushes all looked wilted in the heat.

Syd Parker wiped a hand over his lips.

He was not a particularly large man; but he had plenty of muscle and knew how to arrest a drunk. He sighed.

'The King's Arms is wide open – and we're out here, Ray.'

'We can stop for a tea along at Rosie's – yes?'

'Yes. And we can pick up the latest score. With the pitch as hard as this the seamers should have a field day – maybe break a few heads, too . . .'

The police car passed along the street and turned into the Avenue. From the King's Arms the voice of the TV cricket commentator pitched out into the street, excited, burbling away, reeling off the statistics with the competence that came from having a scorer with Wisdens back to Grace at his elbow.

'That's it. The last ball, leaving 203 runs ahead and an almost certain win. We now return you to the studio.'

In the pub the barman, Freddy, switched off the TV set and turned to his customers. They were all regulars. Freddy beamed at Fitch, who wore a sports blazer and who now spoke up.

'I said it! I told you 1971 was going to be our year. Marvellous. Anybody want to wager against them?'

The King's Arms was a classy pub, with horse brasses and old sporting prints, and an air of ease. It had been built in the early 1930s and carried that square-edged appearance of buildings of that date, offset by cornices and brick patterns. The clientele were all pretty well-heeled. They were all dressed casually, for it was hot enough to call for light sports shirts and slacks. Only Fitch looked out of place, still dressed smartly in a regimental blazer. His face shone with excitement. The glasses ranked over the bar on their brass rails did not gleam as brightly.

'Anybody take a wager? I'll give five to one –'

A heavy voice spoke at Fitch's elbow.

'And if you lose, what will you pay with?'

Fitch's happy face lost all its humour. His mouth closed sharply. He looked abruptly shrunken.

Bill Haydon stood against the bar. Haydon was big, tough, around forty or so. He wore expensive slacks and hand-tooled cordovans. His fancy shirt was open to the waist, revealing a powerful and hairy physique. He liked to think he looked good dressed like that. The gold coin twinkling against his chest, and the gold chain around his neck, added just that air of hot Spanish sunlight to his appearance that made people notice him. As a member of the criminal fraternity, Bill Haydon had come a long way since his Old Kent Road days. He had lost almost all his Cockney twang. He was in the big time, the really big time, and he flaunted his wealth and power so as to be seen. And, best of all, no one could touch him. He always kept his nose clean.

But nothing could disguise the menace he exuded. In even the simplest of movements, the most casual remarks, he always conveyed that depth of power, that menace, that impression of a man whom it would be sure-fire death to cross.

Fitch was only too unhappily aware of Haydon's enormous power and toughness. He licked his lips and fought the smile back on to his shining face.

'W – why, hallo, Haydon.'

Haydon leaned forward. 'Pay 'em with the money the cops gave you. Is that right, Fitch?'

Fitch looked frail, and, somehow, faintly ridiculous in his regimental blazer.

'I – I'm not sure what you mean.'

'No?'

Haydon gripped Fitch's arm, his powerful fingers digging through the cloth. Fitch looked agonised. Freddy, the barman, leaned over the bar and put a hand on Haydon's arm.

'Haydon – ' Freddy started to say.

Big Bill Haydon appeared to shrug. He pushed Freddy. The barman staggered back, catching his foot, landed heavily against the ranked bottle and glass display before the glinting mirrors. Glasses broke. Blood spouted in a greasy line from the back of Freddy's hand. He winced with the sudden stabbing pain.

Haydon ignored the barman. He bent his lowering face on the cringing Fitch.

'I've been looking forward to this little talk, Fitch.'

Freddy lumbered upright. He put the back of his cut hand against his mouth and tasted the salty tang of blood. He moved forward with a nasty look in his eyes and pressed the bell under the bar. Someone had to sort this guy Haydon out, and quick . . .

'So you don't know what I mean?' Haydon gripped Fitch's arm. 'But I think you do.'

'No – honestly – '

'Oh, you know. We all know. You're the information king, Fitch. But this time you made a big mistake when you grassed on *my* boys . . . *my* operation . . . that's why . . . ' he pulled Fitch closer, shoving his squared-off chin into the smaller man's face, 'I'm going to deal with you personally.'

He hit Fitch. When Big Bill Haydon hit a man, that man knew he had been hit. Fitch crashed backwards against the bar which gouged him cruelly in the back; but he couldn't gasp. His mouth was a mass of blood and four teeth were broken and the bits gritty against his tongue. He did not fall down, but hung against the bar like a bird pinned to a tree by an arrow. Haydon moved in.

The landlord appeared in answer to Freddy's summons on the alarm bell. Harry Scott was as big and as tough as Bill Haydon. About forty, like Haydon, he had a large well-formed head and a pugnacious face. And he didn't like people having punch-ups in his pub.

'You're out of line, Haydon.' He jerked his head. 'I don't care what goes between you and Fitch. But not here.'

Haydon kept his grip on Fitch, holding him jammed against the bar. 'Keep out of this, Harry.'

'You're in my pub. In my area.' Haydon appeared to hesitate at this and Scott went on speaking. 'I can back it up.'

The customers in the bar were subtly sorting themselves out. Haydon was an astute man; he recognised the heavies Harry Scott could rely on. And he was out of his own area.

'It's rain check time, then. But I'll be seeing you again, Fitch. I'll be seeing you.'

As he spoke he struck Fitch again and this time he released the little dandified fellow who somersaulted back to crash to the floor and lie motionless. Haydon strolled to the door, apparently unruffled. He turned to shout back at Scott.

'*Your* area? Only by the grace of God – and Bill Haydon! London belongs to me, Harry. I just tolerate small timers like you – because you don't amount to anything.'

Harry Scott's pugnacious face empurpled. He pushed up to the bar flap and lifted it. He was shaking with rage. 'Why, you – ' He crossed the bar after Haydon who went out. 'Come back here!'

As Harry Scott plunged out like an avenging fury after Bill Haydon, Fitch moaned and rolled over. Freddy leaned down to look at him. 'Haydon? Harry'll soon settle *him*!'

Fitch swallowed down and realised that was a mistake. Blood and bits of splintered teeth gagged him. Freddy looked up as Harry Scott re-entered the pub. A change had come over the landlord. Although still boiling with anger, he looked as though he had just had a very bad scare.

'Harry?' said Freddy. The concern in his voice was genuine. 'What's wrong?'

Scott was shaking. He waved a hand before his face, vaguely.

'We've got to fix him, Freddy. We've got to fix Haydon!'

Freddy wrapped a handkerchief around the cut in his hand. His face became suddenly unreadable.

'Yeah,' said the barman. 'We've got to fix him!'

Back on duty for the night Parker and Doyle were just preparing to leave the local station for their waiting prowl car and the nightly patrol when the desk sergeant called them across for a last word. He was a biggish man running a little to fat and, like them all, was in shirt-sleeve order. Big black patches of sweat stained under the armpits of his blue shirt.

'Fitch called in – scared.' The desk sergeant told them. 'Thinks Bill Haydon is after him. Fitch lives in your area, so keep an eye out. Any questions? Parker? Doyle?'

Both policemen indicated they had no questions.

'Oh, and another thing Fitch mentioned. Haydon and Harry Scott had a run in. Odd, according to Fitch. There could be trouble brewing there, too.' The desk sergeant smiled, knowing these two. 'Have a nice, quiet, pleasant night.'

'A hot one, that's for sure,' said Syd Parker as they went out to their patrol car.

Tooling along Broadway with Parker driving they settled in for the night shift. They checked their equipment thoroughly and then Doyle said: 'How's Susan?'

'About the same.' Parker sounded discouraged.

'She should see a doctor.'

'What I keep telling her. She's afraid to.' Syd Parker sounded vexed and apprehensive – and tired. 'I think she's just – tired out. Two kids in four years. Tired out.'

They drove in silence for a space, and then Ray Doyle rapped out: 'Slow down!'

At once Parker, alert, eased off the accelerator. 'What?' He glanced out through the passenger window at what had taken Doyle's attention. 'What is it?'

Parked at the kerb stood a gleaming motor bicycle, brand new, superb, a magnificent machine. Doyle looked at it avidly.

'Moto-Guzzi. Classic bike. Light frame. Big engine. Big, big price. But I'm going to have one some day.'

'Get your priorities right, Ray. First you make sergeant, maybe inspector – then the bike. Okay?'

Doyle nodded, knowing what the words really covered up, liking Syd all the more. The patrol car hummed quietly through the hot nighted streets, and the two patrolmen watched their beat with attentive, all-seeing eyes.

Past the end of a street lined by good-quality if not top-class apartment blocks the patrol car tooled gently, a ghost prowling the night. Suddenly Syd Parker hit the brakes and brought the car to a halt under the drooping trees, masked in shadow. He nodded off to a side street where a car was parked, a large, opulent car, American, with a deal of chrome.

'That's Haydon's car.'

Doyle looked, and then checked the apartment block where most of the windows were mere black rectangles, only a few showing lights.

'And that's Fitch's apartment block.'

They regarded each other. Then Parker switched off the engine. His face revealed nothing save the simple desire to do his job as best he could.

'Worth a look, don't you think?' As Doyle started to open his door, Parker went on: 'No. You stay here.'

Although the apartment block was a reasonably high-class residential building, it had not been equipped with a lift. Parker decided to go on up the stairs to Fitch's flat. He had a funny kind of premonition. As he went up the treads the caretaker, Gilbert, shuffled out of his ground-floor door carrying a garbage disposal bag which he intended to dump out in the area for the morning's collection. He looked up to see Parker just heading around the bend in the stairs. Gilbert wondered what was going on; but it was no business of his. He was still trying to get over the surprising fact that a week ago he'd celebrated his sixtieth birthday. Not that celebrate was the right word. He didn't feel so good, and he was tired all the time, and life didn't get any easier. He shuffled off, dismissing the policeman from his mind, concentrating on his aches and pains.

Parker panted up the stairs to Fitch's door. He was about to knock when the unmistakable sound of a gunshot boomed through the wood.

There was no hesitation. Parker kicked the door open and burst inside. As he did so he shouted: 'Police!'

Inside the door a dark shape lay sprawled on the carpet. No lights were on in this room of the apartment and it was difficult to see; but Parker saw at once that this dark shape was the body of Fitch, and he was probably dead. A scraping sound brought his head up. Against the lighter rectangle of the window the silhouetted shape of a man was climbing out and jumping down on to the landing of the fire escape.

'Police!' bellowed Syd Parker. 'Hold it!'

As he spoke the man in the window turned. His upper body leaned in at the opening. There was no making out his face in that erratic light. The gun in his hand belched flame.

Ray Doyle heard the first gunshot and instantly he was out of the car and sprinting for the flats. He went in the door and up the stairs like a scalded cat. Halfway up he heard the second gunshot. It rolled down the treads like a thunderclap.

Flinging himself the last flight Doyle fairly hurled through the open door to Fitch's flat.

Trained reflexes prevented him from tripping headlong over the sprawled body by the doorway. A single glance in the random illumination from the window told him this was Fitch – a dead Fitch. Doyle saw the second dark shape, saw the uniform, the blue shirt, the fallen uniform cap, saw the face, saw . . .

The window! Doyle blundered across, his co-ordination for the moment completely gone. That was Syd Parker there, Syd Parker, with a sick wife, Syd Parker with a ghastly great hole blown in him . . .

He glared down the fire escape. A man was just leaping off the bottom rungs, the metal ladder swinging. Doyle turned back. It would be quicker down the stairs. He did not look at Syd as he passed. He went out the door and he felt his guts, his chest, his very being swelling and choking him. He wanted that man who was now running through the area. He wanted him very badly.

In the area the caretaker, Gilbert, crouched back with a hand pressed to his heart as the dark figure with the gun leaped off the fire escape. Gilbert wanted none of that malarkey. He saw the man, saw the gun, saw fleeting erratic shadows. And then the man was gone and Gilbert could breathe again.

Doyle hit the street and rushed out across the road to the patrol car. Haydon's car started up with an over-revved engine. The lights snapped on. Tyres screeched. The big car squealed as it spun away from the kerb.

Doyle smashed his way across the road, riding invisible barriers of air. He was panting. He got under the wheel of the prowl car; but Haydon's car was gone, and by the time the road junction up ahead was reached, long gone. Doyle snapped on the radio and grabbed the mike.

'Charley Victor Four to Control.'

'Come in Charley Victor.'

Doyle felt his chest was on fire. But he was a copper, and coppers had jobs to do.

'Shooting at twenty-four Ambury Mansions. Police officer.' He had to struggle to go on. 'Police Officer Parker is dead. Suspect heading south west to junction – ' Here Doyle rattled out a brief description of Haydon's flash Yank car. All the coppers in the area knew it – and knew Big Bill Haydon. Anyway, Ray Doyle wasn't letting any-one else get there first. The radio squawked and the duty officer said: 'Are you in pursuit?'

Doyle said: 'No. That's Bill Haydon's car. He lives south-west, doesn't he? I'm going to pick him up there.' The car started and Doyle slammed her into gear, racing through the cogs until he had her roaring along the asphalt. He spoke into the mike again, for the last time, before he got down to business. 'I'm taking the short cuts!'

Ray Doyle knew his patch. He knew where he was, he knew where Haydon lived, and he knew the quickest way there. The prowl car howled along the streets, cut through alleyways, scattering dustbins, sending scared cats jumping. The tyres burned rubber. Doyle sent the car savagely along a one-way street, disdaining the signs, hurtling along like a banshee.

Bill Haydon's car also drove fast, slicing around corners on her big soft tyres, squealing with that infuriating way of

American cars on even the gentlest of corners. The car halted with a sliding skid in front of a big house facing the Common. Haydon leaped out and started for the garage doors, coming into the light from the wrought-iron lantern on its bracket shining over the archway.

He was almost there, almost safe and dry – a lithe and furious form burst from the shadows by the bushes. Doyle simply slammed into Haydon in the fiercest kind of rugby tackle. The big man went over gasping. Doyle knelt on him, gripping his shirt front. He stuck his hating face down.

'William Haydon, you murdering bastard! You're busted!'

William Haydon went to trial. He went full of hope that his story was watertight. William Haydon was disappointed. No one loves a cop-killer. William Haydon went down. The Judge's words rang in his ears.

'William Henry Haydon. It is the sentence of this court that you serve a life sentence with the recommendation that you should serve at least thirty years for these terrible crimes.'

There was, of course, an appeal.

Haydon sat across from his lawyer and heard the result of the appeal.

'I'm sorry, but that's it.' His lawyer acted with the precise, stuffy way lawyers have when they bring bad news. 'Your appeal has been denied.'

Big Bill Haydon shrivelled then. He sat, stunned, not really believing.

'Then the sentence stands?'

His lawyer nodded gravely.

'Thirty years!' burst out Haydon. 'Thirty years!'

Chapter Six

Even though Ray Doyle was selected for CI5 and teamed up with Bodie and spent his life in hair-raising escapades, he never forgot Syd Parker. Memory of that last ride with Syd, and seeing that gleaming Moto-Guzzi parked by the kerb, and his promise to himself, coiled around Doyle even now as he worked in the open space in front of his mews garage. He was smothered in grease. He wore filthy old clothes. But he was a happy man. Stripped to the frame and therefore scattered about in what appeared to be complete disarray, his very own Moto-Guzzi slumbered before him.

He thought of the bike as slumbering. Once he had her back together again, perfectly tuned, raring to go . . .

A shadow fell across Doyle as he lovingly wiped oil away and readied himself for the first steps in the restoration.

'You,' said Bodie, 'have this terrible decision to make.' Bodie stood at ease, immaculately clad, his dark suit in perfect taste. He looked like a million dollars, and Doyle looked like a crushed fag packet. 'Sue – and this terrific girl she has lined up for you – or this old bike.'

'It's not old! Well – it is. But it's a *classic* old bike. And when I've finished she'll be like new.'

'This girl *is* new. Tall, nubile, accommodating. And we're off duty.'

Doyle looked with deep affection at his bike. Well, at the scattered parts of his new old bike. He wiped his hands on a scrap of cotton waste. 'Always promised myself one.'

Bodie's lips wrinkled. 'A man can't live on promises

alone. Shall I run through the vital statistics again – in greater detail?' His hands made interesting shapes in the air. 'Imagine a goddess – hair like silk – deep, deep eyes – a mouth . . . Did I say mouth? A poem!'

Doyle stood up. 'Okay. Okay. But I'll bet she's not as cheap to run as this beauty will be when I've finished her.' He brisked up with the cotton waste, his mind made up. 'What time?'

Bodie glanced at his thin platinum watch. 'About thirty minutes from now.'

'Better hurry, then . . .'

As they walked briskly towards the entrance to Doyle's mews flat a girl sauntered past. Both men looked at her. She repayed the look. She appeared to be about twenty-five, with legs, and a waist, and a trim style of clothing herself that spoke eloquently of money and of taste. She was staring at Doyle with an intensity he found slightly disconcerting. Her oval face was set into a serious, intent look, and her eyes appraised Doyle. As his own eyes met that gaze she turned away sharply, and walked on, no longer sauntering. Her rear view was just as rewarding as her front. Bodie lifted his eyebrows and regarded his partner with an acerbity that bordered on the demanding.

'Someone you know?'

Doyle shook his head. 'No. But I wouldn't mind.'

Bodie looked back along the mews. The girl had stopped and stood at the entrance on to the street, staring back. Her pose in those exquisite clothes, the way her thigh thrust against her skirt, entranced Bodie. But he went into the flat after Doyle, saying as he did so: 'Nor me.'

The Argive Room was an intimate, restful, Lucullan place of soft lights and shaded alcoves and sumptuous food. Bodie and Doyle had supped well, and the two girls had enjoyed the meal right along with them. Sue kept looking at Bodie as though she wanted to eat him as an extra dessert. And the girl she'd brought along, Eve, outdid even Bodie's enthusiastic and lascivious description. Now Doyle hauled an empty bottle of champagne out of the bucket and proffered it to Bodie.

'How about another bottle?'

Bodie smiled, leaning back, feeling good. 'Taken care of.'

'No, no,' insisted Doyle. 'This is *my* round.'

He laughed as he spoke and glanced up for the wine waiter.

The girl who had scrutinised him so intently in the mews stood by the table. She wore an evening dress that cupped beauty, that clung sensuously to thighs, that put two vertical dints between the impeccable eyebrows of Sue and Eve. From the girl's hand an evening wrap trailed to the floor. A diamond bracelet caught the light and flashed.

Doyle, rocking back, looking up, said: 'I've seen you before. Outside my place.'

'Yes, I followed you. You are Ray Doyle, aren't you?'

'Who wants to know?' Doyle didn't believe in giving away too much all in one go.

But Bodie, never able to resist a woman, was on his feet. 'Yes, he's Ray Doyle. And *I'm* Bodie.' He whipped a spindly chair from under the next table, reaching swiftly out of the alcove and to hell with head waiters. 'Will you sit down?'

The girl sat smoothly, and the dress slithered to fit. 'I – I didn't mean to disturb you.' She glanced at the girls. 'And I'm not a girl friend or anything. But it is important.' She moistened her lips. 'My name is Haydon. Jill Haydon.' Jill let her intent gaze rest on Doyle meaningfully. '*Haydon*. You arrested my father. William Haydon.'

Doyle stood up. His face was compressed. '*That* Haydon!' His napkin crushed in his fist. 'Good-bye.'

'Please –'

'It was a long time ago.'

Jill blurted the words out as though they were forced from her by an anguish she could not contain. 'Seven years, two months and five days.' She was breathing unsteadily now. 'If you've forgotten . . .'

Doyle said harshly: 'I remember very clearly. I remember *exactly*. Good-bye.'

Bodie said: 'Ray . . .' on a rising inflexion.

Doyle turned away, looking at Eve. 'Weren't we going on somewhere? You mentioned a disco . . . ?'

Doyle's companions looked on the scene intrigued, only faintly embarrassed – after all, it was not their situation – and then they all started to ready themselves to move off to the disco. Doyle regarded Jill for the last time. 'I remember exactly.'

Back in Doyle's mews flat after the evening, Ray Doyle punched a cushion and said nastily: 'She ruined the whole evening!'

'She did?' Bodie hated to see his partner wrought up like this, and yet he couldn't see any reason – not yet, at least – and that girl Jill Haydon, really had class. 'Look, she just wanted to talk to you. That's all.'

Doyle rounded on Bodie. The words spilled out. He told his partner of that hot sticky night back in 1971 when Syd Parker had been shot to death by Bill Haydon. The memories gushed up, sick and hot and foetid. Bodie was shaken. He moved the curtains and looked down into the mews.

'I dunno. But she's still there.'

'What!' Doyle pushed past and looked down. His eyes regarded the lonely figure waiting under the lamplight. Bodie said nothing. Presently, Doyle went down and opened the door. He couldn't really understand his own motives; but he signalled the girl and said: 'You've got two minutes. Two minutes!'

The talk that followed in the flat between Jill and Doyle was listened to in fascination by Bodie. 'He's done more than seven years,' said Jill. She sat a little hunched, trying to keep back the tears, looking down at the floor. 'Usually, after seven years, you at least get the chance at parole . . .'

'Not,' said Doyle in his grimmest way, 'not cop killers.'

'That's the point. My father's done crooked things – yes,

he admits that. But he didn't kill Fitch, or your friend. He's stuck by that for years. For seven years . . . Now – all he asks is that you go and see him.' Doyle did not move or change his forbidding expression. A little more anxiously, Jill went on: 'You were hurt, yes, I can understand that. But doesn't it bother you that you may have got the wrong man? Doesn't it bother you at all?'

A silence hung, to be broken finally by Bodie who spoke with a big smile towards Jill. 'Doyle, old chum. I think, I really think, if you're to have any peace – you have to go and see the man.'

Prisons were places where the hollow slam of a cell door cut off years of a man's life. Ray Doyle had never been enchanted by the places. Grey walls, grim bars, the eternal stinks of disinfectants and stale cabbage and old socks and the penetrating odours of human sweat and urine – all haphazardly masked by the eternal damned disinfectant.

He sat across from Bill Haydon and saw how time had marked the big man, greying his hair, sagging his jaw line, setting deep lines, like scars of a futile battle against time itself, into his forehead and cheeks. His mouth looked gaunt.

'I know you think I'm a cop killer, and that's what it's all about. A cop gets killed, the pack's unleashed after blood, not caring who they bite as long as they bite someone.' Haydon pushed a broad hand that trembled through his grey hair. He looked a different man from the arrogant crime boss of yesteryear. 'I was set up.' He did not look up, and Doyle regarded him attentively. 'Harry Scott. He had a score to settle. I was set up. I got a call –'

Doyle interrupted, speaking with a controlled passion that made Haydon, this time, look up. 'I heard it all at the trial,' said Doyle. '*You* say you got a call to go to Fitch's place. You arrived and found Fitch dead – and Syd Parker, too . . .'

'I didn't kill either of them!'

'I saw you drive away.'

'Of course.' Some of the fire sparked in Bill Haydon. 'I knew it was a set-up, didn't I? All I thought about was getting away from there. It was a frame, a dirty frame.'

'The caretaker saw you. Saw you stepping off that fire escape with a gun in your hand. He saw you.'

Haydon pulled a hand down his face. He made a familiar, insolent gesture. 'He was bought. I've had plenty of time – years! – to think about it. He had to be bought. And that means he's the weak link . . . ' Haydon shot a hard look at Doyle, who maintained his impassive air that hid the passions within him. Haydon went on: 'If I killed 'em what did I do with the gun? Didn't have it when you grabbed me, did I? It wasn't in the car. So what did I do with it? Where did it go?'

'You,' Doyle told him, 'ditched it.'

Haydon snorted. 'Driving through the streets? Hell, I *couldn't* have had time to stop and bury it. You know that. So if I ditched it, why hasn't it ever been found?' At Doyle's abrupt lifting of his chin, and the sideways glance in his eyes, Haydon pressed on. 'I've heard about you. Working for some new outfit, gone up in the world. You could help me. If you wanted to. If justice is what you *really* care about . . . ' Doyle stood up. He'd had about all he could take. He began to move away and Haydon shouted after him. All the old fire and passion were vented in the harsh words. 'The caretaker, Doyle. He *had* to be bought. The caretaker.'

There was an obvious way to get this bug out of his brain. Doyle sent the car in the direction of old haunts, familiar streets and avenues. They drove past the King's Arms. Around the Avenue. Along towards Ambury Mansions.

'I haven't been back here since Syd – haven't been back here in years.'

Bodie said: 'Seven years, two months, five days.'

Doyle brought the car to a gentle halt. He did not park under the trees where Syd had parked before his death. He regarded Bodie challengingly. 'He did it. We got the right man. Come and listen to the caretaker confirm it.'

They walked into the apartment block and Doyle leaned on the bell. 'He did it,' he said, again, no doubts now in his mind.

Mrs Wilson came halfway out of her groundfloor flat and called across in her pleasant voice. 'The new man won't be here until Friday.'

Doyle swung about, staring blankly, surprised. 'New man?'

'Yes. Poor Mr Gilbert. He died. You didn't know that? Died of bronchitis. So sad. He was two years past retiring and was so looking forward to getting away at last.'

'No. I didn't know,' said Doyle.

'We'll miss him,' said Mrs Wilson, going back into her flat. 'Poor Mr Gilbert. He won't see that Cape Ferrat sunset now.'

'Cape Ferrat?' Doyle's surprise was shared by Bodie. Caretakers in this class of apartment block rarely found themselves retiring to Cape Ferrat.

Mrs Wilson hesitated. 'You didn't know? You're not friends of his then, otherwise you must know. His dream. To sit on the cliffs overlooking Cape Ferrat, sip his brandy, and watch the sun go down.'

Bodie's eyebrows drew down. 'An impossible dream.'

'Oh, no. He had the exact villa picked out and everything.'

'A villa!'

'Yes.' Mrs Wilson nodded in utmost certainty. Bodie got the idea she'd a hankering to go off to Cape Ferrat with the caretaker, Gilbert. 'I think he was planning to go and view this week. But he told me all about it. It sounded wonderful. The pool, and a splendid view of the sea.'

The two CI5 men reacted to this. This kind of information made the nose twitch.

'Are his personal effects still in there?'

'Yes, I think so. He was a bachelor, you see. They're still trying to trace relatives. Poor Mr Gilbert . . .'

Mrs Wilson retired with a graceful inclination of her head.

Bodie said : 'Cape Ferrat.'

Doyle looked at the door marked 'Caretaker'. He drew back. 'Poor Mr Gilbert,' said Doyle, and kicked the door in.

In George Cowley's spartan and extraordinarily utilitarian office the Chief of CI5 pushed his heavy-rimmed glasses on his nose and looked up from the papers spread out on his desk.

'It's fascinating, quite fascinating. You,' he said to Doyle and Bodie who stood in front of his desk, awaiting the great man's reactions, 'had no right to rifle the man's apartment. But, what you've come up with – fascinating.' He lifted and dropped a slip of paper. 'Particularly this, so obviously secret and important taped to the underside of the table.'

'Just numbers,' said Bodie. 'Like a Swiss Number Account.'

'It would certainly seem so, Bodie. Yes,' said George Cowley in his best plummy manner.

Doyle's face was set in lines of honest conviction tinged with the first shades of doubt. 'Well, sir?'

Cowley looked at him. He had to be careful and precise in what he said to Doyle, that was very clear.

'From what you've told me, your original arrest was perfectly correct. On circumstantial evidence Haydon was guilty. But, let us just assume – *assume,* mind – that Haydon is telling the truth. He didn't commit those murders.' He waved a hand and went on speaking, detailing Doyle's account of running up the stairs after the gunshots and seeing a dark shadow of a man running down the fire escape. He finished : 'A man. Bill Haydon?'

Doyle said, swiftly : 'I assumed – '

'You assumed. But you could not *swear* it was Haydon?'

'I wasn't asked to. The circumstances – '

Cowley cut in tigerishly. 'And that's what we keep

coming back to, isn't it? The circumstances. Circumstantial. Before you went on duty you were warned – *preconditioned* – that Haydon was after Fitch. Then you saw his flash Yank car parked nearby – '

'And he took off like a bat out of hell right after the killings!'

'Precisely. That ties in with *his* story. He was panicked. He knew he'd been set up. What would you have done?'

'I suppose,' said Doyle, and he tried to speak with honesty. 'I would have got out of there, sir.'

'That's what I mean. Haydon's story seems to have as much validity as yours.' As Doyle's jaw set and he looked as though he was about to burst out with some trenchant remark, Cowley waved him down and said: 'But I'm still backing your instincts. Just the same . . . Suppose Haydon is telling the truth? Where are we? The real killer could have been hiding in that apartment. You didn't have time to check the other rooms. It's possible. You take off after Haydon's car heading south-west while the real killer slips away in the opposite direction.'

Doyle followed Cowley's pointing finger as the chief gestured on the spread map. 'On foot, perhaps. Across this parkland here. Dispose of the gun, and – ' He made a small dismissive gesture. 'It's all theory, of course.'

'That Swiss Number Account isn't theory,' said Bodie.

'We'll check it out. You're both off duty until . . . ?'

'Wednesday.'

'That's as long as you've got, then. Until Wednesday. Then I want you back in this office ready to tackle some *real* work.' Cowley pushed the map away and drew a thick folder to him. He looked up. 'Best of luck.' As the pair turned to go, Cowley said with all his bite softened by his rare but genuine smile: 'And, Doyle – I'll have a look at the official report. Purely academic. But I *still* think you were right.'

Chapter Seven

Ray Doyle had to acknowledge that there was more to this business than trying to help a pretty girl in trouble. So okay, the girl's father was a crook; but that didn't make her a crook as well, did it? He was passionately devoted to the idea of Justice. He'd been a policeman and now he worked for the toughest outfit in the country waging war against crime. If Bill Haydon was innocent, then Doyle would be the first to protest; but he just was not sure. They had a few days leave left and that meant leg work. He told Jill that she could tell her father he was checking. Bodie wrinkled up his lips and smiled.

'Oh, thank you!' exclaimed Jill, and she leaned forward and kissed Doyle's cheek. After she had gone, radiant, Doyle touched his cheek.

'All I said,' he told Bodie, feeling a little disgruntled, 'was checking.'

'Yeah. But with a different hat on. You're looking at the case now to prove Haydon innocent.'

'No. I'm dispassionate. I have to stay dispassionate.'

'Well, where do you dispassionately go now?'

'Scott.' Doyle had it mapped. 'If someone set Haydon up – and I'm not saying anyone did, mind! – it would have been Scott!'

The years had not been kind to Harry Scott. He sat in a wheel chair and looked shrunken from the big ebullient man he had been. He tended to thrash about in an irascible way with a rubber ferruled stick; but it was painfully clear he had been broken in his spirit. All the old fire had gone.

'It's all different now, Doyle,' said Scott. He drank as he sat in his private room of the King's Arms. Bodie and Doyle shook their heads at the offer. 'Different a few years ago. I had Jock McKay and Lenny, then, Big Charley.' He drank down quickly. 'All different now. I took a fall.'

'You were pushed,' said Doyle. 'It's a matter of record. You were pushed out of a third storey window, busted your pelvis, both thighs and your spine. And in my book it couldn't have happened to a nicer feller.' Scott's eyes wouldn't meet Doyle's. 'When I was a copper on the beat I picked up a fellow you'd worked over. Compared with him, what you got was easy.'

'I don't give any trouble now.' Scott gripped his glass. 'I co-operate.'

'That's right. You will. So tell me about Bill Haydon.'

'He's inside – '

'Since the day you had a quarrel with him here, right in this bar. You remember. Haydon came in and roughed up Fitch.'

'Fitch, yes, that was – '71. That hot summer. Watching the cricket. Freddy rang the bell for me – trouble. Haydon was here showing off his hairy chest and leaning on Fitch. I told him to get out. He did; but he said something – can't remember – but all I knew was I had to make a stand. I mean, in front of my own boys, had to make a stand . . . '

Doyle and Bodie listened. Scott half-mumbled, a broken wreck of a man, harking back to the days when he pulled muscle.

'I took off after him, grabbed him behind the wheel of his flash car, told him to lay off or else.'

'Yes?'

Scott licked his lips, thinking back. 'Then suddenly he produced a gun. Out of nowhere. Out of nowhere, I swear it.'

Scott trembled a little, and drank again. 'I had to back off.'

For a moment a little silence clung, then Scott burped

and fumbled around for the bottle to refill his glass.

Doyle said: 'So he made you look small? And that's when you decided to pay him back? That when you planned the set-up, Scott?'

'Set-up?'

'How much did you pay the caretaker?'

'What caretaker?'

Doyle bore down. 'You killed Fitch, didn't you? Killed him and planted it on Haydon. And then my partner came along and – '

At this Scott looked up, the bottle slopping dangerously. 'Are you crazy? Kill Fitch? Why would I kill Fitch?'

'To stick it on Haydon.'

'You *are* crazy. I'll co-operate all you want. But I don't have to listen to this. I don't want any trouble. Please go – *please*!'

Bodie and Doyle stood for a moment regarding Scott and then Doyle turned to leave. As he went he said cuttingly: 'You may not want it, Scott. But that's no guarantee you aren't going to get it.'

As soon as the door had closed after the two CI5 men Freddy the barman came in. He looked concerned. 'Who was that?'

'CI5. Wanted to know about the old days. When Haydon and me were eye to eye – bad days.'

'What in particular?'

'That day Haydon came in here chasing after Fitch. Do you remember that day, Freddy?'

The barman half-lifted his hand. He turned it over. The scar was there, white and like a centipede across his sinews and veins. He recalled it, slashed against the broken glasses, dripping blood. 'Yeah,' said Freddy. 'I remember it.'

At Doyle's mews flat Jill reacted as Doyle told her that he just did not think Harry Scott could have done the murders.

'It had to be him,' exclaimed Jill.

'No way,' said Doyle. 'He hasn't got – ' He altered what

he was going to say, glancing at Jill, and finished, ' – the machismo.'

'Then who?'

Doyle said it as gently as he could. 'Your daddy's still number one.'

'No! I don't believe that – and neither do you!' She stared at them, at Doyle and Bodie, half challenging, half appealing. 'What about the caretaker? How do you explain the villa, the money? You can't just bring it all to a halt now. You've got to go on . . . You have to . . . '

Doyle put the palm of his hand to his forehead, pushed his spread fingers up through his hair. He looked like a hunted animal seeking a safe lair. 'For God's sake! Just give me time to think!' He looked about, and then slammed out of the door. 'I need some air.'

Jill and Bodie exchanged worried glances and then Bodie nodded, gently, as much to answer her unspoken question. Jill nodded and followed Doyle out. She walked swiftly along the mews and picked Doyle up leaning on the parapet of the embankment, staring moodily at the fire-wriggling reflections of the lights in the invisible water. The sky lowered; but it was not raining. Sounds came muted, distant, as though to isolate these two on the grey stone embankment.

Jill walked up and leaned on the granite alongside Doyle.

'Do you mind?'

'It's a free country.'

His tone did not discourage her. With an evenness that betrayed a great deal, she said: 'My father might disagree with that.'

Doyle started chucking little pieces of gravel and grit into the water. They made tiny plops, like startled fish.

Jill said: 'I know what he was. But that was a long time ago. You've seen him – he's an old man now and every day older. I honestly think he regrets what he once did. The fire's gone out of him.' Her words had grown breathy, chopped up as she went on. She had difficulty in speaking the last few, near-broken words. 'And I'm afraid what more years will do to him. Afraid he's going to . . . Going to die in there . . . '

Doyle saw her face, white, shadowed, saw the mouth trembling. Jill broke down. As the tears poured from her eyes he moved towards her and quite naturally took her into his arms. He held her close, trying by the pressure of their bodies, one against the other, to offer her an assurance of comfort.

'Hey, hey . . . ' said Ray Doyle. He spoke very softly.

'I'm sorry . . . sorry.' She lifted her head, trying to blink away the tears. They glistened thickly on her cheeks. She sniffed and felt for a handkerchief, failed to find one, and Doyle took his own square of hand-stitched linen out and handed it across. She wiped her nose and then, in that pose, their eyes met. Jill managed a smile. 'Thank you. I shouldn't have cried.'

'You've got a right.'

'No, no.' Jill spoke with a new firmness. 'I have to stay strong. Strong. Somebody has to. Somebody on the outside who believes in him.'

Slowly, gently using his handkerchief to brush away the last vestiges of the tears, feeling this girl's nearness, Doyle said: 'Maybe I believe in him, too.' He was very conscious of the nearness of her face, her perfume. 'I don't know – I'd like to if only for your sake. But I don't know. Who does?'

Jill's voice sounded small but very clear. 'What about that man you work for?'

'Cowley?'

With a touch of incisiveness, Jill said: 'Yeah. Cowley.'

Many preoccupations weighed on the mind of George Cowley. He ran CI5 and was sometimes almost hopelessly aware that he attempted to stem the rising tide of violent criminal activity like that little Dutch kid sticking his thumb into the hole in the dyke. The conceit did not amuse him. His men needed breaks from the hard slog of the fight against crime. They needed respite. But Bodie and Doyle were gallivanting off trying to overturn the findings of a seven-year-old case that was shut, closed, finished. And yet, despite all, Cowley owned to an interest in the case. Simple logic told him that justice *could* go wrong, sometimes. Not often; but sometimes.

Enquiries had quickly established that the numbers on the slip of paper found taped to the underside of a table in Gilbert's room did refer to a Swiss Number Account. Further enquiries, of course, were fruitless in that direction. When Bodie and Doyle checked in Cowley spoke harshly to them, for the image had to be maintained. His damned leg had been playing up, lately, and the bullet lodged in it wanted to play scherzos up and down his nerves.

'So Gilbert the caretaker *was* a crook,' said Doyle. 'He *was* on the take.'

'We don't know that, Doyle!' Cowley cut in sharply.

'We know he had a secret account, Goddammit!'

Cowley simply stared. In a moment Doyle said in his huffy voice, 'I'm sorry, sir.'

Cowley nodded understandingly. 'You were just a witness, Doyle, not judge and jury.'

'I helped, didn't I?' Doyle could still see the tear-stained face of Jill Haydon. 'I helped put a man away for a crime he didn't do.'

'Perhaps I was wrong, Doyle. Perhaps you are judge and jury. Perhaps you know better than British Justice and the eight centuries it has taken to get it as near perfect – '

Not quite shouting, Doyle said: '*Near* perfect!'

'Aye.' Cowley paused. Then, 'That's all we can hope for in any human endeavour, Doyle. Near perfect. Translated, that means, "As damned near perfect as we can make it . . . " God and prevailing winds permitting.'

Cowley stood up and, favouring that gammy leg, paced off across his shabby carpet. He came back and rocked back on his heels, his eyes sharp and very hard. 'The gun. The gun is the crucial, missing evidence. Haydon – quite rightly – asked you what did he do with it. Well, perhaps he never had it. Perhaps it'll never be found. But – if you forget Haydon and plump for another man, well, then, would he take it away and hide it, would he calmly take it away . . . ?'

Doyle, abruptly eager, said: 'He must have known I was close by.'

'Precisely. So he would be panicked. Let's say he's on foot, running away, with the murder weapon in his hand. He starts to cross the open parkland. He has to get rid of that gun!'

'Yes . . .'

'The gun is the key.' Cowley sat down and pulled another one of the eternal fat folders towards him. He looked up, as a hunting cat looks up at the smell of game. 'If it could be found . . .'

Ambury Mansions appeared just the same as they had done seven years ago; yet the subtle differences forced Doyle into the present time. A different paint scheme, the shrubbery overgrown in different places, the feel of difference about the place. He went up the stairs, as he had done after hearing the gunshots, but he did not knock on the door of what had been Fitch's apartment. Shaking his head, unsure, wondering, he went down again and around into the area.

If there had been a miscarriage of justice then he was deeply involved. Cowley might say what he had said. Doyle remembered Jill's tear-streaked face, the way she had sobbed in his arms. And the caretaker and his Swiss Bank Account. And the gun . . . The gun had not been found. Find that somewhere where Bill Haydon could not possibly have been on the murder night, and Doyle, for one, would sleep easier. The thought of injustice was not an abstract notion to him, justice itself was what he believed in and fought for, and whilst he agreed with Cowley's practical assessment of its chances, he knew that he had to do everything humanly possible to ensure that justice was indeed not only seen to be done, but done.

The idea that Ray Doyle had shut away an innocent man to do thirty years bird itched at him, nastily.

Across the rear wall the parkland stretched out. The grass and trees looked more grey than green and the light lay long and level. Doyle looked around, started to run towards the wall from the fire escape. Then he hauled up. If he was an escaping murderer – a damned double-murderer – what would he do? Where would he run? He must know that the copper would be after him. So the two men in one, the Ray Doyle of CI5 trying to get under the skin and into the mind of the murderer, and the Ray Doyle sweating in shirt sleeve order chasing down the stairs, separated. The police officer had run to his prowl car. The murderer – over the wall and into the park?

Probably. Almost certainly.

Doyle scrambled up on to the wall and leaped down.

He set off in a reasonably straight line away from the apartment block. He was just following his nose. Following that professional policeman's nose of his.

A clump of trees across the park appeared to be a logical place to make for. The murderer would walk and run as fast as he could for cover. There was a road over there, too, far enough off. Doyle covered the ground in even strides, looking about, trying to get under the skin of the man who had run along here seven years ago – if there had been a man.

Stopping under the trees for a breather he became aware of someone else near. He spun about.

Jill stood there, her fingertips brushing the coarse grey bark of a tree, her form indistinct in the omnipresent overcast. She stepped forward after a moment.

'You're not just out taking exercise.'

Doyle wore his old combat jacket and jeans, and he knew he was in good shape. Jill looked marvellous, beautifully dressed, immaculate. Yet shadows haunted her cheeks.

In explanation of his presence, Doyle nodded to the

road. 'Road over there. Dozen places to park a car.'

Jill understood at once and moved closer. 'It would be dark and if he kept to the grass . . . No noise . . .'

'That distance, wouldn't even hear the car start up.'

'And if you did what would that matter? More than half a mile from Fitch's place.' She stared at Doyle and her lips trembled. 'That's what happened. It has to be!'

'It's probable, that's all. The gun. He has to get rid of the gun. If we could find that gun –'

'You're going to try, aren't you? You're going to try?'

Doyle nodded, the determination plain in his face. Jill reacted. With a half-stifled cry she flung herself forward, into his arms. 'Oh, Ray . . . !' She kissed him. At first the kiss was a simple statement, a way of saying thank you, innocent. But Doyle felt himself aroused by the soft warm pressure of her lips, and he felt Jill respond as the kiss deepened and lengthened. There was an art to kissing, and Doyle had been a painter – painting all them there noods, as his fellow coppers had said, smiling lasciviously. Doyle kissed Jill and he felt her supple body melt and flow in the curve of his arms.

It was some time before they broke apart. Both were panting a little, and Jill's kiss still burned on Doyle's lips.

Later on Jill went to see her father and told him the news. He had been given a new hold on life by the fresh interest in his case. They agreed there was now a strong element of doubt and they thrashed out the details again for the hundredth time.

'This is what we hoped for from the start,' said Haydon.

'Even Doyle now believes there is doubt. But they still haven't found the gun.'

Big Bill Haydon's jaw firmed up. 'They will. They have to.'

A professional search was made of the parkland on a spreading line from the back wall to the area of Ambury Mansions. Police lined out and began prodding and prying. Everyone knew this would be a long and arduous job.

That evening Doyle, who had been able to put in a couple of hours on his beloved Moto-Guzzi – or, at least, on the scattered parts of the bike – looked up to see Jill waltzing down the mews towards him. As always, she looked fabulous. Doyle shook his head. 'No news.'

They went up to Doyle's flat where he switched on the lights and prepared to go into the bathroom to clean up.

'Help yourself to a drink.'

'I don't want a drink.'

Doyle cocked his head on one side. 'That's selfish.' As her head went up, he said quickly: 'Because while you were helping you, you could be helping me.'

Jill studied him and then he smiled and went out. She poured two drinks and called: 'Ray?'

Doyle's voice floated in from the bathroom. 'Yeah?'

'Where are they searching?'

'Straight line, fanning out, in the park, from Fitch's flat to the main road just past where we were.'

'I went out to that park again –'

Doyle appeared, stripped to the waist with a fluffy towel in his hands. He quizzed her as he dried off.

'I tried to imagine I was that man.' Jill looked at Doyle's torso; but she persisted with what she was saying. 'I tried to imagine it at night. It would be different then. All shadows, trees . . . I have a gun. I want – *need* – to get rid of it. I wouldn't go directly north. That way I'd be too close to the main path, almost in clear view. No, I'd veer over to the left, towards the trees, where it was dark, and then, then I'd see it glinting, shining. The water. The pond.'

Doyle lowered the towel. He stared at Jill, at her tense pose, supplicating, one hand held out. The colour burned in her cheeks. Her eyes were brilliant. She was breathing unsteadily.

'I'll tell them first thing tomorrow,' said Ray Doyle.

Betty was, as George Cowley would admit, just about as perfect a personal assistant as any man was likely to find.

But she couldn't always halt a Minister of the Crown in full flight. She thumbed the intercom swiftly and as Cowley answered said: 'Excuse me, sir. The Minister is here. On his way to see you. I tried to delay him, but – '

From the open door of Cowley's office on the tail of Betty's words over the intercom, the Minister said in his booming platform voice, 'She wasn't quick enough!'

Cowley looked up. He kept that lined craggy face of his set into a pleasant mould. The Minister strode to the desk, spoke into the intercom mike: 'Nice try. That will be all. No interruptions now until I leave.'

Betty said in her meek voice: 'Yes, sir.'

The Minister rounded on Cowley. 'A slip-up in protocol; but I'm prepared to overlook it because she has nice legs.'

Cowley was as well aware of that as the next man; but he felt it politic to say: 'Has she?'

The Minister beamed and sat down. 'When I am in your office it means there is trouble. And there is. George – I seem to remember you keep an awfully good malt scotch . . .'

Cowley responded to the friendlier approach. 'Of course.'

As he poured, Cowley listened to the reason for the visit of the Minister to the shabby offices of CI5.

'Doyle.'

'Doyle?'

'Doyle.'

'A good man. One of my best –'

'I've no doubt, George. And if I'm ever hi-jacked in mid-Atlantic he'd be the first person I'd ask for. This business of stirring up old mud . . .'

'The Haydon case.'

'Thank you, George. I'm very pushed for time.'

'What about it?'

'I thought that summed it up.' As Cowley regarded him much as a child regards the rabbit whipped from the conjurer's hat, the Minister went on: 'Haydon was tried,

George. Tried, convicted. The trial lasted six days, cost the tax-payers a lot of money. A number of responsible policemen gave evidence, including Doyle. A learned Judge listened to them. *Three* learned Judges heard the appeal. He was found guilty.'

'But he might not be.' Cowley's flat statement made the ebullient eyebrows forever question-marking the Minister's face rise fractionally. 'Doyle has doubts.'

'Doyle? Raymond Doyle – ex-Detective *Constable*!'

'He's a good man,' said Cowley. He's *my* man. I back my men to the hilt.'

'Even if they're wrong? Is there anything to all this?'

'Until they're proved wrong. And – possibly.' The answer was guarded. Cowley had handled Ministers before.

'When will you know?' Now the velvet was off the glove.

At Cowley's elaborate and over-Gallic shrug, the Minister leaned forward and spoke seriously. 'You have two days, George. I'll keep them off your back for two days. After that – well, there will be questions asked about the resources of CI5 being employed on mere criminal cases –'

Cowley kept his voice level; but he was aware of pain from that bullet-laden leg, and he spoke forcefully.

'This is a question of justice. Justice is within CI5's brief. It should be everyone's concern.' Now Cowley spoke very very carefully; but he said it all the same. 'Even Ministers of the Crown.'

The Minister leaned back in his chair. He looked at George Cowley with a straight, steady regard that did not discompose Cowley – or not by very much. Then: 'You used to beat me regularly at tennis, too.' He held out his glass. 'Do you think I might . . . ?'

Cowley let his smile grow and broaden and went to fetch a refill of the special malt scotch.

Doyle scraped some time together to have another go at the

Moto-Guzzi. He was, as usual, smothered in grease; but he manoeuvred the wheel into the frame with exquisite care. A car horn began to blast, and the sound of a revving engine cannoned up the mews. Doyle jerked and the wheel clanged and dropped. Doyle made an unladylike remark. He turned, furious, to see Bodie leaping out of his car.

'They found it! *They found it!*'

Doyle forgot about the wheel.

'A .44 calibre, seven shot revolver. Two empty chambers.' Bodie moved his hands expressively. 'It's got to be the murder weapon.'

'Where did they find it?' Doyle spoke with passion.

'Somewhere under the trees by the pond – '

'Then she was right.'

When Doyle was cleaned up they tooled around to tell Jill, who showed enormous relief. Excitement buzzed between the three of them. Then they went off to see Merton, CI5's forensics expert.

Merton, a balding, no-nonsense man who knew his business, confirmed that the revolver had killed Fitch and Parker.

'Then,' said Doyle with conviction. 'That's enough for me.' He felt the relief in him mingling with the disjointed feelings that he had been instrumental in putting away an innocent man. 'Haydon couldn't have planted that gun by the pond. He was in his car and away that night – he didn't have time.'

'So Cowley's theory of that "other man" holds up.'

'Yeah.'

Bodie said: 'Then it had to be Harry Scott.'

'No. Maybe. I don't think he ever had the bottle. There must have been a dozen people wanted to put Haydon away.'

'And one of them killed your partner.'

'Yes. And now I know what I have to do.'

In Cowley's office Doyle was stubborn.

'It's not conclusive, Doyle,' Cowley pointed out.

'But it changes things. I know I can't get a retrial for Haydon; but I can start the ball rolling. I can file a new statement saying I could have been wrong. Look – at the trial I *knew* Haydon had done it. That must have coloured my evidence.'

Cowley tapped the file he had called for. 'I've read the transcript. Your evidence was detailed, accurate and, as I would expect of you, scrupulously fair. I can't stop you setting the ball rolling. But have you thought of the implications?'

'Implications?'

'You won't only be saying you could have been wrong; but that your colleagues were wrong, too. Good solid coppers – like your partner, Syd Parker.'

'I still want to make that statement.'

'You know this is a bombshell you're handing me?'

'But you'll see it goes through the proper channels, won't you, sir?'

Sighing, Cowley nodded. 'Aye.'

When Doyle had gone, Cowley rang the Minister. It was late; but he had no difficulty in being connected.

Cowley explained the position. The Minister sounded concerned.

'Damn. As soon as it's signed you'd better send it over by special messenger.'

'No,' said Cowley, and he passed the back of his hand over his forehead. 'No. Tomorrow will be soon enough. I think I'll hold on to the statement until tomorrow.'

'You think he may change his mind?' The sharpness of the Minister's tone was not lost on Cowley.

'Not a chance of that. But I think I'll hold on to it for a wee while.'

'Very well. Good night, George.'

'Good night.'

Cowley buzzed the intercom and spoke to Betty, who was hanging around unwilling to go home at this point.

'Get on to Central Filing. Wake 'em all up if necessary.

I want every piece of paper on the Haydon case. Every word written about it, right up to date.'

Doyle's mews flat looked as though a motor cycle spare parts shop had blown up and deposited all the stock haphazardly over his tables and chairs and carpets. He worked lovingly on the carburettor as Bodie wandered in with drinks held casually. Bodie plonked one down beside oily waste and said: 'We can leave about half seven. Be there before nine. Great way to finish the last day of our leave. Mind you, not that it's been a leave exactly, with you chasing after Haydon.'

'I didn't think, Bodie,' said Doyle, 'that you were such an outdoor type. Fishing? And Bodie? Don't go together somehow.'

'That's very wounding. I'm a deeply sensitive man with an enduring interest in the countryside . . . also . . . Just down the road there's a pub with two *beautiful* barmaids . . .'

'Ah!' said Doyle. '*That* kind of fishing.'

'Both kinds of fishing. First thing tomorrow. What do you say?' At Doyle's okay, Bodie finished his drink, saying: 'Pick you up around seven-thirty, then.' He glanced out of the window. 'Better bring a warm coat, better still, a blanket. That's no heat wave out there!'

When his partner had gone Doyle was aware of a question hanging unanswered in something Bodie had said. Pubs? Barmaids? Fishing? No – not those. Something else. Some vagrant memory niggled at Doyle as he tried to sleep. He lay awake and voices, ghosts, memories crowded up in a jostling host to parade before his eyes and whisper in his ears.

Scott's voice: 'Haydon was there. Showing off his hairy chest – and leaning on Fitch. I had to make a stand . . .'

And Harry Scott again: 'I told him to lay off or else. I grabbed at him. Then he suddenly produced a gun from nowhere . . .'

Doyle could see the ghostly images, of Scott leaning into

the flash Yank car and of Bill Haydon bringing up the big .44 revolver. 'Out of nowhere,' the ghostly voice of Scott continued. 'I swear it. He suddenly produced a gun out of nowhere.' Again and again that ghostly voice repeated itself. 'Out of nowhere, a gun, I swear it . . .'

Abruptly, Doyle sat up in bed. He leaned across and switched on the bedside lamp. The something hanging unanswered had come up clear as a bell. He went to make a cup of tea and think all around the question of the problematical answer.

He could still hear Scott's voice, echoing as though booming in a railway tunnel. 'Showing off his hairy chest . . . produced a gun out of nowhere . . . hairy chest . . . out of nowhere . . .'

In Cowley's office just about the same time the chief of CI5 sat intently reading the mass of documents Betty had brought. He'd told her to clear off home; he wondered if she'd gone. But the papers revealed a great deal, and the latest of all held his attention. Slowly, he read it through again, and then sat back and took off his glasses. He pinched the bridge of his nose.

At last he snapped on the intercom and was not at all surprised that Betty answered.

'Doctor Davis,' said Cowley. 'Call him. Ask him to stand by for an immediate autopsy.'

'He'll be asleep now, sir.'

'Call him.'

'Yes, sir.'

'Also the Home Office. Get the duty man over here right away.' Cowley's voice might have blown off the polar ice cap. 'Tell him to bring an exhumation order with him.'

'Yes, sir,' said Betty.

Cowley started to shuffle the papers into a neat pile. Ray Doyle, ex-Detective Constable, had lost Cowley a night's sleep. But for an intriguing and fascinating item like this, that was a plus in George Cowley's book.

Chapter Eight

Bodie tooled his car into Doyle's mews bright and early and honked the horn. Looking out of the window, Doyle took no notice of his partner's arrival and went on speaking into the telephone. He looked none the worse for his sleepless night, and after he had arrived at what he considered had to be the answer to that dangling question, he had slept, and slept well. But not for long. Now he spoke quickly, nodding as he spoke.

'That's as far as you can trace it?' He jotted down the address. 'Thanks anway – I'll take it from there.'

Bodie's car horn sounded again, an impatient blast.

Doyle smiled and hung up, then he hurried down and out into the mews. Bodie lay back in his car seat, his eyes closed, his whole pose elaborately indicative of a man fast asleep.

Doyle's smile remained and he went around the car and climbed into the passenger seat.

Very artistically, with a yawn and a stretch, Bodie woke up. He turned his head. 'Oh, my goodness,' he said, and yawned again. 'What time is it? Must have slept half the day away.'

'Come on,' said Doyle, not rising to the bait. 'Move it.'

Bodie started up and swung the car through the mews. He looked supremely self-satisfied, his lips in that typical little crinkling smile. 'I called the pub last night. Reserved a couple of rooms. With double beds. Those barmaids live on the premises and – '

'We're not going.'

'Do what?'

'We're not going fishing.' He looked at the address he'd scribbled. 'We're going to Fillerton Street.'

'Now what,' exploded Bodie, 'has Fillerton Street to offer compared with a couple of luscious barmaids panting for – '

'You'll see.'

The sign in the tatty, fly-blown street with the open lots and the broken-down fences and the railway embankment beyond leaned as though held up only by one and a half rusty nails. It read: FILLERTON STREET CAR SALES.

Bodie prowled among the cars, seeing their condition which ranged from runners to heaps. He was aware of Doyle talking to Keller the car salesman by the wooden hut with its garish signs proclaiming the virtues of the cars on display and the ease of credit terms available. Keller at last wrote down an address and handed the slip of paper to Doyle. Doyle motioned to Bodie and both men got back into the car. Bodie sighed.

'Would it be too much to tell me what this is all about?'

'I'm looking for a car.' Doyle showed the address. 'That's our next stop.'

'A car?'

'Haydon's car. The one he was driving that night. It's been through half a dozen hands since then. Let's hope we get lucky.'

The showroom at which they parked had cars in a slightly different class. Doyle saw the car at once, parked at the end of a double vista of bonnets. It had been done up and looked to be in reasonable condition, the flash swank of its chrome still shining. The two CI5 men walked down the lane of cars. The salesman fussed, extolling the virtues of the car, mentioning its clean condition, not rising to the one about the little old ladies who never drove faster than thirty, opening up the hood. He stood up front as Bodie and Doyle stood by the driving side door.

Bodie said: 'You're going to tell me now, aren't you?'

Doyle smiled. The fishing this morning had been great, just great . . . 'Summer of '71', he said. 'Few weeks of it there was a freak heat wave. Even we cops were in shirt sleeves. So was Haydon. Scott remembers him showing off his hairy chest. That'd mean a shirt, wouldn't it, open to the waist?'

Doyle leaned into the car as he spoke and started looking around. Bodie regarded his partner's rear end as though that was where he did his thinking. *'Doyle!'*

Doyle turned half-around. 'They had a run in – and suddenly Haydon produced a gun from "nowhere". He's wearing shirt, slacks, but he produced a gun from nowhere. Get in.'

Bodie got in. He caught on at once. 'It had to be in the car.'

'Right. And if Haydon produced it from nowhere then, perhaps, on the night of the killings, he put it back into nowhere.'

'You told me they turned the car inside out.'

'They did. The usual places – what about unusual places? It's a Yank car, remember . . . ' He started to get out the other door.

'Let's try it,' said Doyle. The salesman, coming around, heard this and perked up with a big smile.

'Certainly, sir. I'll just get the keys.'

'You're Haydon,' said Doyle to Bodie, both men completely ignoring the salesman. 'I'm Scott. Follow you into the car, grab at you . . . ' They suited their actions to the words. Doyle grabbed at Bodie, who reacted. 'Bodie, now you – '

'Wouldn't be my right hand, you'd see it straight away. Left then . . . ' He began to feel under the dash. 'Got to be within arm's reach . . . ' He felt around. 'No.'

Doyle frowned. Then: 'I'm leaning on you, right? You'd lean too, wouldn't you – an inch or two . . . ?'

Bodie leaned. His hand crept along under the dash,

fiddling, pulling screw heads, pushing. 'Nothing,' he said. 'Nothing but – '

The click sounded sharp and high, like a violin string breaking. A small flap opened out and downwards, like a cassette holder upside down. It vibrated. The two CI5 men looked at the revealed cavity, and then at each other. In the compartment, which was very shallow, had been fitted a liner that was the exact shape of a .44 revolver.

'Jackpot!'

The salesman strutted up jangling the keys. 'The keys – '

'Thanks,' said Doyle. He got out, took the keys, and then, shattering the composure of the salesman, locked the door. He took out his I.D. Card with a flourish. He felt good.

'We're impounding the car.'

The salesman's face would have done credit to an old lady at Cap d'Antibes; but Doyle knew his feeling of rightness did not come from this petty display of power. It came from far more deeply rooted feelings that almost – almost – he had allowed to be swamped by newer and sharper impulses.

George Cowley also shared those deeply rooted feelings. He, too, felt good. But there had to be protocol and ways and means. The work had been done and, because it was CI5 talking, it had been done swiftly and thoroughly.

Cowley spoke on the phone before going out. He was in a hurry; but this had to be said.

'Yes, doctor, yes, I have the report here. Yes, I'll be attending to it personally – right now. And sorry again for dragging you out of bed last night. I'm deeply appreciative. Bye.'

Cowley replaced the receiver and stood up. He moved around his desk and then glanced down again at the file.

A photograph was pinned to the manilla, a photograph of an elderly, weak-looking man. The words were typed in that Ministry typing that is almost but not quite illegible on a machine surviving from the Boer War:

MARTIN GILBERT – DECEASED.
EX-CARETAKER, AMBURY MANSIONS.

Cowley allowed himself a single perfunctory smile, and then went out of his office. He shut the door with a firm slam.

Bodie drove. He drove because it was his car; but also he drove because Ray Doyle was not in a fit state to drive.

Doyle sat, tense, angry, wondering at the way the world wagged, trying to understand Jill Haydon's actions and succeeding very well, succeeding only too well . . .

'It was a set-up,' he said. He sat looking through the windscreen and not seeing his way clearly, not seeing the road ahead. 'Always a set-up . . . With me the pigeon.'

Quietly, Bodie said: 'Least you found out in time.'

Doyle sat, looking through the screen. He could see Syd Parker. See Syd at the wheel of the prowl car. See Syd trying to be cheerful with a sick wife and all his worries. See Syd doing his job as a copper. And, most horribly of all, seeing Syd as a crumpled heap on the floor, dead, murdered, shot to death by a big braggart of a murdering bastard . . .

And yet, yet you could understand Jill, couldn't you?

But understanding Jill wouldn't bring Syd Parker back to life, not after seven long years . . .

Mrs Wilson was a pleasant plump lady. She had done well. The two interfering men had believed her story, and she'd been quite thrilled when they'd kicked the door of Mr Gilbert's flat into flinders. Now she held out her hand as Jill Haydon counted out the beautiful ten pound notes.

'That's it,' said Jill. 'You did well.'

Mrs Wilson looked at the money in her hand. 'Any time.' She clutched the money, suddenly, holding it, gripping it. 'Any time at all.'

This was the room in the Haydon house where Ray Doyle had broken the news that the enquiry was to be re-opened, the room where Jill Haydon had learned to welcome new hope. The furnishings were in good taste, for her father's money, ill-gotten though it was, had served Jill very well. As for Ray Doyle – she felt a strange ambivalence there. If he hadn't been a copper – well, a kind of copper – she could have been quite fond of him.

She turned back to Mrs Wilson, smiling, and Mrs Wilson clutching her money suddenly lost her smile.

Jill swivelled quickly, looking towards the door. Mrs Wilson let a tiny gasp push past her suddenly shaking lips.

In the doorway stood a tough, compact man with a mobile mouth and a lined, craggy face. His sandy hair stood defiantly away from his scalp. He walked in with a limp.

'Good morning,' said George Cowley.

For Cowley, he spoke very gently. Very gently indeed.

To anyone who did not know the chief of CI5 it would seem he spoke in sorrow.

Mrs Wilson let out a sudden shrill shriek. She collapsed backwards into one of the comfortable armchairs. Jill Haydon just stood looking at the intruder. She guessed who this was from Doyle's remarks. She guessed; but how much did Cowley know?

Cowley turned his guns on Mrs Wilson for starters.

'You are obliged to say nothing at this time. But you *are* a material witness – '

No – no, Jill Haydon could see it all. They had nothing – nothing. Her confidence returned and with it her poise and self-possession.

'To what?' she spoke contemptuously, ready to turf this one out and clout him with trespass and attempted rape if he wouldn't go quietly. 'To what? Public nuisance?'

Voices and footsteps from outside brought the attention of Cowley and Jill to the door. Cowley forebore to answer the girl. Mrs Wilson sat in the armchair and hugged her plump self, completely lost in the world of her own misery.

Doyle and Bodie walked in. They saw Cowley and were suitably surprised. But not really surprised. No one ought to be surprised at the capacity of George Cowley.

Cowley smiled at them. His face transformed itself, as it always did when he smiled.

'Great minds think alike . . .'

Doyle wasn't going to wait to break the news.

'The gun was a plant. They – ' he turned to stare at Jill. There was no love in that look now. There was sorrow, there, right enough, but the sorrow curled around memories of Syd Parker. ' – *She* buried it!'

'I imagine so,' said Cowley. 'But you interrupted me.'

He turned back to Jill, who stood looking at Doyle as though he had attempted rape. She had to force herself to turn her attention to Cowley.

' "Public Nuisance"? No, I think not. You see, Miss Haydon, I began where you began – with Gilbert, the caretaker. Plant the first doubt there and you knew Doyle would be sure to follow . . .'

Cowley let his glance flick across to Doyle. Bodie, watching intently, was shocked to see a soft kindness in that look, as though Cowley had stripped the outer coverings of his brain bare. The experience was profoundly moving. And Cowley continued his sentence ' – any man would. It worked because the caretaker was conveniently dead. *Very* conveniently. An attack of bronchitis . . . ?'

Slowly, almost playfully, Cowley shook his head. But there was no play-acting here; not with one dead policeman and an ex-policeman almost – but not quite – hoodwinked by a clever and ruthless criminal. 'No,' said George Cowley, shaking his head. 'No.'

Bodie felt it incumbent on him to ask the question.

He asked.

'What,' said Bodie, 'do you mean?'

Cowley beamed. 'I had his body exhumed last night and an autopsy carried out. CI5 can move the mountains of bureaucracy when the motives are right. Gilbert died of suffocation. Probably a pillow pressed over his face. He was old and frail.' Cowley was looking at Bodie and Doyle; he did not move either his head or his eyes to look at Jill Haydon. '*A woman could easily have done it.*'

When he had finished speaking the silence in the room was broken only by the ponderous tick-tock of the ormolu clock on the mantelpiece. Then, one by one, they looked at Jill: Cowley, Bodie – even Mrs Wilson – and, last of all, Ray Doyle.

Jill stood absolutely still. Then she lifted a hand and pressed it to her mouth. She stared at the men. The horror was beginning, now, beginning to claw and gibber at her. Her façade began to crumble. Her mouth opened and her teeth, those beautiful pearly white teeth, began to chew and gnaw at the back of her hand like the teeth of hounds pulling down their quarry.

Cowley went on speaking in a calm composed voice.

'It will take some proving. Circumstantial. But the police have done that before.'

The psychological farce had played itself out. Jill and her father had played for high stakes, using the psychology of honesty allied to a need to achieve justice that they knew existed in most people – if not in their friends or themselves. And that pressure had almost worked. It *had* worked, for Ray Doyle had gone to bat for them simply because an honest doubt had been planted in his mind. Now it had all gone smash.

A ghastly animal retching noise slobbered up from Jill Haydon's delightful throat, burst out shockingly through those perfect lips. She cracked. The real Jill Haydon was revealed. Screaming abuse she hurled herself forward. She struck straight for Cowley. Long painted fingernails ripped down his cheek, missing his eye by a shaving, leaving gouged crimson lines that oozed blood. Cowley went back with the attack and, just for a moment, the shock held them in stasis.

Then Doyle jumped forward and grabbed Jill and hauled her off his chief. Jill had turned into a frenzied, screaming, kicking fury. Her hysteria stank in the room.

Bodie moved, and was still. Cowley took out his handkerchief and dabbed his cheek. He looked remarkably cool for a man who has just had his face lacerated by painted fingernails, and almost lost an eye.

Speaking mildly, Cowley said: 'Someone should tell her father, don't you think?'

Wordlessly, Doyle thrust the kicking squirming form of Jill at his partner. Bodie took her into his capable grip and she quietened, staring about with bright eyes that saw nothing. Her lips kept on writhing, trying to speak, and spittle dribbled.

That same old prison aroma, the same grey walls and iron bars, the same hollow resonance of gates thudding shut, all struck Doyle differently now. He walked along almost jauntily – almost, for walking jauntily in prison is an art form practised by very few, and they the privileged crime barons of the underworld. Doyle felt contempt for them all. One of their number had reached the end of a very important road.

Big Bill Haydon looked up through the wire mesh of the interview room. Doyle had not requested a private room for this one. That, he felt, would spoil a certain charisma he wanted to obtain – wanted to obtain very badly. Syd Parker . . .

Haydon looked hopeful and happy. His face although still lined and sunken, still the face of the old lag and not that of the underworld king he had once been, reflected an inner spirit that looked forward with confidence to his release eventually. His wonderful daughter Jill had fixed it all, with his help and contacts. She had told him a retrial would take time; but now he was confident he could summon the courage to wait a little longer. Just a little longer . . . And then he would be *out*.

'It's special news, isn't it?' he began, eagerly, bubbling. 'Good news? Soon as they told me *you* were coming I knew. That statement of yours has stirred 'em! Stirred 'em up good and proper.' He smiled, a big beam that turned thc lines into good-natured wrinkles. 'Well? Well, tell me. When am I going to get out of here?'

Ray Doyle regarded him.

This – thing – had murdered his partner, Syd Parker. Syd's widow had not lasted long after that . . .

'I don't think,' said Doyle, 'you'll ever get out of here.'

Haydon's face began to draw in. His eyes widened. His mouth opened, suddenly, and he began to pant, like a hunted beast, driven into its lair.

Doyle went remorselessly on: 'Conspiracy with your daughter. Accessory to the caretaker's murder. When they add that to your thirty years they'll probably decide to throw away the key.'

Haydon's face broke up. He tried to speak. There was a drilling pain in his chest, cutting through him like the old thermite lance cut through a safe. He stared at Doyle, beginning to shake, beginning to fall apart.

Doyle turned away, ready to go, not caring to wait around to see a man dying in front of his eyes.

'No,' Haydon managed to croak out, at last. 'No . . . NO!'

Doyle went away and left him there.

Outside the grey walls Cowley and Bodie waited for Doyle in the car. He got in and leaned back, breathing deeply. His Adam's apple jumped in the open neck of the shirt.

Bodie and Cowley exchanged looks.

Cowley cleared his throat. Bodie put the car in gear and they wheeled out.

'Well, cheer up, Doyle,' said Cowley. 'You can't win 'em all! Especially those you already won seven odd years ago!'

Chapter Nine

Heathrow was at the eternal business of funnelling people in and funnelling people out. The sun smoked down brassily and the big jets spewed their long trails as they lifted off. In regular ordered sequence they lifted away and others drifted down out of their stacked orbits to drop down with spread undercarts and more people. The bars and baggage handling facilities and toilets and ticket offices were going full blast. The foyer looked like an overturned bee hive.

All in all, the situation was tailor made for the latest operation of the Myer-Helmut Group.

Myer stood in a casual attitude with a folded newspaper under his arm, his narrow eyes watching the foyer exit. He was a narrow man, with a narrow strip of chin beard, narrow waist, and a look about his close-set eyes, the set of his head on his shoulders, that spoke of a narrow view of life, a dedicated view, a view wrapped in passion like ice-cubes.

His smart unobtrusive clothes did not mark him out as a German; but when he spoke English the unmistakable accent was there, like a deep stain in a stream.

Across from him Inge Helmut waited and watched with her partner. She was around thirty, five years or so younger than Myer, and her body had been kept in trim shape. Her clothes, too, would mean nothing to any observer. Her face, sallow, with a mouth a little too small for real beauty, and eyes that had forgotten how to laugh in real joy, revealed nothing of her thoughts. But her passion, too, was like Myer's – chilling, completely absorbing her whole life, an arctic breath from a glacier.

When Sir Derek Forbes appeared, Myer and Inge gave no indication that the quarry had come walking daintily down to the waterhole. Forbes looked to be what he was, a middle-aged, wealthy business man on a profitable trip. He carried a tooled leather briefcase. His face bore the marks of good living of the standards of the Mansion House luncheons. He walked purposefully. He paused to check his ticket and Myer and Inge, with the slightest of nods, one to the other, converged upon him. Their movements blended with those of the other passengers.

In the hand pressed flat against his thigh, Myer carried a hypodermic needle. He could feel it, hard and round and his fingers did not tremble. This was an operation that would be carried out flawlessly. Once the success had been achieved the world would know the Myer-Helmut Group had pulled off another coup. That was the way to deal with the rotten and corrupt establishments of the world. Treat them with the same force and violence, the same contempt, with which they treated the millions of dupes who so spinelessly acquiesced in that mind-distorting government.

Inge reached Forbes first as he smiled at the inspector and began to stow his wallet away. Inge bumped him. She halted for just that length of time that would ensure the body contact was made, and no longer.

Quite naturally Forbes turned towards her, ready to make an apology for the collision, still thinking of the business appointment ahead, hardly seeing her.

As Forbes' head turned so Myer moved in from the blind side.

The hypodermic needle snouted like a gladius. It went in without resistance, piercing through smart Savile Row cloth, penetrating skin, sinking into flesh. The contents jetted.

Instantly, withdrawing the needle and once more concealing it skilfully, Myer started to move on, his stride not broken.

Death crossed Sir Derek Forbes' face.

He jerked his head back to see Myer, who merely looked through him, walking on, walking out of Forbes' life – walking out of his death.

Inge faded the other side.

Forbes collapsed.

He dropped his briefcase. His hands raked out and caught at Myer's coat, holding the other man for that brief timeless instant. Inge caught the falling briefcase. They both looked at the dying man, the swirling people all about coming and going oblivious of this central drama. Then Forbes' grip slackened. Spittle slobbered from his mouth. He could not speak and paralysis began to harden over his face. He fell.

Myer and Inge walked away – just simply walked away.

Only when Forbes slumped to the floor and lay motionless among the forest of legs was any attention paid to him.

By the time the first onlookers realised the man was dead Myer and Inge were long gone.

The blown-up photograph of Sir Derek Forbes showed his body sprawled in death on the airport foyer floor. Betty pinned it up on the board. She moved with all her accustomed grace; yet she was uncomfortably aware of the tension in her boss. George Cowley, chief of CI5, was a man with a great load of trouble dumped on to him and his organisation – a load of trouble dumped on him from a great height.

Cowley tapped the photograph. He spoke to a group of his men, briefing them. They were not all alike. They were all different. Ray Doyle was there, tousled as ever, casually dressed, storing up the information as it was handed out. There were others there, Tony, Jax, the massive and genial Negro who packed such a punch, Colin Cade, the dynamite artist who could use his plastic to blow apart anything at all. They were all different. But they were all the same in their alertness, their dedication to the reasons for the existence of the Squad, their loyalty to George Cowley. On the shoulders of these men of CI5 rested far too much of the responsibility for the peace and safety of the country.

Bodie was not there.

Cowley spoke in his usual brisk way, a voice brimming with confidence, and, also, a voice of acerbity that made a man's backbone straighten up.

'Sir Derek Forbes. Businessman. Politician. Deceased.'

As an epitaph it was pithy and true. Cowley showed the second photograph. The prick of the needle had left a hole in Forbes' thigh. The hole was ringed in red fibre-point.

'He took a hypo in the thigh, here. Two grains of pure poison. And all the hallmarks of the Myer-Helmut Group.'

Cowley crossed to the second board where the mugshots of the gang were pinned up. The agents followed his movements with eyes alert, storing away lineaments, using their training to trigger the required responses when the time came. If it ever came...

Cowley indicated the faces in the pinned-up photographs as he ticked them off.

'Franz Myer. Inge Helmut. Hans Russeheim. Tony Kristo. There are others, of course. But these are the leaders. These are the most dangerous.' Cowley pulled his glasses off and regarded his men with a stony face. 'The Myer-Helmut Group. Anarchists, fanatics, they've bombed, killed or maimed at least a hundred innocent people in the last two years. Now they're here – in Britain.' His voice remained level; but the force drove home deeply. 'And I want them!'

Raymond Doyle would answer with a friendly smile to the name Ray. William Andrew Philip Bodie would answer only to Bodie. That was the way the guy was. He claimed the most startling history, with all manner of adventures in Africa, from being a mercenary in the jungles to living with an older woman on the Cape. He had been a sergeant in the Airborne, that was true. But he was canny in opening up his past life, and to Doyle, who had been a copper and a detective-constable, and understood the criminal underworld of London, Bodie often posed the kind of exotic picture a flamingo must pose to a sparrow.

Now Bodie looked at his right hand and tried to think of the vilest swearwords he could use and still not come up with half of his feelings.

The doctors CI5 employed were the best.

Bodie tried to close that powerful right hand of his into a fist. He strained. He could feel all the muscles pulling, the nerves screaming and he tried to blank out the pain.

'You see, doc?' he said, and knew it wasn't any damned good.

The doctor shook his head, only half-smiling. 'The bullet tore the ligaments. They heal slowly –'

'But,' persisted Bodie with all the stupid stubbornness in him that would make his partner Doyle smile wryly. 'You see? It's okay now?'

'You can't close your hand.'

'Doc . . . ' The note of pleading in Bodie's voice would have shocked those unfortunates who had been severely struck about their vital parts by that same right fist. Spike McFadden's bullet had done grievous harm to Bodie's right hand, just before Bodie had shot the killer in the guts. But the damage was done. That case was over and McFadden would stand trial. But the evil results were being agonised over, here and now.

The doctor spoke more forcefully.

'If you can't close your hand, you can't hold a gun, and if you can't hold a gun there's no place in this organisation for you.' The doctor allowed a frosty twinkle to kindle for a tiny time in his eyes. 'Quote – George Cowley.'

'Doc, surely – I'm pretty good with my left – have to be in the jungle –'

'Not good enough. You're not a hundred per cent. Do you want to argue it with *him*?'

Bodie's face drew down and his eyebrows formed a

black and hating bar. He did not wish to argue anything with George Cowley, no sir!

'Another week, Bodie, should see it all right.'

'Another week!'

'One week, and I'll certify you fit for duty again. Meanwhile, give it some gentle exercise. But don't overdo it.'

That was that.

Bodie picked up his fashionable coat, perfectly tailored, and had a devil of a struggle to pull the lapel out with that confounded hand. Disgruntled he took himself off to the briefing room. Ray Doyle might serve to cheer him up if he could get in a few good cracks. Trust Doyle to get in first, though, talking about a one-winged wonder, no doubt...

Cowley was still speaking, winding up the briefing.

'At the moment we don't have a single lead – so it's a question of nosing around, staying alert, keeping your eyes open. Okay.'

Bodie walked in as the men started to file out. He had a good look at the board, saw the photo of the dead man, saw the mug shots. He went up to Cowley and stiffened up.

'Excuse me, sir –'

Cowley did not look up. 'One more week, Bodie. The doctor has already told me.' He shuffled papers and turned away, a busy man preoccupied with his job. 'I don't like being a man short. But until that hand heals, you're no good to me.'

With that the chief of CI5 walked with his limping stride out of the briefing room.

Doyle smiled sympathetically at his partner.

'You're not missing much, Bodie. Just a routine stay alert. Myer-Helmut Group.' Bodie looked back at Doyle and made a face and, together, shoulder to shoulder, they walked out of the briefing room with the last of the others. 'Anyway,' went on Doyle, miming envy, using his hands. Your timing's perfect.' He smiled again at Bodie's injured reaction. 'Didn't you tell me the lovely Julia was free this week?'

'Yeah.' Bodie brightened. In all the furore of the last

case and McFadden and the gunshot he'd almost forgotten – almost but not quite. No healthy young man was going to forget the luscious Julia. 'Yeah! I'll take her on the river.'

Just past Marlow the Thames looked particularly lovely under the sun. The sky beamed. The trees hung over the water and their reflections danced. Tiny ripples over the surface of the water responded to the gentlest of breezes, the authentic zephyr. This was a day for relaxing, for enjoyment – and, if your inclinations lay that way – for messing about in boats.

Bodie knew all about leaping out of landing craft and charging up the beach with Sterling blazing. He knew all about paddling canoes up and down the treacherous African rivers. And he could pull an oar with the best. But, now, in a dinky little rowing boat he hauled and lugged and sweated and kept the pain from his injured right hand tucked down and away and submerged in a deep dark corner of his mind.

But that damned right hand of his pained him cruelly!

The little boat trundled along and Bodie kept her more or less on a straight line. The lovely Julia lolled in the sternsheets. She wore a dress that was white, and then wasn't white, and then was white again as the sunlight shifted. Her shape had maddened many a hitherto inoffensive young male. Her face – charming, charming! Petal shaped, with huge brown eyes, and delicately framed hair, that face swamped Bodie and aped his attempts to swamp the boat. Yet Julia, who was around twenty-five although Bodie knew enough about gentlemen not to question a lady on her age, even these days, contained a stillness and a sweetness in her that had nothing to do with glamour. Her beauty went a long way farther than merely skin deep. She was, as Doyle had said, lovely, and she was, as Bodie knew, luscious.

Now, as he strove to row with a nonchalance that became more and more strained with every stroke, Bodie felt the oar slipping from that crooked right hand.

He attempted to hold on, felt the water tug at the blade, gave a spasmodic jerk and almost lost the oar. Only by the most fortuitous of chances was he saved the ignominy of catching a crab and soaking Julia. He could feel the sweat on his forehead.

Julia leaned forward.

'Bodie,' she said with genuine concern. 'Your hand. You shouldn't – '

'I'm okay.'

On the very next stroke he was not okay, was very far away from being okay.

He fumbled at the loom, the oar skittered over the water, spinning bright drops skywards, and the oar slewed away from Bodie's clawed right hand. He made a desperate grab for it. He got it, let the water surge carry it sternwards, and then, ignominiously, hauled it inboard. He looked up to meet those huge dark eyes bearing down on him.

'Come on, let me.' She started to lift up, half-bent in the pose that moving about in small boats engenders. Half-bent like that she looked enchanting. 'It won't emasculate you, you know, Bodie. To let me row for a little while.' Bodie still hesitated. 'The mature man,' she told him, with a playful smile on those sweet, sweet lips, 'knows when to concede defeat.'

Bodie smiled, suddenly, feeling the pressure ease, feeling the pleasure of that relaxation.

'I concede.'

They began to change places, moving with caution. The little boat drifted. One of the many little islands that dotted the Thames hereabouts lay over on the starboard bow and the boat drifted towards the shrubbery-drowned bank. Trees grew inland and a few birds wide-winged aloft. Everything was very still and quiet with the chuckle of the water pleasantly liquid and alive about them.

Moving past Julia into the sternsheets, Bodie twisted about to sit down. He looked across at the island past Julia who was in the act of sitting. No man was going to avoid looking at Julia when she was in so interesting a position; but a movement on the island jerked Bodie's eyes up. Movement would always make a man follow it, and for an old campaigner like Bodie movement might be the prelude to trouble. He saw a thin-faced fellow with a strip of chin beard and narrow eyes ducking down behind a bush. Bodie frowned to himself. Had he seen that face before? The fellow probably had a girl down there, and was embarrassed. Good luck, chum, said Bodie, and settled down to the charming sight of the delectable Julia hauling at the oars.

'How's the hand?'

'Terrible.' He looked at the way Julia pulled the oars, bending and straightening, the white dress exquisite, the face a little flushed, the eyes bright. Her shape had never been lovelier. He smiled. 'But the eyes are having a great time.'

'They're staring.'

'They like – faces. Particularly pretty faces.' He smiled again, seeing pure beauty before him. The thought of faces made a new and altogether different idea occur to him. He lost his smile. 'Faces? Mug shots!'

'What?' Julia almost lost her rhythm. But she had pulled an oar before this and controlled the little boat beautifully.

'I knew I'd seen that face before. Turn back. Back to the island.'

'Wha – ?'

'Come on. Turn about!'

Wondering what was biting Bodie, Julia dug in port and pulled starboard. The boat spun around and then Julia gave way together and pulled over to the island. Bodie stood up on the sternsheets and said grimly: 'Stay here!' Then he leaped lightly ashore and vanished at once into the undergrowth.

Just inside the circling fringe of greenery the ground opened up with taller trees creating small clearings. Bodie stepped through and at once halted, in shadows, and looked out. He drew his Browning auto with his right hand, and winced, and transferred the big gun to his left hand. He could shoot okay with his left; but it was awkward and there was no denying that.

A few paces further on a groundsheet had been spread out and a litter of tins of food, plastic bags, and a small portable heating stove gave the impression of a picnic in preparation. But, among the simple domestic things lay a couple of Uzi sub-machine guns, and alarm clocks, bundles of plastic explosives, batteries and wires – all the makings not of an innocent picnic but of the bomber's means of destruction.

Bodie whistled silently, and then froze, at the crouch.

A man had stepped through from the other direction, was walking quickly past the shrubs up to the groundsheet. He looked displeased. Bodie recognised the narrow face, the thin fringe of beard, the harsh arrogance of the man who believed in a cause past reason, who would kill for that cause without compunction.

The man saw Bodie.

Bodie said: 'Hold it.'

The man went for his gun under his unbuttoned coat.

Bodie jerked the big Browning. He stepped forward as the man remained perfectly still. His eyes, like live coals, regarded Bodie with a hatred that pulsed out with a vibrance that shocked. Bodie moved in and reached out to lift the man's gun from its shoulder holster.

As he did this the man reacted. He made a swift grab at Bodie, angling the Browning away, trying for a pair of fingers in his eyes. Bodie reacted with instinct. His right hand slashed around. It hammered the man down, smashed him flat.

The instant he struck, Bodie regretted the action. White hot pain cascaded up his arm from the injured hand. He stifled his yell. But his mouth opened and he whooped for air. That had hurt – damned well hurt!

Hampered by his injured hand, Bodie managed to get

the cuffs on to the fellow. Then he hauled him to his feet.

He started to prod him along, feet dragging. As they went Bodie took a last quick look at the spread groundsheet and its grotesquely mixed freight of innocence and of death.

'Some picnic,' he grunted. 'And the table's laid for more than one.' He prodded the man more urgently. 'Come on.'

Julia stood up in the rowing boat as Bodie appeared urging the handcuffed man before him. Her eyes widened. She looked startled, and more than startled – upset, off balance.

Bodie smiled reassuringly at her.

'I'm always open for business.' He shoved the fellow into the boat. He fell on to his knees. Bodie casually pushed him down flat. 'Okay. Back to the car.'

Stunned by the unexpectedness of the occurrence, Julia obediently picked up the oars, settled them in the rowlocks, and pushed off. She began to pull out along the river.

'Bodie . . .'

'I'll explain later – come on, move it! He's expecting company. And one's just about all I can deal with now.'

Julia rowed. Her mind was in a turmoil. What had this man done that Bodie should treat him so harshly? And there was a feline cruelty in Bodie she had never observed before.

A bend approached and Julia angled the boat neatly to get around as fast as possible. She was well aware that Bodie was not playing games, even if she didn't know what was going on, even if she was appalled at his brutality with the man in handcuffs.

A power boat sped towards them. She was a nice-looking craft, belting out the knots, the white water flaring from her sharp prow. Blue and white, with a tiny mast and flag, she raced down the centre of the river. The passing of the two craft was a moment of splashing confusion. The power boat's wake set the little rowboat rocking madly. Julia struggled to keep the blades of the oars in the water and to urge them along. Bodie bent an evil eye on the handcuffed man and that fellow knew for sure that if he tried anything just then Bodie would plug him. That was writ clear in Bodie's lean handsome face.

The power boat sliced past very close.

The man looked across and a look of passionate joy flushed across his thin face.

'Inge!' he shouted. He half-rose, daring Bodie and the gun. *'Inge!'*

The power boat sped past and Bodie bellowed over the man in the centre to Julia. 'Move!'

The people in the power boat were looking back and then the curve of the river took them out of sight. The power boat came belting along and then heeled sharply, very sharply. She swung around in a hundred and eighty degree turn, leaning over, the water foaming away from her, splashing waves into the banks, sending ducks squawking. The power boat sliced around in a great skating turn and started off back along the river in pursuit of the row boat, of Franz Myer and the two people who were so unaccountably with him.

Inge Helmut could find only one answer to that question.

Franz Myer had in some way been picked up by the security forces – the presence of a woman rowing the boat puzzled her for a space, and then a sly, pleased and yet nasty smile spread her small mouth. Maybe the footling British had included a woman to take care of her. That was the kind of idiocy they went in for. Well, the power boat would soon catch up and then they would see.

The boat surged around the bend, the water cascading, the flag fluttering. Ahead the stretch of water reached out, empty of boats and ducks, still dancing with the reflections of their earlier passage. Inge stared, hatingly.

The power boat slowed as Hans hauled on the throttles. Inge looked at the banks, turning that small arrogant head, peering.

Then she slapped Hans on the shoulder. He was a big beefy man, most useful in a fight, with a thick square plug-ugly face. He saw where she pointed and shoved the throttles open. Drawn up on the bank and half-concealed beneath a drooping bush lay the row boat. The power boat made another sweeping turn, heeling over, and then Hans cut the throttles again.

With a puttering chuckle the power boat eased towards the bank.

Kristo leaned out, trying to see under the bushes. The mud was marked and greasy with gleaming slippery gouges. People had scrambled out there. Kristo, leaner and more wolfish than Hans, pointed off.

Inge nodded.

'The car park!'

Hans at once shoved in the throttles and spun the wheel. The power boat picked up speed and hurtled off towards the landing stage around the far end of the beach.

Bodie had stuffed his handkerchief into Myer's mouth. The terrorist made snorting strangling noises as he stumbled along the muddy path, away from where they'd beached the boat, heading for the landing stage, the bobbing boats, the restaurant and the car park. Bodie urged him on ferociously. Julia panted along at the rear, wide-eyed, fancying all the Hounds of Hell on her heels.

Myer stumbled and fell, his handcuffed hands raking out ineffectually to save him. He crashed to the mud.

'For God's sake!' cried Julia.

'He's a bomber. A killer.' Bodie reached down his left hand.

'He's a human being,' declared Julia, passionately. 'Maybe if *you* were – '

'I'll be more human when we get back to the car.'

He hauled Myer up and shoved him on. Julia just didn't know the score. As to that, Bodie wasn't absolutely sure. But he did know a terrorist's face wasn't pinned up in Cowley's briefing room without very good cause. Ray Doyle had casually mentioned the watch and ready routine; but the Myer-Helmut Gang was known, and detested, by men who tried to save innocent people from getting blown up.

The red roof of the restaurant showed ahead through the trees. Julia stumbled and nearly ricked her ankle, and staggered on after Bodie. That tough man gave Myer a push, forcing him on. The bomber kept faking it, trying to delay progress. They came out under the trees on the edge of the car park.

The blue and white power boat lay a little offshore, expertly held on throttle and rudder, and a man stood up in her, peering towards the car park. Bodie remained still. Two people prowled among the parked cars.

Inge and Hans moved swiftly and expertly among the lines of cars. Inge stopped beside a Ford Capri Ghia, a red model with gold trim. She looked down on to the seat.

A radio-telephone handset lay there. Black and square and with the silver aerial half-telescoped, it told Inge all she wanted to know. She beckoned Hans over.

Watching from the shadow of the trees, Bodie saw the pair congregate around his car.

He cursed.

'Damn!' he said, and even that made Julia wince and glare at him. His tone, the ferocity of disgust in him, shocked her anew.

'They out-thought us,' said Bodie. 'They out-ran us.'

He could feel the pain in his bad right hand. He felt incomplete, ineffective. 'Oh, damn,' said Bodie. 'Damn, damn, damn!'

Chapter Ten

Dick Braydon trundled his old Cortina into the car park. He wore an inane grin of bliss on his narrow, unprepossessing features. The rubber dinghy atop the car roof swayed and rocked as he hauled up and set the hand-brake.

When he alighted from the car he surveyed the cars, the restaurant, the river, and he let the feelings of goodness flow over him. A man to appreciate nice things with the top of his mind, Braydon, a shallow man without a deep thought in his narrow skull.

The sun felt good and he shrugged off his jacket, to reveal an over-fancy shirt. Then he reached up for the first of the complicated knottings he had used to secure the rubber dinghy to the car.

Looking out as the browny-black Cortina stood there, the driving side door open, Bodie could see into the interior. The ignition keys glinted in the lock.

'We'll take that one,' he said with a firmness he really meant. 'Julia, you stay here.'

Julia gripped his arm in the shadows under the trees.

'No, sir ! I'm coming with you.'

'Julia . . .'

'With *you.*'

He looked at her, a searching, appraising look. She met his gaze with her deep eyes without flinching, returning his stare.

He nodded. 'Okay. We'll be running all the way.'

Now Julia nodded, a return signal, a compact.

Bodie got a good grip on Myer and, exploding from

cover, lurched up and shoved the terrorist ahead of him towards the Cortina. The idiot playing with his knots had undone one and the rubber dinghy canted a little that side.

Julia followed, her breath regained, feeling the itch of unknown dangers up her spine.

By Bodie's car Inge saw the tableau. She saw Myer being propelled forward by a man, and a girl following, and recognised them from the rowboat. She yelled at Hans and started to run across, and as she and Hans ran they pulled guns.

Bodie saw the two running towards him and he saw the guns. He was almost up to the car, and the rubber dinghy flapped on the roof as the fellow struggled with the next knot. He was over on the other side. Bodie swung Myer around. He held him fiercely, facing the oncoming pair with the guns.

'In with you, Julia!'

Julia opened the rear door.

Inge and Hans saw Myer, helpless in the grip of the security man. They did not shoot. The security man abruptly hurled Myer into the open rear door. It slammed. He slid under the wheel and the Cortina started on the first twist and bounded away.

Dick Braydon heard the slam of the first door and looked up.

He saw a stranger getting into his car.

'Hey!' said Braydon, not too slow on the uptake. 'Hey!'

He started to come around the car and then had to skip aside as the Cortina leaped off in a Grand Prix start.

The rubber dinghy flapped and caromed against the roof like a half-erected Big Top in a whirlwind.

Braydon started running after his car, waving his arms, a pathetic and a ludicrous sight. There was no chance he was going to stop the car now.

Inge and Hans picked up Kristo and they pelted across to their red Audi. Inge drove. She hurled the car across the car park like a maniac.

Dick Braydon felt the glancing blow of the red Audi and was hurled full length into a muddy patch, half-dried out. He reared up, his narrow face smeared with mud, his hair in a mess, glaring after his Cortina and the Audi in pursuit.

This was all too much for the brain cells of Braydon. He sat there in the mud and shook.

The Cortina howled along the road. Bodie drove hard and fast. The sun had dried out the hedgerows and trees and the day smiled about them. Bodie's face was set in harsh unsmiling lines. He knew only too well what he'd stumbled on, and the knowledge did nothing to reassure him – not with Julia along, a recalcitrant prisoner and a damned half-useless hand.

His hand hurt.

He used his left hand as much as possible, and more leaned on the wheel with his right rather than gripping when he changed gear. The Cortina picked up speed and smoked down the road.

Looking back through the rear window Julia saw the red car snake around the bend after them. The car moved swiftly along the narrow road.

'They're gaining on us!'

She tried to keep the panic out of her voice. Bodie had enough to keep him occupied; but she did look at Myer, and that hard man stared back with a triumphant contempt.

Inge had her foot hard down. The red car hurtled along.

Hans drew his gun and leaned out the window, trying to get a bead on the browny-black car in front.

He fired.

The bullet cracked past, clearly audible to Bodie, who had had long experience in recognising just that sound.

'Get down,' he shouted back. 'Down!'

Julia crouched as Bodie swung the wheel to slash the car around a sharp bend. The white line in the centre of the road whirled away under the tyres. A shadow fell across Bodie.

He took a raking glance out and then switched back to the road ahead.

The rubber dinghy, its knotting loosened, was slipping and sliding off the roof. Now it hung, dangling and blowing in the wind, hanging down the side of the car.

The red Audi pummelled up the road after them.

Bodie had a Bodie-type idea.

The road unwound ahead, running between trees, with the occasional five-barred gate breaking the line of trees and hedges. They were in the heart of the countryside now. The next bend lay a good distance off, and the red car pursuing them was clearly gaining.

Bodie began to saw at the steering wheel.

The Cortina snaked.

The rubber dinghy flapped and banged against the side window like an insane elephant. It dropped lower.

The bend came nearer. Bodie kept on swinging the car left and right, left and right, snaking up the road. Another couple of shots cracked past. Julia jumped.

Myer sat, rolling with the motion of the car, the acid contempt in him clearly evident.

Bodie wrenched at the wheel with his left hand, see-sawing it back and forth, and the Cortina sashayed up the road. Almost at the bend where a white-painted five-barred gate blocked off a dusty track the dinghy gave a last convulsive heave. The wind caught under the bulbous inflated rubber.

With a final heave at the wheel Bodie slewed the car in a four-wheel skid around the bend.

The rocking, the wind, the slipping knots, that final wild skid, all came together in beautiful combination.

The rubber dinghy humped up, flopped like an overweight wrestler into the road. It sighed a spread of dust as it hit.

Bodie gunned the car away up the road.

Inge saw the dinghy and desperately slewed the red Audi away. The front wheel ran over the rubber, puncturing and lacerating the dinghy on the metal trim. The Audi slewed. It slammed off the road, side-swiped the five-barred gate, crashed on up the roadside bank to come to a shuddering halt. The occupants were thrown about; but they were not hurt. Inge banged her small fist on the steering wheel. The Cortina vanished ahead.

Bodie let a smile of triumph curve his mobile lips.

Around the next curve he let up on the accelerator as a red-painted phone booth, situated at a cross-roads, came in view. The Cortina skidded to a halt by the booth, dust spouting from the locked wheels.

'Hold on!' snapped Bodie and leaped from the car. He flung open the phone booth door and grabbed up the receiver. Then jiggling the pressels and cursing, he saw the state of the phone booth. The receiver was dead. The booth had been thoroughly vandalised.

Cursing as though a red-hot poker was being used on his hand – as, it felt to him, one damned-well was – he flung the receiver down.

Julia yelled.

'Bodie . . . Bodie!'

Bodie exited smartly. Julia was pointing back out of the window.

Inge had simply backed the Audi over the rubber dinghy, comprehensively destroying it, slammed in the gear again and gone haring up the road. Now they were in sight again, and Julia was yelling. Bodie raced for the Cortina, leaped in and gunned her away. He felt the chill and the scorch, and neither sensation in his head had much relation to the pain in his hand.

They hared around the corner and belted along a straight stretch. By the time Bodie reached the next curve his hand was like a branch of fire.

Just before he tooled the Cortina around the curve, the red Audi appeared in sight at the far end of the long straight.

Julia was taking a concerned interest in Bodie's hand; she saw the way he winced if he had to use it.

'Bodie . . .' she said.

'I know.'

'The nearest town's at least six miles.'

'I know that, too.'

Julia said with passionate conviction: 'We won't make it.'

Bodie's answer was to wrench savagely at the wheel and drive the car headlong up the roadside bank. The wheels spun and then gripped and the car bounded over the grass and headed under the trees. They jounced along a pot-holed track, feeling branches whipping against the bonnet and windows, rocking from side to side. Bodie changed to second and they ground along with the track rutting and bushes reaching out imploringly at them to halt. He forced the car on, the wheels spinning, until at last, the woods closed in as though to say he had penetrated their secret recesses far enough with his stinking mechanical monster.

Bodie killed the engine.

He got out, opened the rear door and took a good grip on Myer with his left hand. He yanked the terrorist out without ceremony. 'C'mon, you,' said Bodie. Julia followed, looking nervously back. The three set off through the woods.

This was the hare and the hounds, now. A foot-chase through woods. Well, if he was anything, Bodie was a jungle animal. Even so, he hoped against hope that the terrorists would miss that turn-off into the woods and go screeching on – to hell and damnation for Bodie's taste.

Inge sent the red Audi hurling around the bend and straightened up with a distinct shimmy. The car began to build up speed. It went streaking past the opening to the woods.

Abruptly Inge's memory called back the image of that opening, the way the branches looked more straggly than they should. Straggly? No – broken, snapped – a car had driven down there.

She reversed back savagely, the tyres protesting, and wrenched the wheel over. The Audi lolloped over the bank and into the trees. Hans and Kristo drew their guns as they alighted, and Hans carried a heavy-looking valise. Inge bellowed at them to move and they hurried along into the woods.

Out on the far side of the woods Bodie was urging Myer along with an ever increasing sense that the ruse would not work. He didn't think it would have fooled him, and he was well aware that the Myer-Helmut Gang, for all their fanaticism, were a professional bunch. The land opened out past the trees and sloped away to reveal a broad and spacious valley, well wooded, with the glint of water, and a distant church steeple bowered in greenery. There was no reaching that. Down the long grassy slope the three went, with Julia following on as Bodie shoved and pushed the reluctant Myer.

As they descended they became aware of the glint flashing at them from a grove of trees ahead. Instantly Bodie headed that way. The glint came from the windows of a house, a large brick house with stone facings, set in a wall and garden of some extent. It was isolated; but the place would have a telephone.

Bodie had almost reached the last of the slope and was about to push Myer across a gravel path towards the wrought iron gates set between pillars in the wall, when he heard the sounds of pursuit.

He spun about. Julia went past with Myer. Up the long slope and half hidden by the scattered trees three figures ran out from the woods. They started down at once. Bodie felt the anger rising in him, and suppressed it, controlled it, used it as Cowley taught.

Myer turned and saw his friends running out of the woods. He smiled. He dropped to his knees and Julia almost fell over him. He rolled over, ready to lie there and refuse to run any more.

Bodie turned back from that hate-filled stare up the long slope and saw Myer on the ground. Bodie stalked over.

He bent down and spoke flatly. 'You can walk,' said Bodie. He drew his gun, wincing at the pain and transferred it to his left hand. 'Or I'll pistol whip you and carry you.' He drew back the gun with every intention of striking Myer.

Julia started forward, shocked. 'No –'

Bodie thrust her aside. He had to. She just didn't understand.

'Stay out of this.' He spat the word at Myer. '*Well?*'

The terrorist slowly stood up. His face was unreadable. Bodie stowed the gun, grabbed Myer and hustled him across the gravel, through the gateway and up to the large door of the house. Wrought iron bell-pushes, lanterns, flower buckets – the place was delightful if you liked that kind of olde-worlde charm.

Bodie leaned on the push whilst he looked back up the hill.

Three figures were flitting in and out of the scattered trees. So they knew he had a gun, then...

The door opened.

A well-formed woman, very competent-looking, somewhat shabbily-dressed, stood smiling at them. Her blouse had no doubt been fashionable some ten, fifteen years ago. But her shoes were sensible and well-polished, and her skirt neatly pleated.

Bodie didn't wait for formal introductions. Instantly he thrust forward and using Myer as a battering ram slammed the door all the way open and propelled them into the hallway. Julia ran in quickly after them. Myer fell full length. But he did not cry out. Bodie rounded on the woman.

She had the face that would arouse instant trust in an escaped convict. Large eyes, a generous mouth, a clear skin, and, clinching the picture, over it all a polished, smooth, happy look that came from an inner serenity absent from most of a world living on borrowed time on over-prescribed drugs.

Bodie slammed the door shut.

'Don't be frightened.'

The woman's smile did not alter at this bizarre greeting or the unceremonious irruption of these people.

'I'm not frightened.'

Bodie took out his ID Card and showed it.

'CI5 – ' he started to say.

A voice called from the oak staircase almost drowned in bulbous banisters.

'Sara?'

Bodie swivelled, to see the man walking uncertainly down the stairs, wearing black clothes, wore also a clerical collar.

The man took in the scene. 'Oh my God . . .'

Bodie said: 'Wearing that collar – he should be yours.'

'Who are you?' demanded the vicar.

Bodie slapped out the ID again, and said in his briskest voice: 'I take it you believe in free speech?'

'What?'

'Want to use your phone.'

The vicar was about fifty years old with an ascetic face overly-lined, a worried face, a face with too much misery stored away in it that battled always with a vocation in which he believed devoutly. He was, obviously, a bachelor.

The calm woman, Sara, reacted as soon as Bodie finished speaking. She opened the panelled door to the study and motioned to Bodie to go through. 'Through here . . . ' She was amazingly cool. Julia stared at her, a little envy tugging at her own recollections of panic.

When Bodie went through with a polite murmur of thanks, he left the vicar and Sara to stare, a little helplessly, at Julia and Myer. Julia bent over the man and removed Bodie's handkerchief. Myer started to work his jaws around, feeling the after-taste, all soft and fluffy. Julia looked up and felt she had to make some kind of explanation, although this was Bodie's scene.

'He's a bomber. A killer.'

The vicar put a hand to his mouth. The hand was slender and stringy, with wasted flesh between the sinews, and blue veins wriggling like fat worms across the wrinkled skin.

Sara said nothing.

George Cowley looked up perfunctorily from his desk as Doyle brought in a file. The desk was littered with paper. Cowley shoved his heavy glasses up and slapped the file down with the others. He was about to make a caustic comment when the phone rang.

Well – as he had reflected before – when that phone rang it could signal anything, up to and including the end of the world.

He picked up the receiver, his eyes still tracking across the latest report in the file, and said: 'Cowley.'

A moment later he said, sharply: 'Bodie!'

Bodie said quickly: 'I've got one of those faces. Those faces pinned up on your board.'

Cowley took off his glasses with his free hand and crouched closer into the phone.

'Myer-Helmut... Who? Which one?'

Bodie said: 'I dunno. The one with the strip of chin beard and the nasty habits.'

Cowley blinked. 'With the chin beard – That's Myer himself. Franz Myer.'

'Whoever he is,' Bodie told his chief. 'I need help. They're closing in –'

'Where are you?'

'I'm not sure exactly. A little place nor –'

Bodie had stopped speaking and Cowley, tensed up, listened to a dull deadness. Then he said, his voice raised to a shout: 'Hello! Hello!'

He was holding a dead line.

'Bodie... *Bodie!*'

Inge Helmut looked up with satisfaction. Hans dropped down from the little sloping roof and landed like a cat beside her. He dangled a pair of wire-clippers in his hand. He was smiling confidently. With his other hand he offered Inge about a metre of telephone wire. Beyond them the house slumbered in the sun.

Bodie hammered the phone. The black plastic shivered.

'Hello! *Hello!*'

The line was as dead as 1978 morals – in some people.

Slamming the phone back Bodie looked out of the window. The windows were beautifully proportioned, true eyes of a Georgian house, and revealed a peaceful scene of sloping grass and distant trees, with a tranquil sky beaming above. The countryside was isolated, very isolated.

The view got to Bodie. Lithely, moving from stillness to action as a panther springs, he crossed the study and closed the windows, slammed the shutters and, fumbling with his left hand, locked the bar in place. Then he hurried out of the study back to the hall.

He was already speaking before he was fairly out the door.

'Are there shutters on every window?'

The vicar said in a stuffy, enquiring, uncertain way: 'Look here –'

Bodie shouted over him.

'Are there?'

Sara said: 'Yes.'

'Right,' said Bodie. 'You and Julia close every one.' As Julia started to say something, he carried on heavily: 'Just do as I say.' The two women moved away about their task and Bodie turned to the vicar. 'The back door . . .'

Something about the situation penetrated to the vicar, for he merely inclined his head and motioned to Bodie. 'This way.'

On the floor Myer watched them go. His thin face showed a malevolent hatred, the pent-up hatred of a man who fanatically believes in himself and what he stands for and can see no goodness in anyone or anything else.

Cowley's voice spoke tinnily from the recorder.

'That's Myer himself. Franz Myer.'

'Whoever he is. I need help. They're closing in.'

'Where are you?'

'I'm not sure exactly. A little place nor . . .'

The line went dead. Cowley leaned forward and switched the tape recorder back again. Again Bodie's voice said: 'I'm not sure exactly. A little place nor . . .'

Doyle regarded his chief as Cowley switched the recorder off and sat back in his chair with a grunt. He was not pleased.

'I need help, he said.'

'A little place nor . . . North?' queried Doyle.

'North, yes, probably. But north of where?'

Doyle smiled. 'The lovely Julia!'

He explained. 'Bodie said he'd take Julia on the river. Thames, I think. It's a long river – wait a minute – he took me once, a stretch past Marlow.'

'All right. What car did he take from the pool?'

'A red Capri Ghia with –'

Cowley thumbed the intercom and spoke to Betty, giving her the information. 'Start with the car. APB units to find it. Concentrate around the Marlow area.' He stood up and limped around the desk, and Doyle did not miss the instinctive pat to the neatly-tailored suit, a pat to a suspicion of a bulge under the armpit.

'Come on, Doyle.'

Chapter Eleven

Bodie sweated heaving the big bulbous old furniture up against the doors. He tried to make a good job of each one; but his hand was giving him the very devil. He blocked off all the doors save the study door which remained open and the front door and the squared-off stairway leading to the upper floors. He wiped his forehead and then tried to inject an optimism he couldn't really feel into his voice. He had to put some heart into the troops.

'We're lucky. This is an old house. Stout shutters, stout locks – '

'Bodie,' said Julia, exasperated, still deep-down scared and not liking it one little bit. 'Bodie – they're armed!'

'So am I.' Bodie took out the Browning and held it in his bad hand and made a sorry mess of it. 'So am I.'

He prowled to the shutters over the window, and started in to tell the vicar and Sara the meat of the situation. 'They want him.' He nodded to Myer. 'But he's their leader, so they want him alive. Now, all we have to do is sit tight.' He smiled. 'Sit tight and wait.'

'Wait for what?' The vicar's face wore more lines than ever.

'I made a call. I got cut off. But they can put two and two together and make four. They'll find us eventually.'

'And suppose one of my parishioners comes along?'

Bodie swung away from the shutter to glance at Sara. 'Is that likely?'

'Not on a Monday – '

'But it is possible,' said the vicar firmly.

Bodie considered. Then: 'Deal with it when it happens.' He looked again through the crack in the shutters. Difficult to know which way the bastards would come . . . He turned back again and once more tried to inject a note of sanity into an insane situation.

'In the heat of the moment I forgot my manners. I'm Bodie. This is Julia.'

Most grudgingly, the vicar said: 'Edward Turnbull. My housekeeper, Sara.'

Bodie smiled. 'I'm glad to see you're not a teetotaller. Sara, why don't you pour us all a drink? I think we all need one.'

At that Myer began to laugh. Although the laugh was wild, there was nothing mad about the fellow. He mimicked them. 'Have a drink, vicar – so polite, vicar, let's have a little party – you English are all mad.' His smile turned into a grimace of hate. 'Enjoy your drink, because undoubtedly it will be your last.' Bodie moved and stilled as Myer said with scathing venom: 'Do you think they are going to let you hold me here?' He turned to the others. 'Sit tight and wait, he said. Well, he may fool you –'

Bodie said: 'Shut up.'

Myer went on, his voice rising. 'He may even be fooling himself. But there is nothing to wait for – except death –'

Bodie moved. He said: 'Shut up!' and cuffed Myer across the face with his right hand. As Myer fell back and the vicar stepped between them, Bodie felt the lightning bolts go shooting up his arm. His face paled.

'I won't tolerate this –' began the vicar.

'I'm sorry, vicar. But I'm running this show.'

Myer sneered now, sitting up. 'Running the show? Oh, yes, you are armed. You have a gun – but no hand to hold it with. You are dealing with the Myer-Helmut Group and we are not trash. We're a political force –'

Bodie snarled: 'Forget the political – concentrate on the force.'

'Surely,' said the vicar. 'These people outside. If we talked to them – '

'They'd reply with bullets.'

'We should at least try to *talk* – we should at least – '

His uncertain voice was cut short by a harsh bellow from outside. Inge shouted. She sounded angry and tense.

'Hey! Hey – you in there. We have you like rats in a trap.'

Bodie scuttled to the crack in the shutter and peered out. He could see no one. Inge's harsh voice continued.

'It is just a matter of time. But don't listen to my words. *Listen to this!*'

The vicious clatter of a submachine gun burst shards of violence against the golden glowing day.

'We have the power to shoot the door right off its hinges,' shouted Inge. 'To decimate it!'

Bodie acted. He snatched up Myer from the floor and fairly hurled him against the front door. He crouched to one side, holding Myer down as he would hold down a beaten wrestling opponent on the mat.

'Yeah?' bellowed Bodie. 'Well, now, you listen to me. You decimate that door and you decimate Myer along with it. Because I've got him spread right in front of it!'

Inge's voice took on an urgent note. 'All right, all right. So it is stalemate.'

At this Bodie relaxed his fierce grip a little. Inge went on: 'But why be foolish? Release Myer and we'll be quietly on our way. We do not want to hurt innocent people.'

Bodie remembered the submachine gun shots. He remembered the Uzis he'd seen spread on the picnic groundsheet. The bitch probably had her own SMG cradled in her arms now, right now . . .

The vicar was listening to the talk, his mouth open, panting as though he found it difficult to breathe.

Inge said: 'Open the house to us. We will take him away. You won't see us again. You have our promise.' No one answered her. Finally she half-screamed: 'Is everyone in there pig-headed?'

The vicar moved through the study to the window. He moved almost as though he went in a drunken stupor, hardly aware of his actions, knowing that what he did was the right thing to do. He began to throw back the shutters. Julia saw him.

'No,' she cried and ran across. The vicar pushed her aside with a gesture that would have horrified him in other circumstances.

'I'm a man of God,' he shouted, clambering up on to the broad windowsill. He knocked a bowl of flowers flying, the blue and yellow petals and the silvery water cascading like confetti. 'They'll listen to me.' He called out of the window, poising to let himself down outside. 'I'm coming out.'

Poised in the window, one hand gripping the frame, the other reaching out, he looked suddenly powerful, in command of himself, doing the right thing in an impossible situation.

Julia screamed, staggering up from where she had fallen.

'*Bodie!*'

Bodie heard that frenzied scream, the imploring, disbelieving note. He belted in through from the hall.

A submachine gun cut loose from the garden.

The vicar jumped. His body twitched and jerked. Bullets stitched across his torso. Julia and Sara were screaming. The SMG sounded loud and yet feline, a wicked hissing rattling screech of oiled metal and exploding powder.

Bodie catapulted into the room.

The vicar swivelled in the window.

His chest, his stomach, his face were chewed away, shining with blood, gruesome. He stood there, his hands clawed, his legs buckling. Then he toppled outside the window. Bullets chipped through and gouged into the ceiling.

9

Bodie tried to get his bad hand around the Browning and fumbled and cursed and switched hands. Supporting his left with his right he triggered two quick shots through the window as he jumped forward. Outside Inge and Hans dived for cover with the bullets spanging about their ears.

Trying to close the shutters with a gun in his good hand and the bad hand virtually useless was a hopeless task.

He banged away at the shutters and lock and shouted over his shoulder: 'Help me!'

'The Vicar – ' Sara's voice sounded breathy and squashed.

'Already dead . . . Help me . . . Help me . . . '

Between them they got the shutters closed and locked and even as Bodie slammed the bolt home he pushed Sara to the floor. The next instant SMG bullets rattled against the stout wood like flung pebbles.

Outside among his beloved flowers the vicar lay sprawled in death. On his face his last expression was implanted with the violence of his death.

That expression was one of shocked surprise.

Bodie rose to his feet. He looked hard at the women and saw what he expected to see. His lips firmed. This was not going to be an easy ride; yet there was nothing else he could do – not now.

'Round one,' said Bodie.

The APB found Bodie's car and the local police told Cowley of the report of a stolen Cortina – with attached inflatable dinghy – and Doyle at once realised that Bodie had stolen the car. When the rubber dinghy was discovered the area of search was narrowed down. Somewhere north of that point. The country stretched, isolated, bowered in greenery, with a few villages which had hardly changed since William the Conqueror had missed them. Perhaps a hand-cranked petrol pump made a difference.

Cowley told his C15 men: 'Bodie's near here somewhere. Holed up. And we have to find him – fast!'

Julia drew the bandage tightly around Bodie's crippled hand.

'Tighter.' Bodie's face screwed up. 'Tighter!'

'You won't feel anything –'

'That's the idea, isn't it?'

Bodie hefted the Browning auto into his left hand. He could just about manage to give some support with his bandaged right. He was about to put the gun down when a faint scratching noise reached him from the shutters. Quiet as a stalking cat he crossed to the window and peered through the junction of the two shutters. He saw a black round hole poking at him. Instinctively he ducked and the gun blasted over his head. The bullet smashed into a mirror on the other side of the room.

Grimly, making a thing out of it to halt the others' reactions, he said: 'Seven years' bad luck.'

On a sob, Julia said: 'If we've got seven years.'

'Sh . . .' Bodie listened. Then he put his eye to the crack. He was just in time to see the man called Hans turning away to the rear of the house.

Bodie went back to the table and was about to help himself to a stiff drink when the thought occurred to him. He rounded on Sara, like a tiger.

'The cellar! Does this house have a cellar?'

'There's a coal chute – but –'

Bodie was already running out the door.

Now he had to heave aside the furniture he had so laboriously piled up. He savaged the chairs and tables away, breaking through into the corridor that led to the cellar steps. He scrabbled along towards the door, a dun-coloured flimsy affair that wouldn't stop a kitten.

Even as he reached forward the door opened abruptly. Hans was revealed, festooned with cobwebs and smeared with coaldust. On his face a wild look of triumph glittered. He brought the Uzi down to waist level and Bodie triggered a shot clear through the terrorist's chest. Hans stood upright, reaching for the sky. The Uzi under his constricting finger let rip with a long shattering burst, upwards, the bullets punching through the ceiling and scattering plaster like a snowfall. Then Hans toppled backwards and crashed back down the cellar steps.

Silhouetted in the door, Bodie felt the claws of agony strike through his bad hand. He had to open his convulsing fingers. The gun dropped to the floor by his feet.

Julia said, in a soft, scared voice: 'Bodie . . .'

He ignored her, slammed the door shut with his shoulder, and then started to push a handy table against the door, still using his shoulder. Julia moved to help him. When that was done he looked at the fallen automatic. He tried to pick it up with his bandaged hand, and could not. Finally, angrily, he snatched it up with his left hand. He met Julia's eyes. They were filled with a compassion and, also, a strange repugnance and regret.

The situation was rapidly getting out of hand. At that thought Bodie grimaced. Out of hand! A one-handed man against a bunch of sub-machine-gun-armed fanatics – well, he'd damned well do all he could right up until the very last. That was what this was all about.

At the shuttered window in the hall Myer had been slowly and carefully edging back. With all the excitement and the loosing off of an Uzi he was able to reach the shutters. He lifted and let his handcuffed hands bang against the painted wood.

'Inge,' he bellowed in German. 'Inge! The cause is all. You have my permission to attack. Don't mind me. Attack!'

Bodie was there. He slammed Myer away from the shutter, even as the terrorist screamed out a fresh stream of German. Bodie slammed his forearm across Myer's throat and pressed, choking off the shrieked words.

'What did you say?' demanded Bodie, glaring down on Myer.

Sara said: 'He told them to attack. "You have my permission to attack. Don't mind me." I took German at school.'

'Attack,' said Bodie. 'And they will.'

Inge hunkered down in hiding by the bushes watching the shuttered window to the side of the large front door. She could hear Myer's voice, still, in her head. It exhorted her. Like a stirring call of the trumpets, it demanded she rise up and follow where it led. The cause was all. Their lives were nothing beside that.

Kristo sneaked across from the next bush and slid down beside her. He looked grim. His Uzi was slung from a shoulder and he kept his finger lying along the guard.

'Inge,' said Kristo. He paused and then, in a rush: 'Hans is dead.'

Inge was still with the cause, with Myer, with the great plans. 'Did you hear him?' she whispered. 'Attack . . .'

'Inge! He's dead. Hans is dead.'

'We are all dead. In a world like this we are all dead. Just the manner of death has to be decided. Franz has chosen.'

Kristo took a breath and looked hard at the house. He saw its size, its bulk, the stoutness of the walls, the shutters over the windows.

'The house is old – well built. Like a fortress.'

Inge's narrow face tightened and her small mouth formed the words as though she spat out pebbles. 'A fortress is as strong as its weakest gate.' She stared at the front door . . . That large, ornate, opulent-looking front door with the wrought-iron bells and lanterns. 'Franz told us to attack.'

Kristo protested. 'Inge!'

'Are you faltering now, Kristo? Do you want me to do it alone?'

Kristo could not meet her eyes. He fingered his SMG. Then, not too sullenly, for he, too, believed in the cause, he said: 'What do you want?'

'The car. Can you bring it down here?'

Kristo looked startled. He had not expected this. 'I don't know. It's possible, I suppose, but . . .'

Inge nodded with a new and purring satisfaction. 'Bring it.'

As Kristo set off up the rise to the woods, Inge returned her gaze to that front door. She nodded to herself. Softly, speaking under her breath, she said: 'As strong as the weakest gate.'

Cowley's sleek white Rover 3500 sped along the country road. A deal of dust whipped up in the passage of the car; but Cowley drove fast, covering the area, searching for one of his men with a busted hand, holed up somewhere, and facing God knew what in the shape of armed fanatics and assassins.

But he wanted to talk to Doyle, who sat in the seat beside him.

'You've never told me about Bodie.' At Doyle's sudden drawing down of his mouth in surprise, Cowley went on: 'I made you a team – what? – two years ago?'

'Two years, three months.'

'That's long enough.'

'Long enough,' said Doyle, with the patience Cowley demanded. 'For what?'

'For him to get up your nose. Irritate you.'

'Oh, he does that. Every day, he does that.'

'Chalk and cheese, eh?' Cowley smiled with the small satisfaction he sometimes allowed himself when he thought of his aptitude in teaming men. When his damned leg didn't pain him, into the bargain . . . 'It's worked well, though?'

'I've minded his back, he's minded mine. That Wimbledon thing – you remember.' At Cowley's nod, Doyle said with a sudden heaviness. 'We're both still alive.' He had a sudden and devastating thought. His fists bunched, white and glistening. 'At least, this morning we both were.'

Cowley felt an outburst overtaking him, words spilling

out he couldn't control. Bodie and Doyle! Doyle and Bodie!

'I tell you to stay alive!' he broke out, passionately.

After a space he quietened and tooled the Rover around a curve and into another long country road. 'Bodie gets up my nose, too. And so do you! But I want you both to stay alive!'

The white Rover 3500 howled up the road, searching for a holed-up ace agent with a busted hand.

They were sitting in the study, Julia, Sara and Bodie. Myer lay on the floor, handcuffed, his thin and hating face somehow made more malevolent by the thin strip of chin beard.

They were drinking. Bodie fancied he'd have to keep a tight hold on the drink; they had at the very least to stay alert against the mob outside. There was the woman – Inge – and at least one other fellow. One of them, Bodie held in his mind, one of them was already dead.

He forced a parody of a smile, and, really, that smile was not too bad, not bad at all.

'This is where I show my qualities of leadership.' The two women looked at him as though he was going to pull down his trousers. 'I organise games, singing, keep us all occupied, *interested,* so we don't die of exposure. This is the bit where I – '

Flatly, Julia said: 'Shut up, Bodie.'

Bodie's smile did not waver. 'Ah! You've seen that film, too? The dissenter . . . The mandatory coward who cracks, runs wild and – '

Sara's words came smoothly and evenly, interrupting Bodie effortlessly.

'Climbs out of a window and gets himself killed.'

Bodie shut up. The vicar had been wrong – been dead wrong.

Julia said: 'Shut up, Bodie.'

'Yes.'

The silence sat uncomfortably in the study with its panelling and comfortable armchairs and cluttered desk and the vases of flowers. Sara had tidied away the bowl scattered from the window sill. The sun had shifted around and the thin cracks of light from the shutters, like pencils of gold, crawled across the Persian carpets.

'They're a long time coming,' Sara said, after the silence had stretched too insufferably long. ' "Sit tight and wait?" "Put two and two together, and eventually make four?" They're a long time coming . . .'

Bodie hesitated to answer at once, searching for the right words. The silence grew alive with the distant sound of a car coming closer. The note kept changing, revving and sinking, as though the car did not drive over the approach road but across rough and uneven ground.

Bodie crossed to the shutters and swivelled his eyeball about trying to get a comprehensive view through the crack.

'Who is it?' Julia stood up, her breast moving quickly. The hope flared in her that the police had arrived.

Bodie said in a harsh tone: 'Not the Seventh Cavalry.' He straightened from the shutters and headed for the door. 'Stay here.'

He gave a cold hard glare at Myer as he passed and then crossed the hall at a run. The wide letter box had a high-polished brass flap on the inside, the gleam a lustrous reminder of the care lavished by Sara on this old house. Bodie lifted the flap and squinted outside. The gravel drive stretched away, a yellow brick road in the sunshine. The wrought iron gates between their flanking pillars in the wall were closed and he saw the red Audi trundling down the long grassy slope towards them. He watched.

The car bumped out and over the far gravel and halted by a mass of bushes.

The slim form of the woman, Inge, leaped from the cover and entered the car.

What those two bastards out there were up to hit Bodie instantly. It was obvious. The car engaged gear and then started with a screeching roar, wheels spinning, hurtling straight for the wrought iron gates and the gravel drive.

Bodie let the brass letter-box flap fall and raced back to the study.

He roared in, skidding on the Persian carpet, and yanked Myer up.

'Upstairs!' bellowed Bodie, giving the terrorist a savage shake and launching him forward towards the door.

The two women started up.

'What . . . ?' said Julia. Her eyes opened wide. Sara said nothing but started for the door.

Bodie yelled again, dragging at Myer.

'Upstairs. Now. *Now!*'

The engine note of the racing car reached them, screaming higher and higher. Kristo was really pouring on the power and the red car must be picking up the knots.

Bodie hustled Myer out of the study door. He cast a quick glance at the front door and then bellowed at the women to go on up the stairs. They scampered up. Bodie forced Myer ahead of him, shoving him, ready to be brutally swift and merciless if he had to.

The engine noise from outside sounded like a squadron of jet bombers. And it increased, and increased . . .

The squared-off stairway turned a right angle at the first flight.

This was the place Myer chose to stage his protest and his attempt to halt the security man Bodie.

He slipped on the staircarpet which smoothed over the nose of the tread. He fell to his knees, his handcuffed hands dragging. Bodie was wrenched down by him.

'Up!' snarled Bodie.

He yanked ferociously at Myer and heaved him up. He forced the terrorist ahead of him around the bend in the stairway and let fly a tremendous kick. He kicked Myer on up the second flight. The women were scrambling on up to the first floor landing, from which opened a second and much narrower stairway leading up to the attics.

Bodie bellowed them on. The note of the car reached crescendo proportions. He gave a quick look back and then shoved on, up the flight, pushing Myer ahead of him, desperate to reach the landing and the next flight of stairs.

Kristo clamped his foot down on the accelerator all the way to the floor.

The red Audi leaped on, gathering speed like a discharged rocket, jounced over the gravel path with the bushes blurring past.

'Hold on!' screamed Kristo.

Both he and Inge wore their safety belts yanked up tightly. The car rocked over the flower beds. The wrought iron gates reared up, sunlight splintering back off the worn edges. The ornate pillars flanked them – the bonnet of the car struck, the wrought iron folded away, like double doors opening to the entrance of a butler. The car howled through, staggering like a drunk, straightened up as Kristo fought the wheel.

The car shattered through the front gates and belted straight for the front door.

Kristo and Inge held their breaths.

The gravel churned away as the tyres spun. The red car launched itself like a javelin.

The doors looked impressive, solid, with their wrought iron furniture.

The letter box gaped like a wide mouth in a welcoming grin.

The car speared ahead.

The car struck.

The door fountained up in a showering spray of splinters. It sagged back. Hinges squealed and ripped free. The locks snapped. The bars broke. The door smashed back in ruin and the car thundered through, shaking, the windscreen gone, the front wings crunched into red-streaked tissue-paper.

Kristo and Inge were flung about like beans in a grinder.

They gasped with the shock; but they held on, and the steering wheel did not spear through Kristo's chest. The car waltzed half-way up the hall, scattering chips of wood and splinters of glass, collapsed on to punctured tyres, and the engine expired with a long bowel-movement, a groan of extinction.

Inge saw the security man mercilessly beating Myer and making him rise and go on up the stairs. Her sharp features hardened like those of a hawk.

The doors opened as one, unjammed in the smash, and Inge and Kristo leaped out. They unlimbered their guns; but the security man and their chief were gone.

They leaped for the foot of the stairs.

Aloft they heard the voice screaming: '*Keep going*!'

Inge put a foot on the first tread. She smiled, a wolfish smile. 'It is good, Kristo. Now we have them trapped!'

Chapter Twelve

'Keep going!' screamed Bodie.

Somehow they tumbled up the narrow attic staircase and bashed through the door at the head. Bodie slammed Myer through and kicked him headlong. He whirled to the door.

'Julia . . .'

He had the gun gripped in both hands – wrong! He had the gun gripped in his left hand, his right merely touching and the pain flowed over him as though imps from hell raked up every nerve ending with white-hot wires. 'Lean, Julia.' Bodie shoved the gun through the door and Julia pushed the door hard on to the gun, jamming it, holding it level and steady. 'Lean hard!'

With the Browning auto fixed in this emergency clamp, Bodie triggered off a couple of shots down the narrow staircase. The noise blammed out, concussing with doubling and re-doubling echoes. The smell of fired powder rasped up. The bullets spanged off the walls, ricochetting. Below on the landing Inge and Kristo flung themselves back, hiding back of the staircase opening. Their faces bore expressions suitable for witch-doctors at tribal sacrificial orgies. The space was so narrow they knew that the gunman up there must hit something when he shot . . .

Bodie put his eye to the crack and peered out. No sign of the terrorists . . . He sighed and shook his shoulders and then looked about the room in which they found themselves. It was just a musty, fusty, dusty old boxroom, filled with trunks with broken hinges and smashed chairs and rolls of mouldering carpets and items that might have been dredged from the wreck of the *Titanic*. Up above nothing lay between them and the sky but a layer of tiles. Bodie surveyed the bric-a-brac.

'Hell of a way,' Bodie expressed himself lucidly, 'to spend an afternoon.'

On the landing below, Inge and Kristo crept back until they were safe from any random shots that might spang out from the security man aloft. They were both breathing heavily. The shock and smash of the crash when they'd punctured through the front door still rode them. Their nerve-endings still jumped.

Inge cocked her face up, and her eyes showed the impression of a feline satisfaction. 'Up there – '

Kristo protested. 'Inge, they command the stairs!'

'But,' said Inge, with a purring note of triumph. 'But not the roof.'

Kristo nodded, understanding.

A small dormer window afforded a view from the attic room. A distant and, at other times, a most pleasing prospect of open rolling countryside filled with greenery and sunshine extended away. A dusty road laid a track of golden yellow across the scene, appearing and disappearing behind stands of trees and the low rolling hills. Bodie looked out, and his face betrayed nothing as he swung back to regard the others.

Bodie, in a hard, accented voice, said: 'I've made it, ma! Top of the world!' Julia and Sara did not respond. He went on, defensively aggressively: 'Well, didn't you ever see that old Cagney movie?'

Julia said: 'I saw it. He died.'

The fuel tanks had gone up in an almighty conflagration from a sniper's bullet. Cagney had shouted with exultation – but he'd died – in the movie . . .

Bodie was brought to earth with a bump.

The big and genial Negro CI5 man, Jax, reported in that at long last the stolen Cortina had been located. Cowley sent the white Rover hurtling along the country lanes, swinging around corners as though at Brand's Hatch. Doyle hung on. He trusted his partner to be able to handle a tough situation; but he did not forget that Bodie had an injured right hand, and that Bodie was a rifleman rather than a hand gunner. The hunt was taking too damned long, altogther too damned long . . .

Inge commanded the stairway with her SMG and Kristo had gone outside to climb up on to the roof and attack from above. All in all, it appeared to Inge Helmut that the game was at last going her way. Very soon now they'd have killed the fool security man and rescued Myer. As for the women, if they got in the way, they would die, too . . .

Sara's calmness had not deserted her. The death of the vicar had been an ugly act quite outside her experience; yet her beliefs were strong enough to enable her to handle that obscenity. Now she looked curiously at the man, Bodie, and the girl, Julia. They had brought horror into her life. Now she spoke rationally, calmly, putting forward a sensible point of view.

'Why don't we throw him out?' She nodded at the handcuffed Myer. 'That's what they are asking for.'

Julia nodded, convinced. 'Makes sense, Bodie.'

Bodie said: 'No.'

'Why? If we push him out now, there's a chance they'll – '

Interrupting, speaking flatly, Bodie said: 'No.'

'Why?' Julia was shaking now, her face flushed. 'I want to know why!'

'She's right,' Sara said. 'If we are going to die we have a right to know.'

Myer spoke up from the floor. 'I agree with you.'

'You keep out of this,' Bodie told him. He spoke menacingly. Then he faced Sara and Julia. 'I don't know why. Because I took an oath? Because I hate his kind? Because I don't like to lose? I don't know why. Maybe Cowley could tell you.'

In a scathing tone of contempt, Julia said: '*Cowley*!'

Very quickly, Bodie snapped: 'Cowley's all right. Cowley is . . . ' He paused and wrinkled his lips. 'Why? I don't know why. Because I say so!'

'And what you say goes?'

'As long as I'm holding this gun.'

Even as he spoke, Bodie knew that was only the half of it. There was a greater authority here than that given by a mere gun. He was as much in love with life as the next man – more so, given the lovely Julia in view – but if the world owed him nothing he had been more and more convinced lately that he owed the world something. It might be a stupidly naïve viewpoint for a rough, tough, hairy CI5 man; but it was the oil that made civilisation mesh. And then Julia cut that down to size.

'Holding it!' Her words carried more than a hint of hysteria. 'You can barely feel it!'

Bodie's lips compressed. A silence held. Julia opened her mouth, her lips soft and red, and started to say: 'Bodie, can't we at least – '

He chopped her off. 'Shh . . . '

A tiny noise chinkled from the tiles over their heads. He crossed to the dormer window and looked out cautiously.

Away on that dusty yellow road a white car cruised into view and halted, half-hidden by trees. The sunshine lay long golden streaks over the scene, bringing up the aching beauty of the day.

In the shelter of those trees up the little track Cowley and Doyle stepped out of the white Rover. They walked over to the Cortina and Jax pointed out the bullet hole. They looked about.

'Which way, Doyle?' Cowley's voice was brisk.

'I dunno . . . '

'Two years, three months, Doyle.' Cowley looked hard

and ruthless. 'You know him better than any of us. *Which way?*'

Doyle remembered Bodie in action, he remembered that affair with Krivas and Bodie's jungle sense . . . 'Bodie's a jungle animal.'

'It'd be the woods, then?' Cowley squinted off through the trees. 'Cover?'

Doyle nodded.

'Direct all units into this area. A full sweep.' Cowley issued his orders with a snap. 'Begin at the village. Then right across the valley. Doyle. We'll take the back road.'

Cowley and Doyle got back into the Rover and the car started, began to move out.

Up in the attic Bodie watched the distant white speck start to move. It vanished behind trees along the road and then re-appeared. Bodie's eyes felt hot.

'The wrong way,' he said, so low the others couldn't hear. 'Damn you. The wrong way!'

The car wound along the road which swung past a rolling mound of grass and a long stand of trees. Bodie swung further on. The road appeared again, a stretch open and without trees masking it. It was a good long way off. Over his head and out of his sight Kristo worked carefully and quietly with his knife prising up a tile. The terrorist worked with the sure knowledge of success. He would strip a tile, shoot the security man, and Inge would catch the others if they tried to run down the stairs. It would all be easy . . .

Turning back to the others, Bodie said heavily: 'That's Cowley. I'm sure it's Cowley. Going towards the village.'

Breathlessly, Julia asked him: 'A shot . . . ?'

'In the car, at this distance – he'd never hear it. And if he did it would only confuse. Might come from anywhere.' He thought about it. He checked with Sara that the road that appeared in the open stretch was the same road the car was on. He judged the distance. It seemed to be his only chance . . .

He started to open the dormer window.

On the roof Kristo froze. He hardly breathed. Then, after a space, he resumed his careful prising of the tile.

The big Browning automatic looked purposeful, not ugly so much as an artefact made by man for a particular use. Bodie knew as well as anyone that guns are neutral. It is the men or women who use them who are the partisans, the criminals, the heroes . . .

'Julia, wrap your hands around the gun. Hold it tight. Very tight.' Bodie gripped his own hand over Julia's, his left forefinger alongside the trigger. 'If I can just get their attention.'

'Bodie, it's miles!'

Bodie's eyebrows drew down. 'Sara said nearly half a mile. And this damned gun won't shoot half a mile – '

'Then why – ?'

' – it won't shoot – but it'll *reach*! There was a helluva stink on the range once. Somebody overshot and hit a roof nearly a mile away. The bullet was spent, of course. But it *did* reach.' He took his hand away and wiped the sweat from his eyes. He felt lousy. He gripped the gun again. 'Julia – I told you to hold it tight!'

Julia's lips compressed; but she tightened her grip on the Browning.

Bodie was mumbling to himself.

'Angle . . . trajectory . . . the wind could take it miles off course . . .' He licked his lips. '*Hold it steady!*'

The stretch of open road shimmered in the heat. Bodie shut his eyes and then peered along the sight again. 'Too direct. It has to fall like an arrow catching the wind, surfing on the air . . . Make correction for drift . . . What drift? How much?'

And all the time he was making minute adjustments to the aim of the gun, keeping the shakes down, keeping the sweat out of his eyes, feeling the pain in his hand, and, as he wrapped his left hand around Julia's, feeling the soft smoothness of her skin.

'Steady . . . Ver-ry steady . . .'

Abruptly, Cowley's car burst out into view, purring

along past the trees and appearing in that long open stretch. The sun shimmered off the grass and the trees and blurred a golden haze over everything. Bodie felt the heat prickling into his back and under his armpits. Now!

Bodie fired.

Julia said in the aftermath of the explosion: 'Did you hit it?'

'I don't know. I do not know!'

They did not think to let go of the gun for some time.

Cowley hit the brakes with a fierce stamp and the Rover skidded dead straight, smoking dust, pulled up with a squeal. Both men stared at the side window. It was starred but not broken. They exchanged a single look and then exited from the car very speedily. They went around to look at the starring in the window.

Doyle said firmly: 'Bullet.'

'From where?'

Doyle walked back to where the window had starred under the impact of the bullet. Cowley followed. They looked out over the ditch beside the road, past trees and bushes, keeping a straight line – a line a bullet might have followed. Doyle squinted in a hazy golden sunglow. He saw an ancient brick house bowered in trees. He frowned.

'That house!'

Cowley nodded. 'It's a damned long way – but it's the only place around – Bodie. It's got to be Bodie!'

Both men ran back for the car.

The release of one tension only heightened the continuing sense of oppression, the stifling feeling that they were trapped and merely awaiting the final execution. Julia was beginning to show effects of the strain. Her face looked pinched in. Still beautiful, still alluringly voluptuous, she was starting to crumble. Bodie felt for her. He had tried to sustain her by hard words and a sense that they had to do everything they could to stay alive – and bring in the terrorist. If they surrendered Myer, they lost their ace in the hole and could kiss their own lives goodbye. He was firmly convinced of that.

Julia bit her lips. 'Well, Bodie – perhaps they heard the shot.'

Bodie had to say it. 'I told you. That distance . . . car engine . . . Not a chance!'

'Is that our epitaph, too, Bodie? Not a chance!'

'We're here. We're alive.'

Julia was savaging that lip. Watching these people who held him captive, Myer saw that the girl was near to cracking. He looked at the crude bandage around Bodie's hand, and he looked at the security man's left hand. The skin around Myer's eyes crinkled up. Yes, that would do . . .

Bodie looked out of the dormer window again; there was no sign of the white car. Could the shot have reached? Could Cowley have heard? He had to do something about Julia – and he swung about suddenly as she spoke again, conscious of the ugly note of hysteria in her voice.

'It's ironic . . . Live by the sword? Die by it? You, Bodie, your whole way of life – violent!'

Bodie spoke with a harsh, no-nonsense firmness, the time long gone when he might cajole the girl.

'Fight fire with fire.'

'Violence,' said Julia. Her voice rose. Her face was growing pale and then scarlet, white and red, flushing with the violence of her passions as she screamed out the ugly word. 'Violence . . .'

'To protect you.' Bodie moved closer. 'People like you . . .'

'Violence.' Julia screamed it out. 'Violence.' Her voice cracked and slurred into an astonished, frightened, desperate whisper. 'Violence . . .'

Bodie stepped in and, using minimal force, hating it but vitally conscious of the necessity, slapped her across the face. Her eyes opened wide. She did not even put a hand to her face. She stared at him, as though drugged, abruptly conscious of what was happening. In that breathless silence a tiny ray of sunlight shafted down from the roof. Pencil slim, it hovered on Bodie's forehead. As he moved it focused into his eyes.

He blinked.

He looked up.

A tile was slowly being lifted. Carefully, silently, the tile eased up, as though it was the first page of a book.

It started to swivel around the last remaining nail. The black gleam of a gun muzzle showed in the narrow opening.

Bodie went for his gun.

Pure instinct made him grab with his right hand, ready to yank the gun from the holster. The pain started in his hand, travelled up his arm, belted along his shoulder and into his head, exploded with white hot rockets of agony in his skull.

Bodie dropped the gun.

The gun muzzle above angled around, the black hole looking monstrously big. The sunlight flashed along the barrel. A tatty old broom leaned against a dusty and broken trunk. There were about a dozen hairs still left in the broom. Bodie dived for the broom handle, snatched it up, shoved it under his left elbow. He gripped with his left hand. The broom handle wavered in the air. Sweating, choking back the phlegm clogging his throat, trying to get the broom handle centred on that hole left by the dislodged tile, Bodie shoved up with all his strength.

The broom handle went up through the hole in the roof.

Kristo, crouching on the roof, the gun jammed down through the hole, trying for a clear shot into the security man's head, took the broom handle under the chin.

Bodie's strength exploded the wooden shaft up. Kristo was snapped back. The gun cracked off and the bullet went somewhere away and out. The next bullet from the clip chipped stone from the chimney. Kristo lifted up as though doing a back somersault from the high diving board. He lost all sense of balance. Wide-armed, still gripping the gun and firing the clip empty, he sailed off the roof and pitched out and down and smashed his backbone into pieces across the hard-edged walling of the garden below.

The echoes of the gunfire still rang in the attic room as Myer made the move he had been working himself up to – to choose the right moment – and then to act!

With Bodie for the moment winded and shaken by that last dramatic encounter, Myer rushed him. A smashing body contact charge hurled Bodie slamming into the wall. Pain lacerated him as his injured hand thudded into the wall, and added pain clawed at him as, twisting awkwardly, his side ricked a dagger of agony through him. He gasped.

Using his shoulder, Myer smashed Bodie's body against the wall. A knee raked up. Working deliberately and concentrating on his target, Myer slammed Bodie's left hand against the wall. Once, twice, three times, Myer hammered Bodie's good hand. New pain began and Bodie, twisting to get away, started a slashing blow to Myer's head that – in the split-second instant of delivering the blow – he knew would merely multiply the torture from that useless right hand of his.

Myer ducked the blow. Like a snake his head darted forward.

Strong white teeth fastened into Bodie's left hand.

With a barracuda-grip, Myer sank his teeth into Bodie's good hand. Bodie yelled. For an instant he was thrashing about like a gaffed fish. The terrorist's teeth were fast sunk in his left hand.

With another yell and a twisting, convulsive effort, Bodie got the palm of his bad hand against Myer's face. He straight-armed him. Pain flowed so that he nearly passed out. But he shoved Myer away, feeling the bloody rip of teeth tearing loose from his left hand.

Fighting as a man with no arms fights, Bodie put his head down and shoulder-charged Myer. He got a knee in, barged in like a front-row forward, smashed the bomber away. He landed a hefty kick as Myer went down and almost toppled over on top of him. The room was jumping about before his eyes, and everything was limned in bright scarlet. As for his hands – both his hands – they were somewhere in a mincing machine being ground into particularly small and agonising fragments.

But Myer was not finished. His plan had worked.

As Bodie doubled up with the pain lacerating him, so Myer slammed against the wall and with a thread of blood dribbling from his nose, started shouting. He bellowed in German.

'Inge! Now, Inge!' Myer's voice rose in triumph. 'He is helpless!'

Outside on the landing Inge heard that desperately raised voice. She caught the note of triumph. Her lips ricked back.

'Now, Inge . . . Now!'

She started for that narrow stairway, started to run up, and her SMG was held down and level and the muzzle wavered only by a fraction as she clambered up the staircase.

'Attack, Inge. Attack – '

Myer was still shouting as Bodie catapulted up and flung himself bodily across the attic room. He hit Myer with a hard tackle, without hands, belting the corner of his shoulder into the terrorist's throat. Myer gargled, his last shouted: 'Attack!' dying and being smashed back as Bodie charged him down.

Inge started shooting as she hammered up the stairs. Her spray of shots cut the door lock away. Bullets yammered around into the attic room. Smoke wafted and chips of wood sprayed from the shattered door. The noise bellowed in the confined space.

Bodie dived for his gun.

He could not hold it. Both hands were useless. He crouched there, looking up, and a bright devilish look of murder transfigured his face as the door burst in and Inge appeared cradling the submachine gun, gloating down on him.

The tableau held.

Inge stood in the doorway, tall, thin, the SMG aimed, gloating on what she saw.

The security man crouched on the floor.

Inge flicked her eyes over the others.

Myer was sitting up against the wall. He looked in a mess and he was handcuffed; but he was in one piece and as she stared so he summoned up the vestiges of a smile. She looked at the others.

One woman, middle-aged, stood against the wall, breathing deeply. She looked as though she was not a part of this macabre scene.

The other woman, a pretty girl, looked exhausted, hysterical, on her knees in almost an attitude of prayer. Inge switched her gaze back to the security man, Bodie.

He stared back at her and she saw all the hatred and vengeful ferocity on that face, and she laughed.

One hand was bound in a ludicrous bandage, and the other dribbled blood. Myer had done well. The security man was helpless. Inge slowly lifted the muzzle of the submachine gun.

Savouring the coming kill, Inge aimed the SMG.

She did not see the girl's movement.

But suddenly, from out of some deeply-hidden well of strength, Julia found spirit to say: '*No*!'

She scooped up Bodie's big gun. It was heavy. But she had held it before, over the windowsill, aiming to alert Cowley in his white Rover. Now she held its weight in both hands and pointed the muzzle at Inge.

'No.' Julia held the heavy gun, and she panted and her hair fell forward over her face. Her breasts shook with the passion in her; and her forefinger curled around the trigger.

Inge saw.

She started to swing the submachine gun around. She uncovered the security man and started to bring the SMG around to shred the girl into pieces.

A shot blasted.

Inge looked surprised.

No smoke curled from the muzzle of the gun in Julia's hands.

Inge felt strange. The SMG was heavy, very heavy. She let the barrel sag. Her knees wouldn't hold her. The room was spinning. A pain somewhere in her side was growing, was spreading tendrils of fire throughout her body. She opened her lips; but she did not cry out. Surprise, complete and utter surprise, held her enthralled.

Julia looked no less surprised.

She still held the Browning auto pointed; but her finger had not pressed the trigger.

Inge fell. She slid down slowly, the SMG toppling away out of her lax hands. Her body straightened out along the floor. Her legs abruptly shivered, her feet drumming against the linoleum. Her face shrank, lined and drawn. She fell twisting so that her balance went and her torso toppled over the top step. Flopping down like a rag doll she fell head over heels down that steep and narrow stairway.

Her legs flailed. Her arms flew out. Her head lolled.

She tumbled down in an abandoned heap.

She hit the bottom tread and then she toppled over the last one and thumped into the legs of the man who stood there.

He stood still in the pose, the gun in his fists snouting up. He held the pose for a heartbeat.

Then he lowered the gun and, stepping over the woman terrorist, he bellowed up the staircase.

'Bodie!' yelled Doyle. '*Bodie!*'

Silence.

Then a voice, a voice ground out from under the wheels of the death cart, carried down the stairs.

'I'm – all – right.'

Bodie swallowed.

That was Ray Doyle down there.

Good old Doyle. He'd shot Inge in the nick of time. And in the side. A quick snap shot, loosed off in the moment when she was going to cut Julia into pieces.

Moving with a laboriousness that annoyed him, feeling the tiredness, feeling the pain, Bodie shuffled across to Julia.

'That,' said Bodie, 'will be safer in my hands . . .'

He tried to take the gun from her and could not.

He fumbled the Browning. He dropped the gun. It thudded to the floor and lay there, a weapon, an artefact, a thing of blued steel, oiled and dully gleaming.

Bodie lifted his head and waited as Doyle climbed the stairs.

The terrorists had held the aces, and they'd failed. It had not been easy and it had been touch and go. But, in the end, CI5 had come out on top, and they it was who held the trumps.

As Doyle came into view, starting to smile, hiding his concern, Bodie felt the tiredness and the pain surge up in him. But, all the same, he managed a smile. From somewhere, he found a smile for Ray Doyle.

The chief of CI5, the Squad, the Big A, sat at his spartan desk in his scruffy office signing papers. It was a dreadful chore; but he had to keep on top of the paper work somehow or other.

A knock rapped tactfully on the door.

Cowley did not look up.

He did not look up when the door opened.

Someone cleared their throat, a discreet little shuffle of sound.

Still Cowley did not look up. He signed where Betty expected him to sign, turned the paper over, and started on the next one. A lot of water had gone under the bridge since they'd hauled Bodie out of that house where the siege had taken place, and the work had piled up.

A voice said: 'Sir . . .'

Cowley did not look up. He signed, he turned the paper, and he said matter-of-factly: 'Two more weeks, Bodie.'

Bodie stood bolt upright before the desk, his face like

thunder, his eyebrows drawn down, his upper lip most pronounced. He did not answer.

In the most plummy of his plummy voices, Cowley said: 'That's the medical report.'

'But,' protested Bodie, very formally. 'Sir . . .'

'You *should* have returned to active duty ten days ago.' Now Cowley did look up, to see Bodie's face like a granite carving and, alongside him, his partner Doyle smiling away like a loon. Cowley sighed and went on: 'But if you *will* get yourself involved in extra-curricular activities . . . Two more weeks.'

'Yes,' said Bodie. 'Sir.'

'You, Bodie, cannot hold a gun. No use if you can't hold a gun.'

'Yes, sir.'

'Nevertheless, you did very well.'

Bodie brightened a shade at this. Not a lot, for he knew Cowley of old, but a fraction. 'Thank you, sir.'

Cowley was beginning to enjoy this.

'But the damage to the side window of my car.' He spoke up briskly, turning another paper and only when it had riffled flat realising he hadn't signed it. 'It will have to be deducted, of course.'

Sad, resigned, Bodie agreed. 'Of course, sir.'

Cowley rasped out, fiercely: 'From *my* pay.'

For a moment Doyle and Bodie regarded the chief. He was a right old devil, cunning as a fox; but he was their chief and they got up one another's noses, and they fought to stay alive, and they prized CI5 and each other. But, yes . . .

'Yes, sir,' Bodie said at last.

Cowley looked severely at Doyle.

'Doyle! You are grinning.'

'No, sir.' Doyle fought to get his mouth under control. 'Nervous tic, sir.'

'As long as it's that,' said Cowley. 'Now, run along, the pair of you. Don't want to see you again – until eight-thirty.'

Doyle said: 'Eight-thirty, sir?'

'That's right. In the Red Lion bar.' Cowley smiled. That smile did wonders for the backbones of his men of the Big A. 'I intend getting the cost of that car side window back.' The smile became seraphic. 'In pure malt scotch.'

That, Doyle and Bodie knew, was CI5 to the life.

Craig Thomas's supersonic superthriller

FIREFOX

The Soviet Mig-31 is the deadliest warplane ever built. Codenamed FIREFOX by NATO, it can fly at over 4,000 m.p.h., is invulnerable to radar – AND HAS A LETHALLY SOPHISTICATED WEAPONS SYSTEM THAT ITS PILOT CAN CONTROL BY THOUGHT-IMPULSES. There is only one way that British Intelligence and the CIA can counter the threat it poses: a scheme more desperate and daring than any undercover operation since the Second World War –
HIJACK THE FIREFOX!

'Simply won't allow you to put it down until you reach the last page'
JACK HIGGINS, author of *The Eagle has Landed*

'Sensational . . . all too real'
WILLIAM STEVENSON, author of *A Man called Intrepid*

0 7221 0445 6 FICTION 95p

Joseph Wambaugh
Bestselling author of *The Choirboys*

THE BLUE KNIGHT

Bumper Morgan is a cop, a patrolman with twenty years' service under his belt and retirement looming ominously close. His outlook is old-fashioned; he believes in justice – even when it doesn't conform to the letter of the law. If a judicious bit of violence will give him what he needs to solve a crime, he'll use it. That's the way the game's played. And it usually works. Until the prospect of retirement clouds his judgement, and Bumper finds himself starting to make mistakes. The kind of mistakes that kill people . . .

'Abounds in vivid vignettes of police life and the Los Angeles streets . . . the portrait of Bumper has force and authenticity'
New York Times Book Review

0 7221 8894 3 FICTION 95p

You are Energy

A Practical Guide to Your [illegible]

Henriette Maasdijk
FMFSEM, MAST, Cert Ed

Vibrational Healing Foundation

Published by:
The Vibrational Healing Foundation
London W1A 6US

A catalogue record of this book
is available from the British Library.

ISBN 978 0 9547569 3 2

Disclaimer
The information in this book is based upon the author's personal knowledge and experience and is not intended to diagnose, prescribe or treat any ailment, nor is it intended as a substitute for qualified medical advice. If you have a medical problem, or emotional, mental or spiritual health concerns, please consult a qualified physician or a medical healthcare professional. This information is presented at this time with no claim of scientific proof.

All information and techniques are to be used at the sole discretion of the reader. Throughout the book, all exercises have been recommended in good faith. Therefore, in the event that you use the information in this book, the author and publisher assume no responsibility for your actions. This book is for personal use only.

Cover Design by Thorben Bertels

For information about courses:
vibrationalhealingfoundation.co.uk

To all those who are starting out on the path.

Contents

Introduction

To have knowledge about yourself, others and the world around you is an essential life skill. Oddly enough, the majority of people only acknowledge that, in addition to our physical body and five senses, we have emotions and thoughts as well as the ability to learn, create and act. However, they do not delve beyond this. Some also recognise their 'gut feeling' that is aptly named the sixth sense, and most understand that happiness, well-being and status in life depend on circumstances of birth, childhood, education, work, personality and other people. All of this is true, but it is only a small part of a far greater reality known since more than a hundred years, that our so-called physical world is nothing else but a complex pool of subtle energies.

It is also a fact that we are hugely influenced by the actions of family members, loved ones, authority figures, colleagues and, to a certain extent, everyone else. What is less apparent is that we are also affected by other people's thoughts, feelings and beliefs, and in turn, we touch others via our own subtle emanations. In addition to this, the energies in our environment have a significant impact on us.

To have an understanding about such energies and, more importantly, to be able to implement this knowledge in modern day life, has become an essential skill. Avoiding undue negativity or influence, feeling more in charge, developing better self-esteem, dealing constructively with relationship issues and adding to one's general well-being, are only a few of the beneficial changes all of us can instigate by being more aware.

The purpose of this book is to provide a general foundation that everyone can use and that can be regarded as the ABC of personal subtle energy for life skills. This awareness, in the author's view, represents important know-how, although only useful when actively applied and experienced. It is, therefore, advised to try the exercises and take on board what proves to be of benefit. We are all different, and what works well for one person may be less effective for another. All the exercises have been tried and tested, not just by myself, but also by a number of students, colleagues and clients.

Those who are experienced in working with subtle energies will already be familiar with most of the content, and I have to stress that this book serves mainly as an introduction. For individuals who have never heard of subtle energies, the concept of it could seem a little outlandish at first, and there are also many who live happily without this information.

I have included a few of my personal beliefs and these are clearly indicated in the text, none of which are to be regarded as any form of religion. If a few words come across as spiritual or religious, such as the word Angel, this is only because there are no other words available.

Many people have crossed my path during this lifetime and I am grateful to them, because they have enabled me to learn, create and grow. A very special thank you to my seven-year-old grandson, Thorben. When I asked him how he perceived energy, he came up with the design for the cover of this book.

1

Subtle Energies

The whole universe can be likened to a sea of energy. This energy is also the basis of the minerals, trees, plants, animals, human beings and everything else that forms part of and lives in our world. Since ancient times, healers, clairvoyants, mystics and esoteric orders have known this and lived accordingly to what this concept means to our existence and our life on Earth. Some were also able to perceive the bio-field that is situated around all living beings and used their abilities and insights to help others. Sadly, this often led to persecution, which is the reason that much of the knowledge was kept secret and therefore unavailable to the general public.

Fortunately, since the detection of atoms and subatomic particles, modern physics has concerned itself with discovering our world at the smallest levels, which gave rise to the field of quantum physics. This field of science now acknowledges that matter is made up of energy and that both are interchangeable. Yes, we live in a world of energy; we are made up of energy and we are all linked by energy. It follows that we affect each other and the world around us through energy. It is a blessing indeed that scientists, by way of their discoveries, are slowly but surely helping to eliminate fear and ignorance, thereby promoting a greater awareness of what is going on around us as well as within us. Even a basic understanding of subtle energies is a huge aid in living your life in a more balanced, healthy and joyful manner.

Human emotions and thoughts are energy, and a good or bad atmosphere in a place is nothing else but a composite pool of energy, made up of the thoughts, feelings and memories of those who have lived there. Most of this energy derives from human interchange. Energy is all around us and if we are able to perceive our world on energetic levels, and have an awareness of the interchanges and dynamics between humans on these levels, we have more control over how we respond to the challenges that life brings. We can also learn how to stay more focussed, how to release negativity that we may have taken on and, in short, how to be more effective in everything we undertake.

Groups of people generate a potent energy, which is why those who work in offices or interact with the public at large, can also benefit from understanding how this can affect them, and can then take the necessary steps to ensure that it is in a positive manner rather than the opposite. Although this is not a book about healing, it may be of value to point out that stresses and illness carry their own energetic imprint, as do qualities of joy, happiness and peacefulness.

It is not necessary to have a highly developed intuition or sensitivity to energy in order to be able to become aware of subtle energies, unless you want to work in the field of healing and related subjects. For everyone else, it is sufficient to acquire the basic information, spot what is going on and then use it to advantage. This makes the knowledge experiential rather than theoretical only, and it also promotes discernment. One obvious example that shows the need to be aware of energetic influence is the world of sales and advertising. Many subtle techniques, involving colour, sound, imitating body language and other methods, are used to promote goods and, if not aware, we often end up buying something which we may later regret.

When being interviewed for a job, similar methods are often employed to help select a suitable candidate. There are still only relatively few people that are consciously aware of the subtle energies that form such a significant part of day to day life. If they were, such obtuse techniques would be instantly recognised for what they are and not have any undue impact. Being aware of your own subtle emanations is also imperative, since this can help you recognise when there is a need to make changes or address issues that are not conducive to your life.

~♦~

The Human Energy Field

As indicated before, thoughts, subconscious thought, emotions, beliefs and memories can be likened to energies, and these energies surround us and form part of what is termed our bio-magnetic or electro-magnetic field, more popularly known as the aura or human energy field. For those who can perceive it with the naked eye it looks like an oval of fluctuating colours that surrounds our physical body and is around three to four feet in diameter. This oval of energy is in constant movement and the state of it is perpetually changing in line with what we are thinking, feeling and experiencing. It is also affected by the emanations of other people and by the environment.

There are two important aspects that must be mentioned before continuing. The first one is that the energies that surround us, as well as those that we generate, consist of different frequencies. Pleasant feelings such as joy are of a higher vibration than feelings of sadness, and optimism is of a higher note than pessimism. The second aspect is that like attracts like. You can perceive this quite easily in the way that like-minded folk often group together. The saying 'misery loves company' is another example.

An in-depth study of the human energy field shows that it is quite complex. Apart from the various layers in this field, a number of other energy systems are contained within it. This subject is known as subtle anatomy, and it takes a certain amount of practice for an aspiring practitioner in the field to be able to perceive it, assess the state of it and then address any imbalance using a variety of tools such as crystals, colour, sound or flowers. For the purpose of this book, it suffices to mention that it consists of several interpenetrating layers that relate to our experiences, emotional and mental make-up, belief systems, memories, and ancestral and habitual patterns.

The well-known energy centres called chakras are also situated in our energy fields. I will briefly mention them here as they are referred to a few times in the book; however, much can be accomplished by focusing on the energy field as a whole. Of these chakras, there are seven major ones situated along the spine which can be perceived as spinning wheels of energy. They relate to our life experiences and, if all goes smoothly, this system will be in relative balance. If there are difficulties in one's life, the relating centres may become blocked, spin too fast or too slow, or go out of kilter to various degrees. Chakras contain all (rainbow) colours, but have one overriding colour vibration. The top chakra, the crown, is situated above the head, a little like a halo. The second one down, the brow, is situated between the eyebrows (where they would meet); the third centre, the throat, is situated in the hollow of the throat. The fourth centre, the heart chakra, is situated in the centre of the chest. Then comes the solar plexus, which is a couple of inches above the navel, followed by the sacral which is a couple of inches below the navel, and finally the root chakra which is at the base of the spine. From top to bottom, the main colours of the chakras are purple (or gold), indigo, sky blue, green (or pink), yellow, orange and red.

Having a basic awareness of the overall state of our energy field, and being able to use simple exercises to help maintain a healthy balance, is something everyone can achieve. This can also serve you to recognise when outside help is needed.

2

Taking Care of Your Energy Field

Daily care of your energy field is a must, and the first three areas to look at are grounding, clearing and strengthening as well as taking care of your space. These subjects are addressed in this chapter.

Grounding

Nowadays, a great number of people spend the most part of their time in front of a computer or mobile phone, and are therefore not all that in touch with their physical body. The same goes for artists, writers or other people who may be less involved with down to earth activities. Equally, there are many who suffer from excessive stress or anxiety, which are all conditions that result in being unfocussed or what is called, in subtle energy terms, 'ungrounded'. Virtually all of us have periods of ungroundedness during which it is a little more challenging to maintain a strong and healthy energy field. We are not always aware when we are ungrounded, and a few of the more obvious signs of being in this state are:

- Constant daydreaming
- Being overly forgetful (but medically healthy)
- Feeling dizzy or nauseous (but medically healthy)
- Having heart palpitations (but medically healthy)
- Over-sensitivity to sound and light
- Being accident prone
- Frequent twitching eyelids or seeing small sparks in front of one's eyes
- Procrastinating beyond the norm
- Feeling spaced out
- Feeling overly anxious
- Inability to concentrate
- Being overly unrealistic

Another less obvious indication of being habitually ungrounded, is that your plans and ideas hardly ever materialise. In order to make something happen, it is essential to be both focussed and grounded. People that are well grounded are rarely pushed around, which also makes this a must in cases of intimidation.

Taking up a hobby such as gardening, going to the gym or doing any form of physical exercise regularly will help you to stay grounded, but there are also energy exercises that can support you with this. Most of the exercises in this book are visualisation exercises. To visualise is the same as to imagine and quite easy to do. If you find this concept difficult, perhaps just 'know'. An example is if someone asks you the colour of your front door – you will either see it (visualise it) or just know it.

~Grounding Exercise~

Sitting or standing, imagine that thick energy roots are growing from the soles of your feet deep into the ground. The colour of the roots can be black, brown or dark green, whichever feels more comfortable. Let the roots spread out, a little like tree roots and just know you are anchored into the ground. You can do this exercise while sitting on a chair or standing. If sitting on the ground with your legs folded, you can imagine that roots are growing from the base of your spine. You can do this exercise anywhere, even while waiting for a bus or when you are at work and feel spaced out. After a while it will only take a few seconds.

If you often walk in nature you can also take the opportunity to lean against a tree and do the same exercise. Large trees have deep roots and you can imagine that yours are as strong as those of the tree.

~♦~

Clearing

As mentioned before, we are constantly surrounded by subtle energies generated by ourselves, others and the environment. You only need to think about taking the tube or bus in the rush hour, thoughts and feelings of colleagues at work, stresses and minor trials and tribulations of every-day life and reading the news. If those emanations are positive this is not a problem, but if not, you can be negatively affected. Although we can clean and refresh our physical body by taking a bath or shower, this does not clear unhelpful energies from our aura. Rather than letting such energies build up, it is advisable to clear them away at least once a day.

A few of the more obvious signs that you need to clear your energy field are the following:

- A feeling of sticky or dirty energy around you
- Feeling overwhelmed
- Feeling unnecessarily tired
- Feeling threatened for no reason
- Feeling down for no reason
- Becoming aware of constant negative thoughts
- Not being able to stop thinking compulsively about something
- Feeling out of sorts after having been in someone's company (for no reason)
- Feeling out of sorts after having met with certain people (or clients)

~Clearing Exercise~

Imagine a waterfall of brilliant white light coming from above your head and let it flow through your body as well as (up to three or four feet in diameter) around you, into the earth beneath you, clearing away all the energetic debris that you may have collected during the day. Let this happen for a few moments and then change your intent in the way that this waterfall of light now replenishes you and fills you up with new energy. You can do this whilst standing, sitting down or even while you are taking an actual shower. It only takes a moment. A variation of this exercise, using colour, is to imagine a shower of violet light flowing through and around you, clearing away negativity, and once this is gone, change the colour to a vibrant gold and fill your energy field with it. If you find three or four feet are not enough, extend this to the level you are comfortable with.

~♦~

Strengthening

The most potent subtle energies that we generate are strong emotional and thought processes. Repetitive thoughts of an unhelpful and negative nature cause blockages in our energy field, especially when accompanied by intense emotions. Thoughts and feelings from others that are directed towards us are also often taken on, and we sometimes mistake them for our own. If you become aware that you are thinking negatively about a person for no good reason, it is likely that the person in question is thinking negatively about you, which you have energetically registered but not fully recognised for what it is. When in company of certain individuals, we can feel drained, with others we can feel energised, and a good or a bad atmosphere in the environment will affect us accordingly. These are all examples everyone will recognise.

When all is well in our life, our energy field is usually strong and vibrant, but when we experience challenges and difficult situations, this may be a different story. It is then also possible to be more open to outside influences, because our field is more vulnerable. It is important to be able to recognise when your field needs strengthening, and a few of the more obvious signs of having a weak energy field are listed below.

- Being easily influenced
- Feeling threatened or overly defensive
- Unable to get your point of view across
- Feeling drained by others
- Feeling overly insecure
- General feelings of unease
- Thinking intensely and negatively about others for no good reason
- Copying other people's mannerisms
- Overly exaggerating

- Acting against your own interests
- Living your life through others
- Getting sympathy pains
- Feeling intimidated
- Gaining weight for no obvious reason
- Feeling unwell after having been in the presence of certain people or clients
- As a therapist, feeling or taking on symptoms of clients

All these signs are easily identified and most of us experience one or more from time to time.

~Strengthening Exercise~

Imagine that you are surrounded by an oval of energy that leaves enough space around you that feels comfortable. For some it may be three or four feet (approximately one metre) in diameter; others prefer it to be a little wider, and you also need to make sure that the bottom part of your oval is situated in the ground beneath your feet. The outside of this oval should be in one of the higher frequency colours such as purple, electric blue, silver or a shiny gold. Just pick the one you like the most and imagine it there. The inside of your oval can be in your own favourite colour or the same as you use for the outside. Those who are very visual could imagine spraying the colour like an energetic and luminous paint around their oval. If you are happy to take a little more time, you can imagine that you have a pot of paint and a brush, and painstakingly cover the whole of your oval with the selected colour. Please take note that your roots are usually much longer than your oval and part of them are therefore situated outside of it which is fine. You only need to do this exercise for a few moments a couple of times a day or whenever you feel the need.

Clarification of the exercise

Since your energy field can be viewed as an oval of energy, you are imagining something that is already there. You need to use the high frequency colour on the outside in order to deflect the lower (negative) vibrations and influences so they cannot enter your personal space. The saying 'energy follows thought' is a fact that is known to most healers and likeminded people, and we will introduce this subject later on. Just know, that by imagining the colour around your oval, it will be there. For the inside of your oval, use one or more rainbow colours, since you want to keep it light. After a few days of doing this exercise, you will be able to determine for yourself if it gives you some relief, or if it makes you feel a little stronger and more vibrant.

A few of my students and clients, when initially learning about this exercise, wondered if it could create a barrier between themselves and others. It is true that by using this exercise you are creating a barrier to help keep intensely negative and unhelpful energies at bay; however, you are not creating a barrier against anything positive coming your way. If you are involved in helping others who may be angry, sad or unhappy, there is no need to take their emanations on. You will be more enabled to help them when you come from a point of wholeness yourself. I have also been asked what happens to these unpleasant emanations from others if one does not 'let them in'. The fundamental answer to this is that they will find their own level (or frequency) in the world, either by staying with or returning to the person they originally came from, or by being dispersed in the collective. It is important for you to know that you are not harming anyone by refusing to take on board negativity.

This strengthening exercise is also meant to help you address issues and move through challenges without undue hindrance from outside influences. Whenever we are undergoing change, such as leaving a relationship or job or deciding that something does not work for us any longer, our energy field will become a little more fragile and then this exercise can be used as well. After we have started to integrate these changes, our energy field will strengthen again and so life continues. It has to be reiterated, however, that you cannot keep out energies that form part of you or that resonate with you, because like attracts like. If for instance you are a hateful person and someone projects hatred towards you, it will be very difficult to keep this at bay since you have this energy already within you. The best way forward, in such a case, is to deal with your own issue first.

Energy Check

One way to find out if you have a strong energy field is to go to a place where there are many people, such as a high street or a shopping centre. Firmly ground and strengthen your energy field, and then join the crowd. If nobody bumps into you, you have created a strong boundary.

Most of my clients and students have reported to me over the years, that their life changed considerably for the better once they started to use the simple exercises in regard to grounding, clearing and strengthening their energy field. They are all easy to do, and after a while, it will not take more than a minute or so of your time. When all is well, you can do it just once in the morning, once when you come home from work and once before you go to sleep.

Your Space

It may sound a little outlandish, but your possessions, including your home and your car, are connected to your energy field. It is, therefore, worthwhile to make sure you take good care of your living space and your belongings not only in practical terms but also in terms of energy.

Clutter is something that can affect the energy flow throughout your home in a negative manner. Your cupboard may be full of clothes you have not worn for years, and your kitchen may be stocked with out-of-date food or spices, broken cutlery or other objects that you know you will never use again. If you have children, there are probably plenty of broken toys around that have been jettisoned by the little ones. It is definitely a worthwhile endeavour to clear out any such redundant clutter from your home from time to time, because apart from creating more pleasant surroundings, you are also making space for something new to come in. If you are a bit of a hoarder, start with getting rid of things that are damaged or broken, and put the rest in your cellar, attic or garage for a while. You could then take this later to a charity shop, clothes bank or sell it on E Bay or in a car boot sale. This will take care of clearing your space on practical levels.

Clearing your space on subtle levels is, however, even more important, since unpleasant subtle energies are counterproductive to say the least. A bad atmosphere in a room is usually generated by (your own and others) negative emotional or thought processes and, if not cleared, these can linger and affect you badly. Any type of suffering, including depression, anxiety, stress and illness also creates unpleasant energies that will hang around unless removed.

There are several ways of clearing unhelpful subtle energies from your home, and it is sensible to do this frequently, especially if you are going through a rough patch in your life. One of the easiest and fastest way to do this is with sound. Tibetan bowls or bells, Tibetan or Nepalese Ting Sha or a single chime are all suitable tools to use for this purpose, provided they emit a high-pitched sound when you strike them. If you wish to clear a room, first make sure you are calm or at least in a positive mood. Then strike your bell or chime with the intent of clearing and direct the sound into the corners of the room. You only need to do this a few times. You can clear your cupboards, storage space and virtually every part of your home with this method. After a while you will become aware when the atmosphere in your space needs attention so there is no need to overdo it.

Flowers and plants emit positive vibrations, which is why it is useful to have these in your home in order to enhance the atmosphere. Peace Lilies are excellent for this purpose and easy to keep. As explained more fully later on, you can also put a few drops of the Bach Flower Essence, Crab Apple, in a container filled with water and then spray the room with this. If you like incense, this can also help with clearing, as can smudge sticks which are bunches of dried sage and rosemary. These last two methods, however, create smoke and are therefore not suitable for everyone.

Computers and similar items generate unpleasant energies. Plants can also help reduce these and one specific crystal, called Black Tourmaline or Schorl, is very effective in this regard. If you have a piece, hold it for a moment and project the thought of absorbing and draining the negative energies from your computer into it. Then place it near or on your computer and make sure you clean it from time to time. You can do this by holding it under the tap for a short while with the focus on clearing it of negativity. You can then put it back, and there is no need to repeat the original intent.

There is nothing like laughter to lift the vibrations in a room as well as within yourself, so watching a funny movie can also help to clear your space. There actually is such a thing as laughter therapy, which is reported to have helped many people.

If you have a practice, it is essential to clear the therapy room between clients, not only to dissipate the (usually difficult) energies that have been released, but also to avoid taking these on yourself. Years ago, I went to a hairdresser who told me she always felt well after styling my hair, but that this was not the case with everyone. She sometimes developed headaches or felt grumpy during the day after having attended to certain clients. I showed her how to clear and strengthen her energy field as well as clear her space, and having tried this out, she informed me that she was delighted with the results.

If you work in a shop, you may find it raises the atmosphere if you clear the space every evening before you leave. If at all possible, you can also do this in your office, even if it is only around your own desk.

Like everything in book, try out what appeals to you and then judge for yourself what works best.

3

Thought

Thought

Once you know how to better take care of your energy field and your space, the next step is to look at the quality of your thoughts. Many of us are familiar with the saying 'You are what you think', which derives from the 'I think therefore I am' statement of Rene Descartes, a well-known French philosopher who lived in the 17th century. Although he was right, and our thoughts do indeed shape our reality to a large extent, our feelings, memories, habits, beliefs, childhood experiences etc. also play a huge part in this. Thought is a highly complex subject which can be divided into several categories.

On personal levels there are conscious thought, inspirational thought and subconscious thought, better known as the subconscious mind. The thoughts of groups of people are termed collective thought; all thought that exists is called Universal thought; and there are also innumerable thoughtforms, both past and present, that in a sense occupy the space around us. For the purpose of this book and its exercises, we will address each of these thought categories separately.

~♦~

Conscious Thought

Virtually everything that we create originates as a thought, and focussed thought is indeed a powerful energy that affects each and every one of us far more than we often realise. Unfortunately, most of us are not even aware of the actual thoughts we think all day long. In order to demonstrate how powerful, the effect of thought (combined with emotion) is, it may be useful to briefly outline what happens to us when we think excessively worrisome thoughts. That this leads to long term stress is a recognised fact.

Stress always starts in the mind as a thought about one or more situations we feel threatened by. We think we cannot cope, and then negative emotions such as fear, worry, frustration or even panic ensue. This causes chemicals such as adrenaline or nor adrenaline to be released in our bodies. Over time, this builds up and will start to affect our immune systems, ultimately resulting in illness. Since illness is stressful in itself, we then find ourselves in a vicious cycle that can be difficult to address. To think all of this started with just a few thoughts!

Another example of the power of thought is how it can affect our entire demeanours. If we think about unpleasant, unhappy or similar issues for most of the day, we begin to emanate this negativity via our energy fields to those we come into contact with. We might then find ourselves avoided and our social lives in decline, since the majority prefer to be around joyful or peaceful people rather than the opposite. This is another reason to start becoming more aware of what you actually think all day long.

Fleeting thoughts, even if negative, do not do much harm; it is when they become habitual that it is necessary to change things. The way to do this is to first become aware of the thoughts that you are routinely thinking, especially the unpleasant or destructive ones. Then start to address these. If you have to reflect on a problematic situation, set a specific time every day to focus on a solution and then let it go. If you find your thoughts returning there again, quickly change them into something pleasant for a moment, such as a beautiful flower, a sunset or whatever else you really like. Then ensure you think about something else which is positive or constructive. After a while this will become automatic and your flower or sunset will come to mind when you are lapsing, so you can re-adjust. Thinking constantly about a problem and focussing on that problem usually adds to that problem. Focussing on solutions is fine, but you can only do this with success once you are in a better frame of mind and have let go of the intensity of it all.

If you are unhappy with your life, start by having a look at your thought processes – you may be surprised. If, for example, you are concerned about some form of lack, it is likely that you think about this often and you may also express it frequently in conversation. By doing this you are drawing more and more of the energy of this specific lack towards you, rather than creating the opposite. If you experience lack, try to focus on something you already have and be grateful or appreciative for it. By doing this you are lifting the vibration of your energy field and opening yourself a little more to receiving.

Another example is if you want to leave your job because you do not like it. If you focus on not liking your job, you create this emanation in your energy field and you also project it outwards. Your CV forms part of your energy field, and those who read it will subconsciously pick up on you not liking a job, and therefore choose another candidate. Even if you manage to get an interview, your vibe 'of not liking your job' will be off putting. What you can do in such a case, is to find something you like about your job, or at least do it to the best of your ability and only focus on anything beneficial about it. You will then come across in a different manner (energetically) and making changes may well prove to be easier.

Thinking frequent negative thoughts about others is not helpful either, since this also affects your energy field. Apart from more upbeat folk starting to avoid you, you risk attracting those of a similar disposition, which may set you onto a downward spiral. Changing thought processes is possible, but it takes discipline. The first and most important step, as mentioned earlier, is to become aware when you are starting to think negatively. Once you can do this, you are already half way there. Decide to deal with your day to day life issues, do your work with focus and ensure you take time out to relax. In the evening take a few moments to reflect on your day, and if you have personal problems, set aside a specific time to think about these in order to resolve them and then stop. Make certain that what you think about most of the time is helpful and encouraging, and always think about something positive before you go to sleep.

If you are dealing with, or are badly affected by, issues of an intense negative nature, it can be of benefit to get some outside help. So-called positive thinking is not about repressing or ignoring what is going on in your life or within yourself, because anything you repress will grow and come to the surface when you least expect it. Positive thought is about dealing with issues and then focussing on the best possible solutions. It is also about making realistic plans and then letting them come to fruition by thinking and acting in accordance.

It is also advisable, in regard to this subject, to practice some form of meditation each day, even if this takes just a few minutes. There are a few guidelines for this later on.

~♦~

Subconscious Thought

The subconscious mind is amazing in the way that it stores virtually all our experiences. This includes most of our thought processes, strong emotions, habits, memories, beliefs and ideals which form most of our energetic make-up. It also takes care of our bodily functions and of everything else we do automatically. We attract towards us much of what we habitually think and feel, be this positive or the opposite, and our responses to our life's challenges are mainly shaped by our memories, including childhood experiences and our habits.

It follows that the majority of what occurs in our lives is orchestrated via our subconscious mind, although many of us are not aware of this. If the content of your subconscious mind is mostly of a positive nature, you are probably quite happy with your life, but if not, it may be a different story. You could liken your subconscious mind to the database of a computer where you can enter specific programs and delete old ones. This awareness can aid you in manifesting your life in a more conscious manner, rather than perceiving yourself as being subject to the whims of fate. The subconscious mind is particularly open to suggestion prior to falling asleep, which is why it is useful to focus on something you wish to experience in the future during that time. Please note that the subconscious mind is not discerning, it will do all it can to help manifest what is stored within it regardless if this is of benefit to you or not.

The actual location of the subconscious mind, in terms of your subtle anatomy, is behind the solar plexus. The solar plexus relates to your ego, as well as to control, personal power, self-esteem issues, fear and anger. It also correlates to thought. The subconscious mind, although linked to the solar plexus because of its proximity, functions in a much more comprehensive manner as is explained in the previous paragraphs. It is interesting to note that a severe blow in the region of your solar plexus could be fatal.

~Subconscious Mind Exercise~

Sit in a comfortable chair, relax, ground and go within. Imagine that you are walking down a staircase at the end of which is a big yellow door. The words 'my subconscious mind' are inscribed on the door. When you open it, you find yourself in a pleasant room. In the centre of the room is a desk with a keyboard, which is connected to a large screen on the wall in front of the desk. This screen represents your subconscious mind. You can write on it, project images on it, delete programmes and so on. Presuming that you wish to be happy and healthy, project an image of your happy and healthy self on to the screen and write relevant words underneath that picture. Then focus on the feeling of being happy and healthy for a moment and press the enter button. When you are finished, leave the room, close the door firmly behind you and walk back up the stairs into your own space and ground.

You can adapt this simple meditation in any way you want but always write your plans in the present tense. Rather than writing on the screen 'I will be abundant', write 'I am abundant'. Also briefly focus on how the outcome of your wish makes you feel. If you are one of many who believes that you have a 'Higher Self', you could change the ceiling of your room to a sliding one and place a button 'Higher Self' on the desk. Once you have finished placing your picture on the screen, you could then press that button and open the ceiling. Then imagine a beautiful Light streaming down and illuminating your picture before pressing the enter button. Before you leave, just press the button again so that the ceiling is closed. The reason for this is that in daily life it is best to be fully grounded.

All the exercises and meditations are meant for you to try out, see what works for you, and leave the rest aside. You are completely in charge of your inner world, and the more you personalise such exercises, also in accordance with your beliefs, the more empowered you become.

~ ♦ ~

Habits

A habit is something that you have gained by repetition, be it actions, thoughts or emotional responses. One example is when you learn to drive a car. You first have to concentrate on every single action, but once you are more experienced, you can do it automatically. Many habits have been ingrained since early childhood by our parents or other authority figures and are therefore not all that easy to change. We can also get stuck in a rut about something and, if unaware, will not make the necessary adjustments. Thought processes often become habitual if we are not careful and so can our emotional responses, such as anger or fear, especially when we are confronted with a challenge.

Habits reside in the subconscious mind, and it is there that you can change them, either via meditation and/or by changing the habit. It worked for me when I decided to quit smoking, although my way of doing this was a little brutal to say the least, and I would recommend taking a gentler approach. I went into a profound meditation and programmed my subconscious mind to make me feel sick whenever I took a drag from a cigarette. It worked a treat, and I kicked the habit with relative ease.

What is so great about this awareness is that you can take more control of your life. You can also use the subconscious mind clearing exercise to help change a habit.

~Subconscious Mind Clearing Exercise~

Let's pretend that you have a habit of eating too much chocolate and you want to change this. See a picture of yourself on the screen eating a piece of chocolate. Become aware of the words underneath the picture I love eating chocolate. Then delete it. Become aware of old files on the computer where it states the same and delete all of them. After this, see a picture of yourself eating an apple (or another healthy food you like) and underneath write, 'I love eating apples.' Also focus on how you feel when you are eating a lovely apple. Then press the enter button. You can also write over all the other programmes you have deleted and enter the positive one.

If you still wish to continue enjoying chocolate, but just less of it, you can adapt the exercise by writing underneath your picture, 'I occasionally enjoy chocolate'. If the exercise does not work immediately, you could repeat it a few times. In brief, picture the old and delete it, then picture the new, focus on how this makes you feel, write a brief affirmation underneath and press enter.

~♦~

Memories

We all remember things in different ways, which is why a large part of history is only of relative truth. If you go on a journey with ten people and ask them to write an account of it, you will get ten different stories. If you ask them to write about it a few years later, their stories will have changed considerably and so will yours. It shows that memory is highly selective. Good memories about your experiences are great, unless you get stuck in these and constantly muse about 'the good old days', rather than dealing with the present. There actually is a Bach Flower Essence, called Honeysuckle, that can help with not being able to let go of the past.

Bad memories can definitely prove to be a hindrance to your life and therefore merit some attention. Having experienced war, horrendous abuse, natural disaster or other traumatic issues is outside the scope of this book and may require professional help such as counselling or similar therapies. There are, however, ways to address unpleasant memories yourself and thereby release related negative energies that are stuck in your auric field. What is more difficult to deal with is that we all have memories from early childhood that we have forgotten. These are, however, still stored in our subconscious and can still influence how we respond to certain situations. At times, such memories may come to the surface, and if they are of a disturbing nature, it is also advisable to seek professional help.

The first approach to releasing difficult memories is to have a look at how a bad experience has affected and subsequently changed you. Many people find that the more difficult challenges in their lives have ultimately instigated a change for the better. If this is the case, the only thing you need to do is to let go of any remaining negativity including any bad feelings towards the people who may have been involved. For this, you can use the 'freeing yourself exercise' which is mentioned elsewhere. If you are angry about something you did in the past, you can use the 'freeing yourself exercise' and take the Bach Flower Essence, Pine, in order to help clear any remnants of guilt. To release old, negative memories, first ensure that you have dealt with these, or in case they formed part of a learning process, that you have fully integrated that lesson and moved on. You do not want a repeat.

~Memory Release Exercise~

First think of something positive in your life that happened after your unpleasant memory; something that is now in your life that you are happy with. Then ground yourself and go within. Form a picture of the unpleasant memory and, when you can see it clearly, take a pot of brilliant white paint and brush or spray this over the image. Make sure it is all gone. Then project the new positive image over it. Focus on this for a moment, and become aware of a beautiful and intense light illuminating your new picture. You can mentally state that this is the new you from now on, or something similar. End the process by letting the picture fade, and ground yourself. If the old memory ever rears its ugly head, repeat the exercise until it no longer has a hold on you.

There is no need to enter a long meditation to do this, or to go into the subconscious mind, unless you prefer it that way.

~♦~

Inspirational Thought

Inspiration is also thought, but it is of a higher note (energetic vibration) than conscious and subconscious thought processes. Looking at a beautiful sunset is inspirational and can lift your mood. The same goes for poetry or a piece of classical music. This is what is termed positive or sometimes heavenly inspiration, and most artists get their ideas via the inspirational mind. Beauty is one of the universal principles, and it is worthwhile when you are feeling down, to place something that you consider beautiful in your environment. This could be a vase of flowers, a painting or sculpture or even listening to a piece of music.

Many years ago, I underwent a painful operation. A friend had given me a large bouquet of wildflowers, which I thought were amazing, and which I was allowed to have in my hospital room. These were placed on a table at the foot of my bed. When I awoke from the anaesthetic, I focused intensely on the flowers and could not tear my eyes away. Every single moment was fixated on them, and my body healed within a record time. It was only after I had entered the world of healing that I realised that, by focussing on the high frequency energies and beauty of those flowers, I had speeded up the natural healing process, which in this case was triggered by the inspirational mind.

~Connecting to the Inspirational Mind Exercise~

It is not difficult to connect to the inspirational mind in meditation. Take a few deep breaths, go within, and think of a stunning sea or landscape. You could imagine you are sitting on a beach watching a sunset. The colours of the sky and the sea are spectacular, and you lose yourself in the beauty of it. Spend some time in this landscape and then come back into an ordinary state of awareness and ground yourself.

You can imagine whatever you like, provided it is beautiful and inspires you. Doing this, even once a day, will lift your mood as well as the overall vibration of your energy field.

~♦~

Beliefs

Most beliefs relate to what is termed our spiritual aspect. Reflecting about spiritual issues lifts one's energy, as does sitting in the peaceful and serene atmosphere of a church, a temple or in nature. If your life is getting a bit too much, spending some time in such a place can help you gain perspective or at least some peace. I personally believe that our world was created by a 'Universal 'Love/Intelligence Consciousness', which I call Light. Others call this by different names, according to their own beliefs. The reason I am mentioning this 'Light', (the highest aspect of our belief system), is that like everything else, it can also be viewed as energy, and can be linked to. Doing this can be of benefit, gifting you with a sense of stillness, harmony and serenity. Most people do this automatically when they pray, and healers do this before they channel healing energies.

~Linking to your Spiritual Aspect Exercise~

For this you need to be alone, in a quiet space. Ground, clear and strengthen your energy field and also affirm that only beneficial energies may enter your space. Then quietly reflect on what you believe is the highest consciousness that exists. You could perceive this as a beautiful Light or as a feeling of unconditional love. Just ask that you may be connected to the highest possible vibration that you can cope with, and then stay in that space for a while. Afterwards, ground yourself thoroughly.

You can do the same according to your personal beliefs. If you are aware of your 'Higher Self', you can link to that, or anything else for that matter. My own belief system and experiences are as follows: I deem that I am a Soul that has incarnated on Earth in order to experience matter, learn, create, balance out any issues from other lives and also do my bit to help the collective. In addition to my physical body and the energy systems that are connected to and form part of this, I also have a 'Higher Self', which has a wider view of what my exact purpose here entails.

My Soul aspect (which is who I really am), forms part of a group of other Souls. This aspect is also evolving towards ever higher notes. You can link to both your Soul and your Soul group. Here on Earth, you can also connect to everything and everyone, because all of it can be viewed as one. My favourite analogy for this is an ocean. The ocean is vast and you are a drop within it; therefore, you can link to any other drop. If your experiences and beliefs are different from others, that is normal because no two individuals are exactly the same. My advice is to always only take on board what resonates with you, in the understanding that theories are just that until they become concrete.

~♦~

Collective Thought

If a group of people think the same way about something, this results in what one can call a collective thought pattern. Collective thought is powerful and one can easily be caught up in it. You only need to think of fashion trends, must-have toys or other objects that are promoted and then take hold. The same goes for anything that involves large groups of people, and this fact is often used deliberately by those want to be in control of or influence something. The result can be something objectionable, such as certain cults or street gangs; or something positive, such as many people all of a sudden becoming aware of the dangers of plastic and then taking helpful action. Nationalism, belief systems and politics etc. are all the result of collective thought. There is in fact very little that is not.

If you do not want to be affected by collective thought patterns, just strengthen your energy field before buying into something, and if you are then still happy about it, go ahead. If you, all of a sudden have doubts, you know you are being impelled by a group of people who are thinking alike. If something important is occurring in your vicinity or on the news, such as an election or people demonstrating about a serious issue, and you start to feel upset, angry or depressed, clear your field and strengthen it. More often than not, you are 'picking up' on the vibe out there, and when you do your energy exercise, the negative feelings will leave.

The term 'out of the box' relates to people who are highly independent, not easily influenced, and who are often innovative. They are also natural leaders and usually have strong energy fields, which allows them to maintain their individuality and not be distracted from their paths. Even if you are someone who prefers to go with the norm, it is always good to know your own mind.

~ ♦ ~

Universal Thought

Universal thought relates to all thought there ever was, is and will be. Some call this the mind of God; others see it as the Universal mind. Universal thought is omnipresent. We can all connect to this Universal mind via our own thoughts; and this connection will correspond to the degree of our own understanding and awareness. If you focus on a subject for a while and link to the Universal mind, more often than not, new ideas and insights will come to the fore, although only to levels that you can comprehend with relevant ease. Try it out and see what happens.

~♦~

Thoughtforms

Thoughtforms are collections of thoughts of a specific nature that 'float' around us in the atmosphere. They are thoughts (energies) that have been created by people since the beginning of time and that are still being created. Thoughtforms can be of a constructive and positive note, or the opposite, and since like attracts like, we are prone to attract comparable thoughtforms, especially if our own thoughts are intense or habitual. If your thoughts are often uplifting or inspiring, you may well attract similar energies, but if they are of a discouraging type, it is possible that you will attract more of the same, which may make matters worse. You are in charge of what you think, and you can change your thoughts at any time!

~Linking to Thoughtforms Exercise~

If you have been depressed or you are generally thinking negatively, you could try the following exercise to help change this, by linking to a positive thoughtform. If, for example, you are a professor or engineer and you are stuck with a theory or project, linking to a thoughtform of your profession could point you in the right direction. If you have difficulty with abundance, you could try linking to a universal thoughtform of success and abundance.

Imagine that a beautiful violet light appears above your head. It begins to flow down throughout your energy field and your physical body, washing away any unwanted thoughts or other negativity. Now change the light to a gold colour, allowing it to replenish you, and have the intent that this light is replacing that which was released. At this point, have the intent to link to thoughtforms of joy, peace, harmony or whatever energies you feel could be of benefit to you. If you are so inclined, you could ask the Angelic to help you with this. Sit with the energies for a while and then firmly ground yourself.

4

Emotions

We are usually far more aware of our feelings than we are of our thoughts. This is because feelings are more tangible, being of a slightly 'slower' vibration. We are hugely affected by our own as well as other people's emotions and in turn we affect everyone else's. An unpleasant atmosphere in a room is largely due to the feelings of those present, and if you are with someone who is unhappy, angry or sad, you feel it immediately and your own mood will suffer. You may also start to feel drained and tired. There are sensitive people who can clearly perceive the state of a person's emotions in his/her energy field.

When all is well, the emotional layer of the energy field is made up of rainbow colours. When there is any form of negativity, these colours become dull or murky and are unpleasant to look at. Most emotions flow through you like a wave of energy, and if strong, have an immediate effect. Joy, love, passion, harmony, inner peace and so on make you feel wonderful. Intense grief, hatred and depression have the opposite effect and, when not addressed, can ultimately make you ill. Such negative feelings, especially if repetitive, tend to get stuck and then start to form part of our subconscious mind, which is something that is best avoided.

Becoming aware of and then addressing any long-term negative emotions is, therefore, as important as doing this with your thoughts. It goes without saying that issues such as intense anger, hatred and similar feelings, especially if they are frequent, are best released rather than repressed. Although not an alternative to medical help, counselling or similar therapies, there are a number of self-help tools that you can use to help deal with your feelings and emotions.

The emanations of potent feelings do not just disappear; they continue to exist in the atmosphere. You could liken this to 'energy clouds' that are present in the environment. Some of these energies, such as peace, joy and happiness have a high vibration, but there are also energies such as hatred, anger and depression around which are the opposite. When you then look at the fact that like attracts like, it becomes obvious that the more we can do to ensure that our energetic makeup is of a healthy and positive nature, the better. The linking to thoughtforms exercise at the end of the previous chapter counts for both thoughts and emotions, and you can adapt this exercise to suit you.

Flower Essences are incredibly helpful in regard to overcoming negative emotional states, and our feelings are also much affected by colour. It is worthwhile to have some understanding of this, so you can use this information accordingly. There is more about these subjects in following chapters.

~ ♦ ~

Human Interaction

The most intense relationships we have as adults, are with our family, partners and long-term friends, and these can cause the most distress when things go awry. Relationships in the workplace come next and then there are the many acquaintances and those we meet fleetingly. It has been established that seventy percent of our communication with others is non-verbal and that most of this is done via (subconscious) body language and facial expression. Counsellors and practitioners of similar therapies are well aware of this, and so are quite a number of business, marketing and sales people, who use this knowledge when recruiting staff or for advertising and sales purposes.

What is, however, less well known is that our subtle energies also play a large part in our interactions with others, even at a distance. Although it can serve you well to brush up on communication skills, it is equally beneficial to have some awareness of what is happening on subtle levels.

Whenever someone thinks about you, they energetically link to you, and if their thoughts are charged with emotion this energy can be quite potent. If the thoughts and feelings are positive, that is fine, but if they are not, you may be adversely affected. Most people do not realise this, because whenever this happens, they believe such energy is their own. An example of this, as indicated earlier, is when you become aware that you are thinking unpleasant thoughts about a person, not just once or twice, but fairly frequently. Reflecting on it, you discover that you have no issue with this person and therefore no reason to think negatively about him or her. What is actually occurring is that the person in question is thinking about you in a negative manner and you have taken this on as your own issue. To address this, you must clear and strengthen your energy field, thereby setting a strong and positive boundary.

This also applies if you have a difficult issue or conflict with someone and feel negatively about them. If the other person feels the same about you, the negativity increases and often ends in mutual enmity. In the workplace or in other groups of people, such interactions tend to also create an unpleasant atmosphere to say the least, even if outwardly there is a pretence that all is well. The best way to handle such concerns, is to first of all, try to resolve it with the other person. If that is not possible, and you believe there is no solution, the best you can do is to look at how you can move forward yourself and cut loose energetically. We cannot really change others; we can only change ourselves and respond to situations as well as challenges to the best of our ability, which includes walking away if that is the only option.

~♦~

Forgiveness

Freeing yourself from someone energetically is akin to what is termed forgiveness. Forgiving someone who has done something bad does not mean condoning what they have done, nor does it mean you have to be friends. It actually means releasing yourself from the negativity that exists between you and the other person and moving forward to a more positive and pleasant vibration. Thinking with hatred, hurt or similar feelings about someone will not help you, and by doing this, you are also in a sense giving your power to that person, especially if s/he operates on a lower vibration than you. If they are on a higher vibration than you, it is possible that they will deflect your negative thoughts and feelings back to you. This does not mean you should compare yourself to others. Just be yourself, deal with your own inner anger or hurt as best as you can, and if this is too difficult, get some help from a suitable therapist or healer. Also, as indicated before, you cannot change other people, especially if they do not wish to change!

Sometimes the freeing yourself exercise results in negative energies being cleared to such an extent that enmity disappears, and that a relationship can be resumed, but that depends on the severity of the situation. You can do this exercise with anyone although it is not recommended to do it with children before they have reached the age of puberty. Please also note that you are not harming anyone with this exercise. You are letting go of negativity; that is all.

~Freeing Yourself Exercise~

Clear, ground and strengthen your energy field and, if you wish, ask your Guardian Angel to help you with this exercise. Then go into a meditative state and imagine you are standing in a landscape of your choice. This can be a meadow that is filled with wild flowers. Just keep it simple. You see a circle of golden light on the ground and step into it. Then, two or three metres away, imagine an identical circle of golden light on the ground facing you. Invite the other person to come and stand in that circle and briefly state that you wish to clear negative energies between you.

Between you, the ground opens up and you can see a large hole which is filled with a purple light. You firmly tell the other person to dump all their negativity towards you into that hole and watch this happening. When the person has finished, say goodbye and see them walk out of the golden circle and away into a brilliant white light. You now have to dump all your own negativity concerning the other person and the situation into the hole. When you have done this, the ground will close up and the wild flowers will reappear. Become aware of a golden shower of light flowing through and around you, filling you up with new energy. You are now finished so let the landscape fade and ground yourself.

If you want to do this for yourself, in regard to difficult memories you are ready to let go of, go into your landscape, place yourself in your golden circle and see the ground in front of you opening up and state that you are ready to let go of all this negativity. You can see or feel this falling into the hole, and know it is transmuted by the purple light. Once finished, see the ground closing up and let yourself be filled with the shower of golden light. Then end the exercise.

If you are dealing with someone you fear, you can ask your Guardian Angel to stand in front or next to you. Also note that whoever you invite into your space will have to do what you say, provided it is something that concerns you, and also provided your intent is pure. You have every right to tell someone to let go of negative energies directed towards you. Obviously, the person may continue to feel badly about you, but it will no longer affect you that much if you do not continue with your own negative thoughts and feelings. You may have to do this exercise more than once, and also remember to keep up with your clearing, grounding and strengthening exercises.

~♦~

Feeling Victimised

We all come across people that tend to be intimidating, manipulative, deceitful and worse. In all such situations, it is important to practice the clearing, grounding and strengthening methods. In case of intimidation by someone you cannot avoid, you could try out the freeing yourself exercise, although you may have to do this more than once. A simple technique to carry out, if someone has a go, is to imagine a (one-sided) wall of mirrors between you, with the actual mirrors facing the other person, who then energetically sees his/her own image. The unpleasant energies are then reflected back, rather than entering into your own field. Also, when you have to communicate with such individuals, rather than looking directly into their eyes, you can focus slightly higher, thereby removing intense eye contact and reducing intimidation. If someone in your office is angry or aggressive towards you, you can imagine your energy field is filled with a vibrant rainbow pink colour. Then project this a little further outwards. It is all a matter of trying out what works.

Three of the many crystals that can help foster a stronger self-esteem are Carnelian, Tigers Eye and Yellow Jasper. These crystals are grounding and Yellow Jasper, especially, stills any fears. If you are low in energy and need something uplifting, you could add Citrine and then tune your crystals for the purpose of strengthening your self-worth.

The Bach Flower Essences, Larch and Mimulus, are appropriate for a lack of confidence and fear, which can be caused by intimidation. It is also worthwhile to remember that bullies are ultimately cowards. Someone who has good self-esteem and who is comfortable in their own power will not need to intimidate others.

Nowadays, it is also essential to be aware of positive manipulation. As indicated in the first chapter, marketing folk are excellent at this and have many techniques at their disposal. The only thing you have to do when being bombarded with such 'positive' vibes, is to focus on what it is you really need or want and ensure you are well grounded and protected. The saying 'what seems to be too good to be true', usually applies, so take a step back and do the necessary energy work before making decisions. I remember an incident when I was much taken with an advertisement for a rather expensive product. I was on the point of ordering it and felt a mild hesitation, which made me wonder if I was being cleverly coerced into a desire. Therefore, and I always do this when such doubts hit me, I grounded and strengthened my energy field. And, lo and behold, the interest left me completely.

Another personal example is from when I started out in this field, and an opportunity was presented to me for a new project. It seemed exciting, and I became very enthusiastic when discussing it with the person who had approached me. Once alone, and reflecting upon the whole concept, I lost all interest and wondered what the excitement had been about. I then realised I had been manipulated and took this onboard as a very valid lesson.

Being the victim of any form of deceit can also be difficult to cope with. In my personal view, if you have been cheated or deceived, a good way forward is to take your power back. Deal with practical issues the best you can and stop giving the culprit any power via your thoughts and emotions. Take it all as a learning opportunity and then let go. The freeing yourself exercise can be helpful here as well. Depending on various feelings that come up, you can take relevant Bach Flower Essences which are described in the next chapter. The most important thing you can do is move on with your own life.

~♦~

Grief

Grief is an emotion all of us will experience, be this through the death of a loved one, the end of a relationship or due to significant changes that occur in everyone's lives. Even inevitable changes such as aging or one's children leaving home, just to mention a few, are not always managed with ease. Grief is an emotion that must be recognised and dealt with since otherwise a part of us will be unable to move forward. How long the grieving process lasts, depends on each individual's emotional makeup and the severity of feeling. The realisation that everything in our world will and must change can sometimes help with coming to terms with certain grief processes. The Bach Flower Essence, Star of Bethlehem, is the one for grief (both current and past) as well as shock, and the well-known Essence, Rescue Remedy, is always helpful to have to hand in case of any traumatic event.

If you have lost a loved one, you could reflect on the wonderful times you had together and then send thoughts of love or gratitude and any other relevant positive sentiments to this person. Then recognise and acknowledge that your loved one or friend has departed this world and that you are sad about it. According to your personal belief system or religion, you might then either trust that you will meet again or decide that it is the inevitable that happens to all of us.

If you had unpleasant issues with someone who has died, you could do the freeing yourself exercise, and if you have been able to truly let go of the negative energies, go into a calm and reflective state of mind, imagine the deceased in front of you and just mentally state 'I forgive you, and you forgive me, for all eternity.' Then imagine the person disappearing into light. It is a simple exercise that can bring huge relief.

For other difficult changes, you could honour the good times or search within yourself for the wisdom you may have gained. If the change has come about because of any form of duplicity, or other difficult issues, recognise this and then let go in the realisation that you are now creating a new beginning for yourself. If things are too intense you can also seek help from a relevant therapist or healer.

5

Flower Essences

In the early 20th century, a medical doctor, bacteriologist and homeopath called Dr Edward Bach determined that it was essential to treat the cause of disease rather than physical symptoms alone. He also believed that the energies of specific flowers and trees could help with this and gave up his practice in London in 1930 in order to devote the rest of his life to finding essences that could help address negative states of mind and emotion. The results became known as the Bach Flower Remedies.

These flower essences were, and still are, prepared by picking fresh flowers and blooms from trees, placing them in pure water and leaving them in sunlight for several hours or, alternatively, boiling them in water. Afterwards, brandy is added to the water to preserve the essence, and this is then bottled. The essences work by flooding the energy field with the positive and opposing virtue of specific negative states of mind and emotions, rather than repressing these. For instance, for someone suffering from a fear of speaking in public, an essence that promotes confidence would be appropriate.

There are 38 essences, plus an extra one called Rescue or Five Flower Essence, which is a combination of five essences and is useful in times of crisis. This is a simple system which can be used by anyone, and since it is 'subtle energy medicine', there are no side effects. Those who cannot have alcohol, can obtain essences that are preserved without it. Below is a list of the essences and a brief description of their qualities. The way to take the essences is to place a couple of drops in a glass of water and drink this a few times a day. You can also put a few drops of one or more essences in a separate bottle, fill this up with water and take four drops several times a day. In this case, it would be best to keep it to not more than three or four essences.

If you are unsure about which essences to take, there are many practitioners who are qualified to advise on these. There are also plenty of books available on the subject, and you can buy the essences on line. The keywords below serve only as a brief and initial explanation for each of the essences.

A few Keywords for the Essences:

~courage and confidence~

Aspen: for vague fears. This essence can also be of help if you suffer from nightmares, are afraid of the dark or feel uneasy in general.

Mimulus: for known fears, phobias and extreme shyness. Together with Larch, this essence is excellent for promoting confidence in regard to speaking in public, for a job interview or similar undertakings. It can also be of use if you are afraid of something specific, such as spiders!

Cherry Plum: for when matters get out of control in a crisis. It can also be of use with issues such as bedwetting or when you feel out of control to the point of wanting to scream.

Rock Rose: for fear bordering on terror which is far more intense than Aspen. It can also be of help with anxiety and panic.

Red Chestnut: is for worrying constantly about others. This is something we can all do, and is unhelpful to the one you worry about. Also, an excellent essence for parents, and for those with an ill loved one.

Larch: when there is a lack of confidence. Most of us suffer from this at times even when we know we are capable.

~positivity and cheer~

Gentian: for discouragement and doubts. This can also assist you when taking exams, together with other relevant essences. Basically, an essence for those who perceive the glass as half empty rather than full.

Gorse: for hopelessness. It helps to regain a strong will and not give up hope in difficult, long-term situations. The plant is extremely strong and will grow anywhere!

Mustard: when a dark cloud of depression descends upon you and you have no idea why. Some believe this is a symptom of unrecognised anger, and many suffer from this in countries where sunshine is lacking.

Sweet Chestnut: when you are experiencing extreme anguish and despair, feeling you cannot cope any longer. It can help link to the Angelic or create a spark of light in the darkness.

~coping better~

Hornbeam: for those days when you cannot find your usual get up and go. This is more a mental fatigue rather than a physical one. Some call this the Monday morning feeling.

Elm: when you are temporarily overwhelmed with work or just have too much to do. This essence is for very busy people.

Oak: this is for those who overwork and never take a break, even when they should. They carry much responsibility and refuse to delegate. In the long-term, this can lead to serious burn-out.

Olive: for utter mental, emotional and physical exhaustion. This essence must be taken with care, because you may well get the flu or something similar after taking it, forcing you to stay in bed and rest for a few days!

White Chestnut: eases mental stress. This is for when you cannot stop thinking about something. It can also help to empty the mind in order to get into a meditative state.

~being strong in the here and now~

Centaury: for being too self-effacing. Some call this the doormat essence. It is indicated when you need to do something for yourself, rather than always putting others first. It helps strengthen the ego (in a healthy manner).

Honeysuckle: for those that are living in the past. For when we reminisce about the good old days or find it difficult to deal with the inevitable changes as we age.

Chestnut Bud: for repeating mistakes. This is something we all do, so if you are aware of repeating a redundant pattern, this is the essence for you.

Walnut: for whenever there is change in your life. It can also help you to create necessary boundaries. Whenever you are in a state of change, you need to ensure that your energy field stays as strong as possible, and this essence is excellent for this.

~easing up a little~

Chicory: for those who are overly controlling and who always expect something back when they give. A bit like conditional love.

Holly: for any form of hatred, anger or jealousy. This can also help if such feelings are directed towards you.

Willow: when there is resentment or a sense of victimisation. Deep resentment is actually quite dangerous because it eats away at you and could possibly, after a while, result in unpleasant physical symptoms.

Beech: for being over critical. This essence helps if you find yourself being judgemental about virtually everyone and everything. The positive quality is to be a little more tolerant.

Vervain: for being over enthusiastic. Some call this the missionary essence. It is for when you put your point of view across with a little too much fervour.

Vine: the bully and domineering essence. For if you find yourself being a little too bossy, or alternatively, you could take it if you suffer from someone else's overbearing behaviour.

Impatiens: this is for those who are fast in thought and action and find it difficult to deal with those who are a little slower on the uptake. It can also sometimes help with physical pain or irritability.

~communication and focus~

Heather: for when you cannot stop talking about yourself or if you come across as a little needy. All of us have heather moments.

Water Violet: this can be of help if people find you a little distant, or if they are somewhat in awe of you. You could come across as mildly superior.

Cerato: when you keep asking everyone for advice but never take it. This essence can be of help when you do not trust your intuition.

Scleranthus: for when you have to make your mind up about choosing between two possibilities. It has also often been of use in travel sickness or unexplained dizziness (if medically well).

Wild Oat: when you need focus and direction, or find it difficult to choose a specific path because there is too much choice. A grasshopper mentality.

Wild Rose: the keyword here is apathy. It is when you are virtually uninterested in anything and your spark has gone.

Clematis: this is to help daydreamers come back to Earth. Most of us who are interested in the worlds of energy need this essence from time to time.

~to help cope and clear~

Agrimony: when you pretend to be fine but are suffering inside. The stiff upper lip syndrome. Many unresolved issues may come to the fore when taking this essence in order to be released.

Star of Bethlehem: shock and grief for both current and past issues. Although this is a component of the Five-Flower Essence, taking it by itself has a stronger effect. It can also be of help with shock and trauma from other lifetimes.

Pine: for guilt. I do not know anyone who has not felt guilty from time to time, so it a good essence to have to hand.

Crab Apple: the clearing essence. This can also help with OCD and you can put a few drops in a spray bottle in order to help clear unpleasant energies from your home.

Rock Water: for when you are too strict with yourself, be it in dieting, exercising or anything else. It can also help with relieving any form of shame.

Rescue Essence: also called Five Flower Essence, is a combination of Cherry Plum, Clematis, Impatiens, Star of Bethlehem and Rock Rose. These essences together can be of assistance in any difficult situation, and many people carry a bottle with them just in case.

6

Colour and Sound

Colour

Colour, as we perceive it, is the visible part of the electromagnetic spectrum. It is white light split into seven spectrum colours. Colour moves as waveforms of energy through the universe and these waves have different vibrations. The slower ones are red and the faster or higher ones are purple. We take in colour via our eyes, skin and auric field, and we also ingest it with our food. Colour vibrations strongly affect us on many levels including our emotions, and it is therefore of benefit to know about some of their qualities.

If you feel the need to assert yourself, why not wear something red. This is a colour of action, vitality, passion and, to a certain extent, grounding. It is also highly stimulating and therefore not a colour used much in decorating; a bright red room could prove to be a little too much for most. The colour orange is cheerful and can stimulate creativity. If you are depressed or feeling low, it may help to wear either something orange or yellow.

Yellow is always uplifting and is also the colour of joy, optimism, enthusiasm, high energy and self-worth.

If you are stressed, colours such as green or blue are useful. Green is the colour of nature and therefore one of balance as well as abundance. It is also a colour that promotes stability, and dark green can help you stay a little more grounded. Pink is the colour of compassion, gentleness, kindness, nurturing and it can serve as an antidote to anger. It is not possible to keep up aggression or deep anger when surrounded by pink. Blue is known as a colour of peace, calming, cooling and also that of healing. It helps to release tensions and can also be of use with issues of communication or self-expression.

The colour indigo, which is a midnight blue, can help reduce pain. If you mentally project the colour to where it hurts, you may experience some relief. I use this technique when going to the dentist, and apart from not flinching any longer, I also feel calmer. Indigo also relates to (inner) vision and responsibility, so if you want to come across as serious, this is a good colour to wear. If you want to enter into profound meditation, the colours violet or purple come to mind. Deep purple also relates to power and dignity and can help clear negativity on energetic levels. It is, however, not a good colour to wear when you suffer from depression.

The colour black is one of mastery and can also be useful to lessen pain. In this case you can project a velvety black onto the painful area. Black absorbs light, can drain excess energy as well as help with the grounding process.

White reflects light and is about purity and perfection. It is also considered a colour that can cleanse on energetic levels, and some say that like black, it is one of mastery. Turquoise is a colour of protection and it also refreshes and encourages. It is also stimulating and can aid with clarity of expression. You can try wearing the colours or use them in meditation.

~Colour Meditation~

Sitting in a chair, ground yourself and go within. Imagine a dark pink colour and breathe it around your energy field, close to your body. After a few breaths, change the colour to a pale orange and do the same, but this time, breathe it a little further away from your body. Then repeat this with a sunny yellow, grass green, sky blue, midnight blue and violet. You are now sitting in a rainbow of colour, and just enjoy this for a little while. Then seal the outside of your energy field with a shiny while light, drawing it as close to your body as is comfortable. Finish the exercise by grounding yourself.

~ ♦ ~

Sound

Listening to music affects us hugely. If you are down, it may benefit you to listen to music that uplifts your energies, or when in need of peace you can listen to a piece of music that you find calming.

All sound has a vibration, which includes the tone of our voices. If you are sensitive to sound, you will definitely feel a little uneasy when people are not straight with you, because their voice will not sound quite right. If one of your loved ones is feeling unwell and trying to hide this, you may notice that his/her tone of voice is slightly off key.

You can use your own voice in order to boost your energies. Singing is one way of doing this. You can also create your own relaxation recording; just ensure you do this when you are healthy, well and rested. Listening to it, when you feel stressed or out of sorts, can help bring you back into balance. The following exercise is one way of gently addressing your chakra system in order to bring it into more balance.

~Toning chakras exercise~

Relax, ground yourself and take a few deep breaths. Then gently breathe in, focussing on your root chakra, and on the outbreath, chant the vowel sound U (like you). You could also imagine the colour red entering that chakra on the inbreath, although only do this if it feels comfortable.

Then go through the whole system in the following manner:

Root chakra	–	breathe in the colour red, and chant the vowel sound U (you) on the outbreath.

Sacral chakra	–	breathe in the colour orange, and chant the vowel sound U (you) on the outbreath.
Solar Plexus chakra	–	breathe in a sunny yellow, and chant the vowel sound OH (saw) on the outbreath.
Heart chakra	–	breathe in a green or pink colour, and chant the vowel sound AH (heart) on the outbreath
Throat chakra	–	breathe in a sky-blue colour, and chant the vowel sound EH (well) on the outbreath.
Brow chakra	–	breathe in a midnight blue colour, and chant the vowel sound EEE (see) on the outbreath.
Crown chakra	–	breath in purple or gold, and sound the MMM (closed lips) on the outbreath.

When finished, ground yourself.

There is no need to breathe in a colour on the inbreath, but do focus on each chakra on both the in and outbreath. You should feel somewhat more energised after this.

~ ♦ ~

Affirmations

An affirmation is a statement of intent that you can create to help you focus on a personal goal or anything else you wish to achieve. Always ensure your affirmation consists of one or two sentences, is positive, to the point and in the present tense. You can then repeat it whenever you think of it, and do this silently or speak it aloud when you are alone. You can also repeat your affirmation before you go to sleep. The following affirmation is just one example. If you often lose your temper, you could create the affirmation, 'I respond to challenges in a calm and effective manner'. When repeating this, you could imagine yourself as calm and surrounded by (or wearing) a peaceful colour such as blue or green. This affirmation is short, positive, in the present and easy to remember.

If you want to create an affirmation for your health and well-being, a statement such as 'I am healthy and well' is appropriate, and when repeating it, perceive yourself as being healthy and well. Doing this when going for a walk in a park, while meditating or before you go to sleep is a good idea. This is of course not meant as a substitute for practical healthy living.

7

Meditation

Meditation is an excellent tool to help calm both mind and emotions, and there is no need to do this for long periods of time in order to get results. There are several ways to meditate, and what they all have in common, is that you need to relax and be in the stillness. Before you start, clear, ground and strengthen your energy field. Also regulate your breathing in the way that it is calm and even. The best position is to sit straight in a chair, since laying down may result in falling asleep. You can then proceed with any of the following meditations.

Reflective meditation: you can do this when you need information about something. You may have thought about a new project or plan and you want to find out if it is worthwhile to proceed or if you have already anything in common with it. In the stillness, just ask a question about your plan and let the thoughts enter your mind in a calm manner. You may be surprised at what comes up! This way of meditating can also help with finding solutions to problems.

Creative meditation: do this when you want to achieve something using visualisation/imagination. You have thought about a project and already taken practical steps to make it happen. You can help this along by entering a meditative state and imagining that it is already happening. If you are moving house, and have already organised everything, you can enter a meditative state and just imagine the move occurring smoothly and you feeling happy about it. It is worthwhile trying these techniques with small goals, and when you gain experience, you will become more confident in aiming for something larger.

Stress and tension release meditation: If you are overworked and stressed, it is important to relax your body and mind at least once a day. It is not necessary to do this for more than fifteen minutes. You can buy a stress release audio for this or create your own. The audio will consist of spoken directions to relax your body in stages.

Stillness meditation: This meditation is a little more difficult for the novice, since it requires the ability not to let thoughts distract you. Begin by entering into a meditative state, and let any thoughts that come to mind just pass through and fade away. If they keep coming, breath them away without giving them any power. Then focus on being still. Some people find it helpful to concentrate on just one thing to start with, such as a flower, a candle flame, a crystal, a colour or a word. Others count their breath; either the in-breath or the out-breath. Try out what works for you and then just be in the stillness while fully present.

Breath

We can only live a few minutes without breathing, and although most of us do not even think about it, breathing is an important factor in regard to our health and well-being. Most of us do not breathe correctly or, in other words, deep enough. Equally, when living in a city, pollution has become a major health issue. Breathing deeply while walking on a busy street is not ideal, which is why it is important to be in nature whenever possible. Even going for a walk in a park, and then breathing deeply for a while, can help clear toxins from your lungs. It will also help relax your muscles, which become tense when not receiving enough oxygen. There are some who say that breathing correctly promotes health like nothing else.

For the purpose of this book, it is sufficient to make your aware of a few techniques you can use to enhance your energy field. When in nature, you can imagine that you are taking in beautiful energy with each deep breath, and on the out-breath, you release anything you no longer want, such as negative thoughts, emotions or other toxins. Some folk actually perceive this energy as tiny golden sparks when they breathe in, but just knowing that the air is pure is fine too. Try to ensure that the in-breath is as long as the out-breath.

When you start doing breathing exercises, you may only be able to breathe in for four or five seconds. After you do this, hold your breath for a couple of seconds and then breathe out for four or five seconds. Then wait a few seconds and breathe in again. Do this for a few minutes only, until you become more proficient at it. After a while, you may find you are able to breathe in for ten or more seconds, and do the same with the out-breath. Always start by breathing the air into your stomach and finishing at the top of your lungs; then on the out-breath, empty your lungs first, finishing with your stomach.

8

Stress

Most of us will suffer at some stage from excessive stress and ensuing health related issues. It has become a huge concern in our modern-day society, not just in the workplace but also in daily life.

A few of the more obvious physical indications of long-term stress are tense and aching shoulders, neck strain, lower backache, headaches, palpitations or heart flutter, grinding one's teeth (especially when asleep), stomach ache or ulcers and discomfort in general.

Some of the more intense emotional symptoms of excessive stress are panic, anxiety, fear, anger, hatred and paranoia. Long-term emotional states such as resentment, sadness, grief, depression, constantly doubting oneself and feeling hopeless are other indications.

Mental symptoms of excessive stress are worry, forgetfulness, overthinking things, inability to relax the mind, confusion, inability to focus or prioritise and being irrational.

'Energy' symptoms of excessive stress are a lack of inspiration, loss of belief or ideals, inability to connect energetically to higher vibrations and inability to ground. The energy field as a whole will also be weak.

Different types of Stress

There are many different types of stress, and although the effects of these are often similar, it is helpful to try to pinpoint where the main issue lies before addressing it. Much stress ensues in the workplace, at home, in relationships, in regard to parenting, finances and lack of time.

There are practical solutions to try first, such as joining a gym or at least making sure you have enough physical exercise if your job involves sitting in front of a computer all day. It is also vital to set a boundary between work and time out. You may need to think about getting a hobby, and ensure you do something that you truly like (other than your work) once a day. This will counteract some of the stress.

Energetically, always make sure that you clear your energy field when you come home from work, and if necessary, strengthen it as well. If you cannot stop thinking about work, the Bach Flower Essence, White Chestnut, may give you some relief. It is also important to ensure you are well-grounded, the moment you start to feel stressed out.

~Emergency Tension Release Exercise~

An effective 'emergency' release exercise to do when you feel stress coming on is to take a deep breath while imagining that the air you are breathing in is a pale blue or cream coloured energy. Let this energy rest in your head and lungs for a moment and then breathe out forcefully while dropping your shoulders. Repeat this three times and then ground yourself.

Illness

Long term illness is highly stressful, and stress leads to illness, so it is extremely important when ill or recovering from illness to relax the mind and body as much as possible. A brief stress release exercise, practiced once or twice a day, is definitely of benefit in such a situation.

~Stress Release Exercise~

Please read to the end of the chapter before trying the following exercise.

Make yourself comfortable and start by taking a few deep breaths. Then close your eyes and imagine that you are relaxing underneath your favourite tree in a garden full of beautiful flowers and plants. Just get a good sense of this landscape and know you are safe. Bring your focus to your feet and imagine that they are touched by rays of light, that have both a healing and relaxing energy, and breathe that light around your feet. You then bring your focus to your legs and do the same. Then go to your lower back, continue up your spine, breathing this light around the whole of your back. Then focus on your abdomen and breathe this healing light around there, up to your stomach, including your solar plexus. You then focus on your chest area, throat area and then to the back of your neck. Then breathe this healing light into your shoulders, arms and hands. After this, focus the light to the back of your head, your face and your jaw muscles. Then when your whole body is relaxed, just stay in this relaxed space for as long as you want. After this, let the picture fade and ground yourself if you have to get up.

Most people fall asleep during this exercise and so it is a good idea to do it just before you want to go to sleep. You could also listen to relaxing music during this exercise; just memorise the different body parts you need to focus on, beforehand, and make sure you have enough time to complete the whole exercise, which should take around ten to fifteen minutes.

Some people are under so much stress that they cannot relax, meditate or even listen to a guided meditation without feeling mild anxiety. If this is the case, it is advisable to first obtain outside help such as stress management, counselling or stress therapy before attempting the exercise.

9

The Elements

Our world is made up of five elements, namely earth, water, fire/light, air and ether and every living being is continually nourished by them. We cannot live without air for more than a few minutes, we need water and food to survive and without the light of the sun, nothing can grow. The element of ether imbues the 'physical' world with vitality and also relates to the subtle energies in nature.

Unfortunately, most of Humanity has not treated nature with the care and respect it deserves, especially since the industrial revolution; and if we do not change things soon, the future looks bleak. Many animal species are already extinct and, what is worrying indeed, is that (at the time of writing) bees and butterflies are on the brink of becoming an endangered species. Much of the water on our planet is polluted, the air is toxic and much of our food is contaminated by pesticides or, in the case of animal meat, by antibiotics. There are also substances such as plastic that cannot be recycled, and environmental disasters such as earthquakes, floods, hurricanes and bush fires, that seem to be related to global warming, are on the increase.

On the positive side, it looks like many people are waking up to the fact that we have no choice but to start acting responsibly if we want to continue to live on this beautiful planet, and a number are also taking action to instigate positive change.

It is also useful to have a brief look at how you can use awareness of the elements for your personal well-being.

Earth

Being aware of the element of earth can help you be more grounded, develop greater stability and actualise your plans and goals. If you realise that everything you eat can be grouped under this element, you can use this knowledge to improve the quality of the energy of your food. This can in turn enhance your personal energies. You can do this by expressing a few words of gratitude before a meal or even briefly passing your hand over your food, while imagining that Light is flowing from your palm into it; this will cause a positive energy to be emitted into your food, as long as you also mentally intend this. You can also do this with any ingredients you use to prepare your food.

Other methods of connecting with the element of earth are walking barefoot on a beach or in nature, and doing some gardening will also strongly connect you to this element and keep you grounded.

Water

There is a finite mass of water on the planet which is constantly recycled. It also has a memory as has been illustrated by the Japanese Professor Emoto in his book 'Messages from Water' and if you reflect on these facts, you may feel a little uneasy, especially if you live in a big city. It follows that it can only be of benefit to clear your water before drinking it. On practical levels you can do this with a water filter, but it is equally important to do it energetically. You can clear your water by passing your hand over your glass or jug and briefly imagining that you are putting positive energy into it. The intent is enough. When you have a bath, you can clear the water in the same manner and if you shower, just imagine the water is energetically clean.

Fire

This element relates to our passion, enthusiasm and similar qualities. For day to day living it suffices to just mention that we all need enough (safe) exposure to sunlight in order to have enough of vitamin D. It is well known that those who live in countries where there is not much sunlight often suffer from depression, and not everyone has enough funds to go on extensive holidays. There are certain lamps that can help, and also bear in mind that the colour yellow is uplifting.

The Bach Flower Essence, Mustard, is the one for depression, that comes out of the blue, with no consciously known cause. I mention it here, because this type of depression is often experienced by people who do not have enough exposure to sunlight.

Air

Breath is one of the ways in which our bodies detox, and therefore shallow breathing is not all that conducive to good health. Those who practice Yoga have learned specific breathing techniques, and are also advised to use these techniques in nature where the air is pure. It is also beneficial to have a few plants in your home and not use too much air purifier or other substances that render the air toxic.

As indicated elsewhere, it is worthwhile to spend some time in nature whenever you can, so you can breathe good clean air.

Ether

This element relates to our vitality. It is the first layer of our energy fields and looks like a white misty glow surrounding the physical body. You can energise this layer by going into nature and taking a few deep breaths, imagining that you are breathing in all the goodness and vitality from the environment.

Much has been written in folklore about the energies behind nature such as fairies, gnomes and other nature spirits and elementals. All of these belong to the element of ether and form part of what is called the Devic Realm, of which the Angelic is in charge.

If you are open to this concept, do read the next chapter about Angels, and if not, that is fine too and will not hinder you in regard to any of the following exercises.

10

Angels

Since our physical bodies (in a sense) are made up of the four elements, and imbued with vitality relating to the fifth, it follows that we form part of nature. Then consider that the Angelic is in charge of nature, and it follows that we must have an Angelic presence within us, which in my view is what is known as our Guardian Angel. In other words, we are partly Angelic for the simple reason that our bodies form part of nature and are nourished by nature. Because of this, we are all able to connect to the rest of the Angelic Realm with ease and do not need any intermediaries to do this.

Unlike Human beings, the Angelic have no free will and therefore cannot actively intervene in our destructive attitudes towards nature, which, as indicated earlier, will ultimately lead to our own ruin if we do not change things. It is becoming apparent that more and more natural disasters will happen, until all of us get the message as loud and as clear as is necessary.

Over the years I have met many people with a variety of belief systems, some of which did not recognise the term Angels. All of them did, however, recognise the concept of nature spirits and could therefore relate to what we call the Angelic as these are all part of the Devic realm. We concluded that it was only a matter of different words expressing similar beliefs. It is highly advisable to foster a relationship with your Guardian Angel, since it can often help you. Being not very sporty, I found myself becoming a little stiff-jointed as I grew older, to the point that getting up from a chair, or out of the bath, became problematic. I have a good connection with my Guardian Angel and whenever this happens, I ask for help. So far, this has always been given.

Your Guardian Angel forms part of you and therefore it is easy to connect with it. Mentally asking that you wish to link to your Guardian Angel is all you need to do. You can give it a name in order to make communication a little easier. Energies are subtle, so you may only become aware of a specific feeling within yourself when you are linked to your Angel – this is called a 'signature', and could be the light becoming a little brighter or sensing a presence with you. Once you have practiced this, and are sure about the 'signature', you can then 'chat' about anything you like and know that you are being listened to. Answers usually come as strong thoughts in your mind or, as in my case, help with your physical body may also be given. Why not try this out…

~Getting in Touch with your Guardian Angel~

If you have never done this before, first reflect on the fact that you do have a Guardian Angel, due to the simple fact that you depend on nature to survive. Your physical body is part of nature (in a sense) and the Angelic is in charge of the whole of nature. After this, go within and imagine you are sitting in a beautiful landscape of your choice. Make sure there are flowers there and that you are at peace. Then ask that you may meet your Guardian Angel. Be acutely aware of any possible change in your meditation. The stillness could increase, you could become aware of a colour, a sound or a bright light. If you are visual you could perceive a figure of light. (You only need to be aware of a small change in the atmosphere in order to be able to build upon this and deepen your communication over time). Then begin your communication and finish by giving your Guardian Angel a name or, alternatively, asking your Guardian Angel how it would like to be addressed. When you are ready, you can end the exercise by thanking your Guardian Angel, allowing the image to fade and grounding yourself. Always ensure you are fully grounded after such meditation exercises.

More about Angels

Angels have always been an integral part of humanity, and in this current time of change and upheaval, the interest in these beings of Light has greatly increased. There are innumerable stories about how Angels have helped, protected or healed human beings who found themselves in dire situations, and many books have been written on this subject. Angels have also been known to impart important messages to certain individuals as is reported in religious and other texts.

The Angelic realms consists of a strict hierarchy known as choirs, each of which contains three levels. The reason I am including this information in the book, is that some readers may wish to link to specific Angelic energies. When doing this, you can ask your Guardian Angel to help you to connect.

The highest choir consists of the Seraphim, Cherubim and Thrones respectively. The Seraphim are the Angels of pure love and radiate such Light that one cannot look upon them. The Cherubim are the Angels of wisdom. They have four faces (human, lion, ox and eagle) which also relate to the four fixed signs of the Zodiac. The Thrones can be perceived as wheels and could have to do with time, space and form.

The second highest choir consist of the Dominions, Virtues and Powers in that order. The Dominions are Angels of mercy and grace. They can also relate to forgiveness. The Virtues help those who struggle by instilling courage and also bestowing miracles. The Powers help deflect the efforts of the so-called dark side and can be Angels of peace.

The third choir consists of the Principalities, Archangels and Angels. The Principalities are in charge of countries and cities. The best-known Archangels are Michael, Raphael, Gabriel and Uriel. and finally, there are the Angels who are closest to us and who were mentioned in an earlier paragraph. Please note that you can safely connect to any of the Angelic levels, since you will only receive a tiny spark of the immense energies that these beings epitomise

There are of course also 'naughty' Angels, representing the opposite forces to those of Light. If ever you feel threatened by something very dark or nasty, you can always call upon the four Archangels mentioned for help and protection.

If you do not believe in the Angelic that is fine too. Only take on board what works for you.

11

Manifesting your Plans

If you wish to create something new in your life, it is important to be clear about what it is you want to achieve in as much detail as possible. Once this is done, you then must stay both focussed and positive about your project, as well as be flexible when this is called for. If you already have the skills to carry out your plan, determine how you can best make use of these. If you do not, look for someone who has, or take steps to learn them yourself. You also have to uncover any possible doubts or fears and address these.

Depending on what it is you want to create in your life, you may have to let go of something that is more or less redundant. This is not always easy because many of us are uncomfortable with change. The best way to go about this, therefore, is to first acknowledge that you may feel a little sad for the old to go; then be thankful for how it may have enriched your life, and make the conscious decision that you want to move forward. The Bach Flower Essence,

Star of Bethlehem, can help if you feel any pangs of regret or nostalgia.

An effective method to make something happen, is what is termed one-pointedness (without becoming obsessed). Whatever you focus on for a period of time, combined with positive intent, can lead to great inspiration, and many worthwhile ideas may come your way. Obviously, you must also take action. Always ensure that what you want to create is also of benefit to others. Even with small things, such as manifesting a parking space, which most healers do with ease, I always add 'for the highest good of all'. If someone has an emergency and urgently needs a parking space, I do not want to take it from them. This is not just a case of being spiritually-minded, it is also a case of respecting the laws of cause and effect. Everything we do, will at some stage return to us and it is preferable that this is positive rather than the other.

It is possible that some of your plans may not materialise. This could be because you do not really want them to happen all that much, have not thought things through enough, lost your focus or it may even be counterproductive to you or others. It is therefore useful to set a (reasonable) time limit for your plans to come about. As advised, several times previously in this book, just give the exercise a go, and if you find it does bring you success, you can delve further into the subject.

~Manifesting Plans Exercise~

Before you go to sleep, focus for a moment on the outcome of your plan and imagine how you will feel when it has all been realised. Now bring this feeling into the present moment. Also picture yourself living the result, and bring that into the present too. If you desire a new car, see yourself driving it; for good health, picture yourself in good health and enjoying this. Make the picture as clear as you can and concentrate also on the good feelings. Then thank the Universe.

For the parking space mentioned above, just ask for one and know that it will be there (always for the highest good of all)!

12

Coping with Events

This final chapter is being penned during the pandemic of the coronavirus, while I am at home in lockdown. The fear that was, and still is, generated because of what is written in the papers is tangible. At the start of this event, people began panic buying to the extent that supermarkets did not have enough food left for everyone. After a few weeks this calmed down, but the fear, anger and sadness are still very much evident two months later.

Because so many are apparently dying of the virus, there is much grief, but there is also the notion that this catastrophe could turn out to be an opportunity for much needed change. It is, of course, up to each and every one of us to try and ensure that these changes are for the better, rather than the opposite, although this is easier said than done. It is also possible that during such a time, past emotional or other trauma has come up to be released. The media is mostly spreading doom and gloom, creating further stress as well as fear, which are not exactly conducive to a healthy immune system. There are also many conspiracy theories doing the rounds and some of these appear to be quite valid, especially when expressed by professionals in various related fields.

The first thing to do with any such calamity is to try not to 'hook in' to the fear, anger or worry, however much this is justified. To do this, first of all acknowledge how you feel, and do the clearing, grounding and strengthening exercises. Then if you feel angry or fearful, just imagine yourself to be surrounded by a light pink colour with tiny golden specks and also breathe in this colour while focussing on the quality of harmony or something similar. Do this every time you feel you start to be overwhelmed and also ensure you stay grounded. If you are full of tension, do the same, but this time with a pale blue colour with silver specks and focus on the quality of peace. If you do not like pale blue, you can use pale green. If you are depressed, use the colour yellow with golden sparks and focus on the feeling of joy. Relevant Bach Flower Essences can also be helpful.

Once you feel better within yourself, you can then quietly make plans according to what your possibilities are and what inspiration you receive. Even if this may prove to be too difficult, at least deal with the negative emotions and thoughts so you are not too much affected by these. The more you manage your personal energies and the more you keep these on a high note as possible, the easier it gets. Panic, fear and worry etc. will get you nowhere and can only produce unhappy results.

If at all possible, you could instead think about anything positive that results from such a difficult event. In this current case, it is noticeable that since the enforced isolation, the air in London is clean as never before. Everywhere in nature, indications of restoration are becoming visible. People are friendly (although from a distance) and there is music and singing from balconies, in quite a few areas. Many now also have the time to ponder about their lives and what is important.

It is always a good idea in such a scenario, to picture yourself healthy and well, and to affirm this often during the day and again before going to sleep, so your subconscious mind gets the message.

A Final Consideration

This booklet serves as an initial and basic foundation for those who wish to start using this knowledge in their daily lives, and I hope it will help many to take their first steps into the worlds of energy of which we are a part of. One could write a book on each of the chapters, but the reason that everything has been reduced to the bare bones, is to make it a practical volume rather than expanding on theories. This is also the reason that the exercises are brief and easy to remember as well as carry out.

For those who wish to take it further, it would be more advantageous to join a course or a group on healing or related subjects. More profound theories will remain just that unless there is the opportunity for practice and experience under the guidance of someone who is highly proficient in these fields.

A few of the (older) books that I found initially helpful and that are relevant to the fundamental content of this volume are:

- The Power of the Subconscious Mind, by Joseph Murphy
- You can Heal your Life, by Louisa Hay
- A Handbook of Angels, by H C Moolenburgh
- The Healing Herbs of Edward Bach, by Julian and Martine Barnard
- Science of Breath (and other books), by Yogi Ramachakraka

- The books written by Dr Wayne W. Dyer are highly inspirational and most relate to manifesting your life.
- For any issues with stress, you can contact 'Mindeeze-Wellness in Life and at Work'.

I have written a book about crystals for newcomers which is called 'Crystals & Healing for Everyone', and a larger volume for healers who are practicing or training in these therapies will soon be available.

If you have any questions pertaining to the content of these pages, please do not hesitate to contact the VHF:

vibrationalhealingfoundation.co.uk

With Light

Henriette

Appendix

List of Exercises

ABOUT THE AUTHOR

Henriette Maasdijk is a Subtle Energy Medicine Specialist™ and De-stress therapist, and has completed the certificate of education (Cert.Ed). She is a founder of the Vibrational Healing Foundation and co-founder of the Federation of Subtle Energy Medicine. She is also a member of, and consultant to, several healing organisations. She has taught throughout the UK, Ireland and Europe for over 25 years, leading diploma courses and workshops on Subtle Energy Medicine subjects and inner development. She has always had a keen interest in the so-called unknown, and a great love and respect for the beauty and power of crystals. She believes that inner development and healing are the key to a life of joy, empowerment and fulfilment. Henriette is of Dutch origin and has lived in London for over forty years.

About the Vibrational Healing Foundation

The VHF, formed in 1996, offers expert training in healing and inner development. In the ancient wisdom schools, the dictum 'man know thyself' conveyed best what such training represents; nowadays, it comes under the term 'subtle energy medicine'.

Subtle energy medicine, in a nutshell, is about the exploration of ourselves as complex beings of energy, existing in a world of energy, and how this relates to our life, health and wellbeing. It is also about being able to support others, when they need it, with the skilled use of tools such as crystals, flowers, flower remedies, colour and sound. Such work and study are an ongoing process, because this is also a path towards what is termed enlightenment.

For information on courses in the UK, please visit:

vibrationalhealingfoundation.co.uk

~♦~

Printed in Great Britain
by Amazon

44624581R00066